MATTER OF DISCRETION

DONNA LEE DAVIS

MATTER OF DISCRETION

Printed in the U.S.A

Print ISBN: 978-1-54390-149-8

eBook ISBN: 978-1-54390-150-4

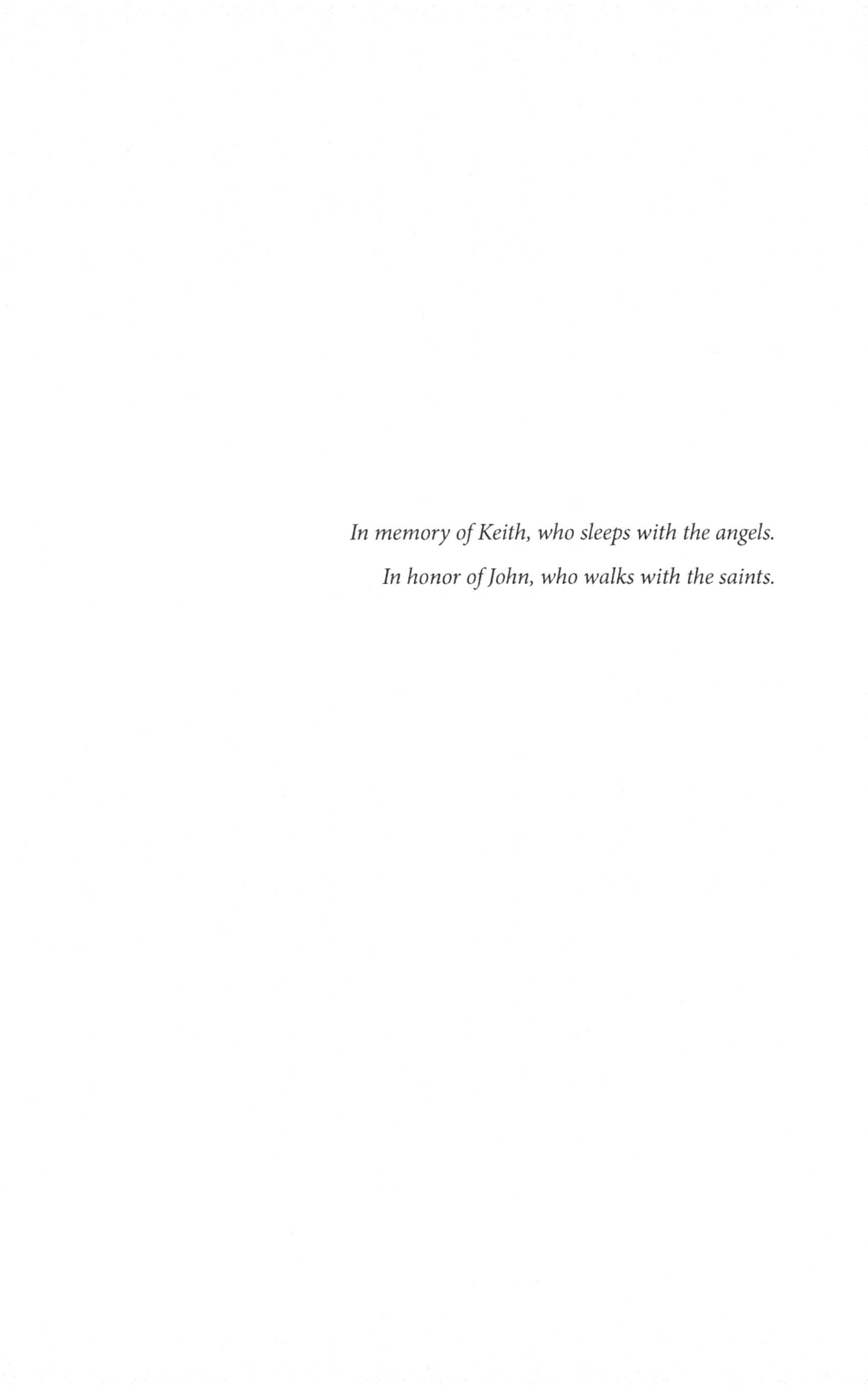

In memory of Keith, who sleeps with the angels.

In honor of John, who walks with the saints.

FOREWORD

I didn't set out to write a period piece. The year in which my story takes place was less than a decade past when the concept of *Matter of Discretion* was conceived. The location setting is the military base at Quantico, Virginia, a place that continues to grow and reinvent itself at a dizzying pace. I should know. I worked there, with the chaplains and later in military justice, for 33 years. The story opens in 1974 because that was the last year I was intimately acquainted with both venues.

In the mid-seventies the Religious Program Specialist profession for Navy enlisted was not yet established. Chaplain assistants at Marine Corps installations were enlisted Marines assigned the 0151 MOS, administrative clerk, usually secondary to another occupational specialty. Military court reporting by closed microphone, performed stateside primarily by a civilian work force, was the accepted—and respected—norm. There were no criminal data bases because there were no computers. There was no DNA analysis available to law enforcement. There were no cell phones, no Internet. It was long before NIS, the Naval Investigative Service, added a C for "Criminal" to its moniker and inspired three television shows.

All that said, it is important to note that *Matter of Discretion* is not merely the tale of a homicide investigation at Quantico in 1974. It is a story of Providence in friendships, souls in peril and hearts in distress. In that sense, I hope it is timeless.

1

He had always loved the sea. From the depths of his natural mariner's heart, he had been drawn to its vastness, to the lonesome roll of deep waters under endless skies. He loved the lore of it, the wondrous lure of it; the essence of it that spoke to his soul. In a naval household where walls were called "bulkheads" and floors were "decks" for his mother to swab faithfully every Thursday night, his childhood had been well seasoned with brine.

For much of his seventh summer, having reached the age of reason, while other boys were outside playing cowboys or riding bikes, he labored under a naked lightbulb in a basement redolent with dampness, struggling with tweezers and glue to build a scale model of Old Ironsides. In sixth grade, after a field trip to the National Aquarium in Washington, his extra credit paper on marine biology earned an A+ and Sister's scrawled prediction, "future oceanographer." With few exceptions, the heroes of his adolescence swaggered tattooed and rum sodden through the pages of Dana and Melville. By the time he was an honor student at Our Lady of the Harbor High, Damon was known to claim an imaginary comradeship with Queequeg and Ahab, and to quote *The Ancient Mariner* one moment, *Mister Roberts* the next. Until a deeper love—a more insistent, more wondrous lure—captured the whole of his being, it was widely assumed that like his father The Chief, young Damon would one day be a career Navy man. And so he was eventually, for he lived his vocation within his first calling.

It was now his forty-first summer, and there was not even a model ship on his horizon. Lieutenant Commander Damon John Keith, Chaplain Corps, U.S. Navy, exited Virginia's stretch of Interstate 95 North at Marine Base Quantico's rear gate and brought his tired Chevy, his dusty, beloved '72 Impala with power everything, to a gradual stop. He lowered the driver's side window and returned the gate sentry's salute.

"Morning, Padre," the MP said. "Visitor's pass?"

"I have change of station orders here." He tentatively fingered a manila envelope on the passenger seat.

"Then you'll be wanting a pass, sir, until you register your vehicle and get a base decal." Eyeing the Florida plates and the accumulation of bug spatters on windshield and grille, the Marine offered, "There's a new car wash across from the PX, sir. Fully automatic."

"Duly noted, corporal, thank you." He pulled away from the squat brick sentry shack with a large yellow visitor's placard displayed on the dash.

The roadway to headquarters was straight and lushly shaded by old hardwoods on both sides. The strong July sun flickered intermittently through the screen of trees, setting colors to dancing in his vision. As he often had during the long trip north, Damon reflected once again on this latest tack in his life's course and, as a practical exercise in recognition of grace, with every flash of sunlight through the trees he counted his blessings.

He was highly regarded by his clergy superiors, both the Bishop of Richmond, Virginia, his home diocese, and at the Military Ordinariate, the Archbishop of New York who oversaw all priests in the military. The Navy had embraced him; he was recently selected for promotion to full commander. There was a Navy Commendation Ribbon on his chest that had nominally impressed The Chief, and one for the Purple Heart that had truly horrified his mother. In cold weather he was pleased to lie beneath the scratchy wool of a souvenir blanket stamped in indelible GI ink with the name of a decommissioned destroyer. Like his brass sextant, some scrimshaw from Mystic Seaport and a framed photo of the Memorial that was USS Arizona, that blanket lent a salty sailor's flair to his quarters, wherever he was stationed.

But as for old seafaring dreams, he might better have fulfilled them by buying a boat. Most of his naval service had been ashore, much of it only a few hours inland from his boyhood home in Norfolk. With the exception of one wartime tour cut short by a Viet Cong grenade fragment, he had not left the East Coast. And although each succeeding billet proved the more demanding of his energies and the more rewarding to his career, it was still a ship that he asked for in each conversation with his detailer and on every fitness report dream sheet.

His sixth-grade teacher's intuition had been less than prophetic. Damon had never wanted to study the ocean. He wished to live on it, to minister to other men living on it; to eat and work and sleep on the ocean, and wake to it in the morning. He wanted sea duty. It was a romantic notion, he supposed. His admiral, the Chief of Chaplains, had somewhat perversely ordered him to a second tour at Quantico—this time, as Assistant Staff Chaplain and senior Catholic priest. A test of humility, perhaps. But in terms of grace, a blessing.

The Marine Corps Development and Education Command, known to the initiated by its acronym, was fancifully touted as a showplace, "the Annapolis of the Marine Corps." Realistically, its brick or clapboard façades were hardly celebrated for their architecture, and the appointments and landscaping were likewise unremarkable. "McDec" was small compared to the Fleet Marine Force camps, Lejeune and Pendleton. It was even considered by those within the Washington Beltway somewhat a social backwater, despite its relative proximity to the nation's capital. Hosting the FBI Academy lent some degree of prestige with civilians, as did the presence of the Presidential helicopter squadron at the air station; but McDec's status among military personnel lay solely in the fact that the Marine Corps trained officers here, making its mission the future of the Corps and its population top heavy with brass.

Sprawled as it was across miles of gently rolling woodland abutting the lower Potomac, McDec effectively surrounded the old village of Quantico, the rather pinched and bedraggled "Q-Town." Its several thousand Marines supported a large post exchange complex, three service clubs, two movie theaters, the Medal of Honor Golf Course, riding stables, swimming pools and other perks; a few nearby brothels; and perhaps less eagerly, three interfaith chapels.

But the familiarity of the surroundings and the duty didn't rule out challenges, Damon reminded himself, and dwelling on disappointment was folly. When first the Marine Memorial Chapel and next the Lejeune Hall headquarters building loomed into sight, he whispered belated thanks to God for yet another shore assignment, and for the opportunity to renew old friendships.

Michael Patrick O'Shea, lifelong friend and sometime challenge, was stationed here as a Marine judge advocate. If memory served, the legal department and the chaplains were allocated adjacent ground floor office spaces in Lejeune Hall. That meant that he and Michael, who had entered life on birthdays only a month apart at homes on the same block in Norfolk, would be neighbors again.

And then of course there was Cassie. Dear, dependable, unflappable Cass. Unquestionably, civilian employees at military posts were living continuity, solid roots for an otherwise transient community. Cassie Martin, the chaplains' secretary, was far more than that. She could quote chapter and verse from Navy and Marine Corps regulations, squeeze a scrawny operating budget until the eagle in the Great Seal squawked, and meet any deadline, the commanding general's or God's. But she was prized most of all for her benignly cheeky irreverence, and for the amazing, ecumenical ability to be everybody's best girl.

He found her there, just as he had hoped he would, waiting to greet him and to deposit a chaste kiss that faintly suggested salami. With mustard.

"Father Keith, your timing is perfect!" She thumbed off the lipstick smear she'd left on his cheek. "Everyone but me is out on lunch break. I can give you the welcome-aboard speech myself."

"Can't think of anyone better qualified," he admitted. Seeing her gave him a true sense of homecoming.

Beaming, Cassie hoisted her coffee mug. "If this is the Navy's idea of recycling, I'm all for it. Cheers!"

He thought she looked much the same as he remembered. A little plumper, perhaps, in her gray sheath dress—more matronly—and her pale hair shorter, different somehow, frosted; but the same open honesty in her eyes, the same impish grin. She was eating lunch at her desk as usual, and was characteristically happy to share. He passed on the offer of office mess coffee but did take a large cookie from the wax paper packet she shoved within reach.

"So how goes it, Cass? What's different? How does '74 here compare to '68?"

Cassie rolled her eyes. "Father, only the faces change in Lejeune Hall, you know that."

She was right. Little else was open to change, save the uniforms beneath the faces, and those varied only with the seasons. He had felt conspicuous and oddly out of place in his Navy whites since passing the gate. With some reluctance he would no doubt surrender them to the khaki tedium prescribed at Quantico until blues came in for the winter, or until he was asked to wear the Marine Corps uniform, which was likely. Marines didn't mind their navy doctors dressing like squids, but the padre they preferred to see as one of their own.

"Actually, we have a pretty solid bunch of chaplains right now. You probably won't be crazy about working for the Cap, but he's harmless enough." She winked. "A great talent for delegating responsibility."

Captain Bill Stannard's reputation as something of a management lightweight and even a brownnose had reached Damon at his former duty station. Stannard was said to be a fair match for and constant companion of the commanding general on the golf course.

Cassie seemed to read his mind. "He's teeing off at 1300 hours. You won't see him until tomorrow. Father Mac will be here this afternoon, though. He's not into playing games, unless it's poker. We're going to miss him," she sighed. "He's one of the good ones."

As Damon drifted away from her desk, Cassie contentedly applied herself to the remnants of her sandwich. She liked her job. Not so much the pay, which could certainly be better, but the work and the company. And the status, even if that existed only in her imagination. The only woman in the department, she reigned here as queen, part go-to girl, part mother hen. Most of the year there were seven officers to keep happy, half again as many more during summer augmentation with Naval Reservist chaplains reporting for stints of active duty. And then there were the chaplain's assistants, the half dozen or so young enlisted Marines. She was their confidante, their sounding board, sometimes their intercessor. After working hours each man, officer or enlisted, belonged to his wife or girlfriend or church, but from eight to four-thirty they were all hers.

The fact that Cassie herself was hardly religious never clouded her workday. If asked, she was prepared to call herself a "closet agnostic," impartial and unbiased. She judged the chaplains on the basis of their sincerity and could readily identify what she termed "the good ones." She smiled with satisfaction as she tossed her sandwich wrapper into the circular file. In her estimation, they didn't come any better than Father Damon Keith.

He was walking around, eating his cookie, peering into rooms, assessing the present and resurrecting the past.

From the outside, Lejeune Hall had always looked rather imposing, a two-story U-shaped red brick structure at the rear of an expansive lawn that doubled as a parade deck. The crimson banner of command with its three yellow stars flew above a wide white wood and glass door forbidden to all but the general's personal staff and dignitaries. That private front entrance overlooked a paved courtyard and tall flagpole. Damon had stood at attention many a morning on that courtyard, watching the flag raising and appreciating the band on special days, canned bugle notes on others. The lawn was kept thriving and green. It stretched beyond the courtyard, all the way to the main road in front and for a good distance to intersecting streets on either side. Bleachers would be set up out there on occasion for pass in review ceremonies, but most of the year the grass was frequented only by gulls and Canada geese.

Except for the amenities of the general's suite on the second deck, all of the interior of Lejeune Hall was the quintessence of utility. The chaplains' spaces occupied the tip of the north wing, main deck. They were allotted six private offices, a central storage room sans ventilation, called for that good reason "the vault," and a reception area outfitted with mismatched chairs, a rack of religious literature, and the requisite coffee mess. The bulkheads were white painted cinder-block, the decks dark asphalt tile. Bald florescent tubing shone overhead, Venetian blinds yellowing in varied stages of decay hung at the windows, and in the rear rooms exposed plumbing pipes serviced the general's private head a floor above.

In a doorway a few paces from the reception area, Damon surveyed the office he would occupy. The priest he was relieving, Pete McLaughlin, had already cleaned out the desk, a serviceable old steel hulk in gunmetal gray topped with battleship linoleum. On the floor two cardboard boxes were loaded to overflowing with a jumble of books and personal belongings. Stripped of all that had made it Mac's, the room was much as Damon remembered it. Olive drab file cabinet and swivel chair, a brown vinyl covered settee; no carpet or curtains to soften the harsh contrast between near-black floor and bright white walls. The starkness of the room was relieved only by a print of The Sacred Heart of Jesus in a gilded frame, an aging piece of chapel property that had passed from senior priest to senior priest. This was a monastic cell compared to the smaller adjacent office that had been Damon's six years before, plastered as it now was with the riotous color of Corita Kent posters. The desk and chairs in that room were cluttered with record albums and unruly stacks of sheet music. A twelve-string folk guitar was propped precariously in a corner atop a portable tape player.

"Sings like an angel," intoned the voice now at Damon's elbow, again following his train of thought. "Looks like one, too."

"Father Roberts?"

Cassie nodded slowly and seriously, fixing Damon with a faux naughty but frankly appraising stare. "How come the Catholic chaplains are always the best lookers?" she demanded. "Is it one of Murphy's laws?"

"Sounds more like Martin's malarkey to me," he laughed. Cassie hadn't changed a bit. "And how's your Joe, speaking of lookers?"

"Mean as ever," she grinned, pleased that he hadn't forgotten. "The big baby is cutting a wisdom tooth, so he's home from work today. Joey's keeping him company, with a sore throat that may or may not be the genuine article." She consulted her wristwatch. "My guess is they're playing Matchbox cars about now, and dripping chicken soup and cracker crumbs all over my clean floor."

Damon swallowed the last of the cookie. A mystery texture, and a taste heavy on nutmeg. "What kind of cookie was that, anyway?"

"Carrot-bran."

"No kidding?"

"I'm into nutrition these days," Cassie shrugged, "no apologies. You know the jar I keep on my desk? Well, now it's for sunflower seeds or sesame wafers. Around here that lasts a lot longer than candy." Her face brightened with a devilish recollection. "Remember the time we put in the rubber gumdrops to fool Chaplain Stutler?"

"Sure I do."

"So does he," Cassie giggled. "He's retired now, you know, but still in the Reserves. He was here last June for two weeks of active duty drill. Wouldn't even trust me to pour his coffee."

Damon walked into his new office and over to the windows that afforded a view of Memorial Chapel across the parade field to the west. The carillon was ringing "Panis Angelicus," signaling the close of noon Mass.

"Chaplain Ramsey came around recently, too, just visiting," Cassie was saying. "Remember him?"

"Um-hmm . . ."

"And I thought I saw that creep, your fanatic friend the dropout, in Q-Town the other day. Looked like him, although that hardly seems possible."

Damon wasn't really listening. The sun had retreated and the sky seemed suddenly heavy, its summer blue washed out; it was characterless save for the fading stitch of a vapor trail. The church from here was a sedate cube of brick red topped with a rocket-like steel spire. The horseshoe drive leading to its door was lined with crepe myrtles taller now than a man. Their blossoms were luxurious in a shade of fuchsia that seemed a perfect blend of the rose and purple hues that were liturgically correct in Advent and Lent. Gulls from the Potomac, scores of them, had settled on the steamy sea green lawn like clumps of manna from heaven. And they were just that in a sense: food for the soul, snowy, beautiful.

"Father?" Cassie plucked lightly at his sleeve. "Of course you're welcome to another cookie, but if you catch Father Mac before he leaves the chapel for Tony's, he'll probably spring for a meatball sub."

She sauntered back to her desk with such an air of smug amusement that he realized his stomach must have been rumbling. Manna from heaven, indeed.

2

Choosing the most direct path, he set out across the parade deck on foot and found Commander Pete McLaughlin outside Memorial Chapel, just as he was preparing to lower his considerable bulk into the battered remains of what was once a respectable Buick. Father Mac was well over six feet tall, massive and solid, with not an ounce of extra flesh on his frame. His face was florid, further reddened by the heat of the day and the heavy vestments he'd just shed. It was a good face; plenty of laugh lines. His sideburns and eyebrows were several shades darker than the hair of his head, what there was of it. Damon had met him once before and remembered him, not unkindly, as a "glad hander," a bit effusive. He didn't disappoint.

"Bless you, Boy-o!" Mac exclaimed, flashing a disarming grin. He clapped Damon on the back with one hand while pumping a firm handshake with the other. "Welcome aboard! You just get in?"

"A few minutes ago. I stopped by the office."

"Cassie said she had a feeling you might show up around noon. I never discount that girl's intuition. You hungry? You must be hungry! Pile in!"

Damon held his breath as Mac propelled them across base, zigzagging the Buick through lunchtime traffic with a zest that did much to explain his car's apparent history. "Tony's okay?" Mac called above the blast of the AC. Damon nodded approval. He remembered Tony's.

There was little more to Q-Town's business district than its main street, Potomac Avenue. Most of that quarter-mile strip, forever in a state of flux, was checkered with chameleon-like enterprises. There was a uniform store that doubled as a factory outlet, a shoe repair shop with a pawnbroker's sign above the door, a tobacconist that fronted a tattoo parlor. There were several small restaurants perpetually under new management, and establishments that were greasy spoons by day, sleazy bars at night. Even durable Tony's Italian Kitchen, by virtue of an elaborate neon sign some former owner had left behind, became The Sentry Box after dark.

They entered Tony's to the din of the jukebox and had to wait a few seconds until their eyes adjusted to the dimness. Like most business properties constructed along Potomac in the 1920's, this one was deep and shoebox narrow. Entrepreneurship had thrived here for decades; street frontage was golden. Anthony Iocona, the proprietor, was a retired Marine master sergeant and proud son of a former New York policeman. He had decorated his particular shoebox with tokens of his divided devotion. The walls were covered in Marine Corps memorabilia mixed among law enforcement collectibles, with here and there a nod to celebrities of Italian ancestry.

Tony himself was ensconced behind the bar at the cash register beneath a sign that proclaimed in clear if less than civil terms his reluctance to extend credit. He hailed Pete McLaughlin with a mock salute. "Hey, Father, how's it going?"

"It's going fast, Tony," Mac acknowledged. "I'm a short timer now." He clapped an arm around Damon. "I want you to meet Father Keith. He'll be taking my place."

Tony stuck out a meaty hand. He was balding, dough-faced, thick around the middle, and had the grip of a weightlifter. "Hey, don't I know you, though? You look familiar."

"That's right! I was stationed here six years ago. Glad to see you're still in business."

The doughy face split with a smile. "Makes two of us, Father." He called over his shoulder to someone named Marie, "A bottle of the best Dago red for the two chaplains here, on the house." To Damon and Mac he winked, "Premium stuff, cork and all. Go ahead, Fathers. Have a seat."

They followed a trail worn in the thin carpet to the rear of the dining room, claimed the booth farthest from the jukebox, and within minutes were attacking some surprisingly good cannelloni.

Between bites they exchanged pleasantries about the drive up from Mayport, the gas mileage of a '72 Impala versus a '70 Skylark, Damon's family in Norfolk, Mac's in Illinois, his leave plans in Michigan.

MacLaughlin said that he had arranged an afternoon interview for Damon with the base weekly. "You know what that's like. The newspaper story will read like your standard bio, no matter what you say. The main thing they're after is a photo, and if it's done today it'll make *The Quantico Sentry* this Friday."

"That's fine. I've got the time."

"Good. And I thought we could concelebrate the last Mass on Sunday, if you don't mind. The choir has worked up something special, and the ladies have planned a little cookies and punch reception." He raised a pinkie to signify something daintier than Dago red. "We'll put up a tent on the grounds. Room for the kids to play."

While they finished their food Mac outlined the turnover process. There would be an orderly transition, and in little more than a week the new senior priest would be on his own. Even finding quarters would be no problem, since they had already agreed that Damon would assume the lease on the snug bungalow Mac had been renting on Fuller Heights Road, just outside the main gate and close to St. Francis of Assisi, the civilian Catholic church in Triangle. Settled and done.

After a long silence Mac said tentatively, "I hope you like admin work."

"I can take it or leave it."

"The Cap *makes* policy, you understand, but he'll leave it up to you to implement. His own contact with the powers that be is primarily social.

Yours, I predict, will be strictly business." He smirked a bit. In fact, if I weren't so happy to be going to Great Lakes, I could probably work up some honest Catholic guilt about the unfinished business I'm leaving you with."

"Such as?"

"We're not due for a change in command for another year, for one thing."

"So?"

"So the commanding general has had me up to here," he snickered, working those dark eyebrows. "He's bound to be laying for you, Boy-o, our being cut from the same cloth, so to speak."

"I don't think I follow you."

Mac seemed to hesitate, apparently weighing his words. Damon noticed for the first time how tired the man looked. "It's simple, really. General Swaggart is a lip-service Christian, no particular denominational preference. He's made up his mind that a peacetime chaplaincy is just so much extra baggage. And his chief of staff is a professed atheist. A stunning combination, that."

"I'm impressed."

"As well you should be." Mac smiled crookedly and replenished Damon's wine. "You'll hear a lot of noise from our fearless leader about the great support we've been getting from the command. Don't believe a word of it. I've known Bill Stannard for fifteen years. He's a hell of a nice guy, but he wouldn't recognize a stab in the back if he had eyes behind his ears. The truth is, we're not supported at all. We don't get the money, we don't get the manpower, and we certainly don't get moral support. Every budget proposal we send up comes back cut to the bone."

"That's pretty much to be expected from the Marines, isn't it?" Damon countered. The Corps prided itself on doing more with less. "The 'lean green machine'?"

"To a certain extent, maybe. But somehow they always allow themselves enough to accomplish their own mission." Mac's genial mood was disintegrating visibly. "The chaplain doesn't rate that. We jury-rig solutions and we supplement our equipment, our office supplies—you name it—from the collection plate. Our Cassie is a talented *cumshaw* artist, but even she can't finesse a box of typewriter ribbons out of Supply once our quarterly allotment is gone." He frowned. "And the kids they assign to us are a hindrance."

"Still no chaplain's assistant MOS in the Corps."

"That's right. They won't dignify the work with one. No religious Military Occupational Specialty. And there's no screening, no training. Traditionally we get the misfits; you know that."

"It does seem that way," Damon admitted.

"And believe me, I have great respect for tradition. But we're getting exceptionally incompetent misfits these days, and some real troublemakers. According to the Table of Organization we should have a gunny, a staff sergeant, two sergeants, a corporal—well, you get the idea. But the T.O. may as well be written in sand at floodtide. What we do have is one noncom—a sergeant—and the rest are non-rated. One of them was just busted to private for assault. By rights he should be in the brig, but Bill intervened." Mac reached for his wineglass and drained it. "Just the sort of misguided maneuver that undermines our credibility as officers," he said tartly. "He has me attend the command briefings, and somehow I've managed to antagonize the general without even trying. One unfortunate flap after another. The more I sound off now, the more I'm ignored. Pat the padre on the head, tell the latest 'a priest and a rabbi walk into a bar' joke, and shove him in the corner 'til Sunday."

Damon pushed his plate away. The cannelloni was beginning to lay like a stone.

"Oh, I know," Mac went on, doleful. "I know what you're thinking. Old Pete McLaughlin has lost all his perspective and most of his charity."

"Not at all," Damon protested lamely.

"They're insignificant concerns, I grant you that. Mickey Mouse, petty annoyances. But they add up." He hunched forward and lowered his voice as though imparting a secret. "They steal the joy, Damey Boy-o. There's little joy in serving people who don't want you."

Damon cast about for a safer topic of conversation and, finding his mind a blank, studied the ornaments on the wall above their booth. An oil portrait of Chesty Puller was centered amid laminated newspaper accounts of heroic acts honored by the Long Island Fraternal Order of Police. And that grouping was somehow less jarring than the sight of a Miraculous Medal hanging from a framed glossy eight-by-ten of Frank Sinatra inscribed, *Tony, keep pouring, FS.*

The busy Marie returned, chewing gum and clattering dishes as she cleared the table. They both passed on dessert.

"I don't know," Mac reflected softly when the waitress was gone. "I'll be making a retreat before reporting in at Great Lakes. Maybe I'm long overdue for it." He lit a cigarette and took a slow, satisfying drag, leaving unsaid what both of them already knew. A couple weeks of prayer and solitude could be like balm on a festering wound. "You're younger than I am, Boy-o. There's a lot to be said for the resiliency of youth."

Damon smiled at that. He felt he had aged a decade in the last six years. Maybe perspective was everything.

"Your combat experience won't do you any harm, either. The general will respect that," Mac predicted. "And on the plus side, we do have some fine people in our congregation. And the Protestant chaplains on the whole really are an exceptional lot."

"Cassie called them a 'pretty solid bunch,'" Damon recalled.

"Did she?" Mac's eyes brightened. "That's one of her more astute assessments. They're a good crew, no doubt about it. We have a couple of charismatic preachers in Hughes and Jack Devlin. Hughes is out at the

Air Station. He's Baptist, a quiet, reserved guy until he takes the pulpit. Before the Chaplain Corps, he marched with Dr. King. Jack's our Officer Candidates School Chaplain. High Episcopalian, very Boston with the accent, the whole nine, very classy." He snickered wickedly, "His family was Catholic before they had money. Shorty Laurence is the most senior of the Presbyterians, and a good writer; his columns for the *Sentry* put mine to shame. He's an especially effective counselor, too, extensive background in psychology. And Fred Siebott is Evangelical Lutheran, old school, from Philly; fluent in German. He's a little older than the rest of us, a grandfather already.

"But I guess my personal favorite and closest pal is the Orthodox priest, Theo Lurakis. His wife Mary, among other virtues, makes a great souvlaki and a baklava to die for. Sweet, generous woman. Theo is a poker player extraordinaire. A born con man, so help me, and droll; I feel gullible when he lays it on. Never know for sure if he's serious."

Mac claimed the tab and lumbered to his feet, leaving Marie a generous tip. "The chaplain assistants I'll let you discover for yourself. They defy description, anyway. Sergeant Diaz is the only Catholic, but he comes to Mass about as often as he writes his mother."

"Sounds normal," remarked Damon.

"Yeah. Oh, yeah," Mac acknowledged wearily.

They found the Buick still un-ticketed where Mac had parked it, perilously close to a fire hydrant. Some wag had written "Your Ad Here" in the dust on the trunk.

"Keep an eye on Father Roberts," Mac advised as they launched from the curb. "He's a good man, a good priest. He'll work until he drops. Not for you, mind—too independent to cater to superiors, thank you—but for Mother Church. He's dogmatic, though, and ultra conservative. A little too . . . well, *zealous* for my taste." He shook his head at the thought. " He reminds me of myself as a young horse's ass, and anybody that rigidly idealistic is probably headed for a fall."

He was smiling but was unmistakably serious. “Just watch him, that’s all.”

“Done.”

3

The interview for the *Sentry* was simple enough. A young female non-com from Public Affairs showed up, and just as Pete McLaughlin had predicted, a photograph sufficed. They posed together at the desk, in fact, the outgoing Senior Catholic Chaplain briefing his relief. One question about Father Keith's opinion of modern liturgical music—"I'm a fan"—and they were free.

Damon spent the rest of his afternoon checking in, following the military's time honored prescription for acclimating a newcomer; that is, sending him in circles with a checklist. The Provost Marshal's Office, the battalion, the company office, the clinic, chow hall, gym, the credit union, even the base dry cleaner. The effortless routine of collecting signatures allowed his mind to wander, to thoughts of his youth in Norfolk and his friendship with Michael.

Michael Patrick O'Shea was his parents' miracle mid-life baby, the youngest of five children and the only son. Damon's early fascination with the O'Sheas had been suffused with boyish pity. The parents had emigrated from County Wicklow, Ireland, and "no sooner than landing" the father found work as a civilian laborer at the Newport News shipyards. The mother was dead, had died indeed little more than two years after the spring both Damon and Michael were born, and the father did not remarry. Only in bad dreams could young Damon picture the bleakness of a home devoid of both a mother and the Navy.

He had found Michael's four sisters especially admirable, partly because they thrived with less pocket money and more responsibilities than his own sister Rose, who simply had her Damey to look after, and partly because they were pretty. He would watch them file into church on Sunday, their coppery hair arranged in identical braids. They wore hand-me-downs that were clean and mended but never quite free of wrinkles. Even their names were romantic and strange, Siobhan, Maeve and Bridie Maureen—except for the youngest born in America, called Lucy after the redhead on the "telly." From the tallest girl, speaking with her father's brogue and smelling of flowers—toilet water, Rose said, causing Damey to sniff in puzzlement about the commode—to the smallest, who favored him with dimpled secret smiles, there was something vaguely entrancing about those lasses, as their father called them. Damon seemed to be forever nursing a hopeless crush on one or another.

Michael, on the other hand, was an irritant, the exemplary altar boy whose carrot top and freckles unfairly charmed the nuns. He was good at everything, equally smart and funny in class. Damey had never disliked him—you couldn't dislike Michael, he was innocent in his perfection—but certainly he had resented him.

As they matured it became apparent to everyone else that he and Michael were much alike, or at least similar enough to encourage comparison. But comparisons rankled. Naturally enough they became rivals, competitors for grades and honors, for girls, in sports, at after school jobs. During their senior year at Our Lady their surging rivalry peaked publicly with a fistfight over a carhop from Ocean View. It ebbed privately weeks later when the girl eloped with a sailor. After that letdown they commiserated like brothers, drowning their disillusionment in illicit beer and sharing another of life's lessons, a first hangover. To the surprise of most of their classmates, Michael O'Shea and Damon Keith were inseparable by graduation. And to the greater astonishment of their families as well as their peers, after high school they entered seminary together.

At the foot of the Blue Ridge Mountains, Saint John Vianney Major Seminary beckoned to young men of their generation like an oasis in a desert of hedonism, a fragrant well of knowledge, serenity and idealism. For Damon, with passing time the place lost its seductive powers, but never its appeal. He discovered the seminary was a flawed and sterile institution, but one that offered truths to be learned, devils to be faced, and a life of service to be embraced. For Michael, it proved to be more prison than haven. By the middle of second term he was ready to leave his buddy and the "sem" behind. He confessed to their spiritual director that he no longer felt called to the priesthood, but to Damon he confided a simpler truth, that having "rediscovered prurience" on the beach at summer break, he wished to hold, savor—perhaps even act on—every deliciously impure thought.

He had crept into Damon's room after lights-out to say goodbye, his face by full moonlight an amalgam of worry, excitement and embarrassment. "They don't let you stick around once you ask out," he whispered sheepishly.

"Bad influence," Damon laughed. The nervousness was contagious. "So this is it, then?"

"Yeah. My old man is coming up to get me." Michael shook his head in disbelief. "Spirited away in the night like a damned thief."

"No thief," Damon told him. "Whatever you take with you is yours. You earned it."

"Learned it," Michael corrected him. "And some of it I hope I can unlearn."

They both laughed, Damon with an unexpected rush of relief that he would remember long afterward. As his closest friend and only link with home, Michael would be missed. But an end finally to the subtle contest that threatened to linger between them could only be welcomed.

"Here, I want you to have this." Michael opened his hand to reveal a small, unusually detailed medallion that Damon recognized at once: Saint Patrick depicted in high relief on the front, the reverse side set with a smooth green stone. "It was my mother's," Michael said, sounding wistful, "brought over from Dublin. And it's all right," he added quickly, anticipating protest. "It's not the one I always wear but another just like it, see?" He fished the duplicate out of his tee shirt. There was the glint of silver as it caught a bit of moonlight. "She's the one wanted a priest in the family, so I'm told." Then sighing, "But you can't live someone else's dream."

That too Damon would long remember. He had wordlessly taken the gift and slid it onto the chain that held the old cruciform medal he'd received at confirmation. He wore it still.

For years after that midnight parting they kept in touch sporadically, with Christmas notes, gag cards on birthdays. It wasn't until Michael had a commission in the Marines and Damon was contemplating the Navy Chaplain Corps that friendship really flourished again. Suddenly their paths were at least parallel, if not convergent. During the latter part of Damon's Vietnam tour they were in country at the same time but repeatedly missed connecting. Then a carefully planned joint R&R had to be scrapped when Damon was medevac'd home. A full year after Michael's return from Nam they did manage one leave together, deep sea fishing off Nags Head, North Carolina, soaking up sun and suds amid memories of Norfolk, Phu Bai and Danang. Since then they had corresponded more regularly.

It was an increasingly comfortable relationship. Michael remained conscientious in his faith, if somewhat casual in his approach to it. He seemed keenly aware of the conflict between the spiritual and the secular in his own life. Often his letters were long exercises in rationalization, as though he wished to justify his choices. But Damon never judged. Michael's path appeared to be right for him, and some of his choices were enviable. His latest news was of marriage plans. He wanted Damon to instruct his bride-to-be in the Catholic faith and to celebrate the wedding Mass. That alone was worth the price of a second admission to McDec. Damon's fervent prayer was for a happy re-acquaintance.

Late in the afternoon, near the air station on the last leg of his check-in circuit, he got his wish as he nearly collided with none other than Major Mike O'Shea, still flushed from a workout at Larsen Gym.

Damon's first thought was that the years had been very kind to Michael. Fine lines around his eyes and mouth only added distinction to that freckled, obviously Irish mug. Thick eyeglass lenses in metal aviator frames and a hairline just beginning to recede ordinarily might have lent his face a scholarly, somewhat owlish appearance, but that was lost now in his unabashed glee. He barraged his friend with what seemed a dozen questions, and nearly as many demands: "When did you get in?" "Why didn't you call?" "Are you staying at the Q?" "Have your personal effects arrived yet?" "You must meet Mia." Time melted away for Damon with the urgent excitement in that familiar voice; they could have been in high school or seminary again. "How's Rose? And The Chief, and Mrs. Keith?" "Have you been by the old neighborhood recently?" "Mia wants to meet you." "When will you be saying Mass?" "Come to Happy Hour tonight. Mia will be there."

By quitting time Damon would have begged off that invitation, claiming genuine fatigue, had it not been for the contagion of Michael's eager insistence—*You must meet Mia*—and his own mounting curiosity, which was considerable.

4

In letters Michael's only physical description of his fiancée had been "pretty as a picture."

She was standing with her back to Damon as he entered Harry Lee Hall, the venerable old Officers' Club. His first glimpse of her did indeed present a picture, one of relaxed and graceful sensuality. The careless posture, the slender curve of flesh in a nearly backless red dress, the wisp of stray hair feathery at the nape of her neck like a dark brushstroke, all were suggestive of a figure by Degas. The analogy was complete when Michael alerted her with a nod in Damon's direction and she turned to approach him, her movement fluid as a dancer's. She was not a great beauty, but the delicacy of her even features was more than pleasing, and there was an almost ethereal quality about those steady gray eyes.

Mia didn't wait for an introduction but announced immediately, "You don't look like a Catholic priest," with a hint of humor playing about pursed lips.

"Oh?" He felt slightly defensive, in spite of himself. "And how does a priest look?"

"Like Pat O'Brien in the movies."

Michael shook his head in disapproval. "It's the Good Humor man uniform," he said with a straight face. "Pat O'Brien wouldn't have been caught dead in it. Or Bing Crosby, for that matter. But then, Damey's always had a penchant for things nautical. You may never see this one wearing a clerical collar."

"Damey?" She looked quizzically from one to the other.

"A boyhood nickname." He drew himself to attention and bowed extravagantly, employing his all but forgotten Tidewater drawl. "Damon John Keith, ma'am, at your service."

She smiled and was suddenly dazzling. "And here I'd thought Keith was your first name. I'm Mia Rodgers."

He took the hand she extended, resisting the theatrical impulse to raise it to his lips. "You don't look much like a Mia."

"Touché, Father," she said, smiling again. "My name is also a childhood relic."

"Short for something?"

"Mary Virginia. I couldn't pronounce the whole mouthful when I was learning to talk, and it stuck." She raised her chin in her fiancé's direction. "So it seems we have more than just Michael in common."

"'Just Michael,' the woman says! Well, 'just Michael' is in need of serious libation. Bourbon still your drink?"

Damon nodded.

"Then I think this occasion calls for some of Kentucky's finest, and a Jameson's for me." He lowered his head and leered at Mia over the rims of his spectacles. "I know just what you like, madam."

They watched him maneuver through the crowd, threading his way to the bar. Damon turned to her. "It's a pleasure to meet the future Mrs. O'Shea, whatever she calls herself."

"Thank you."

"Since I first received the news I've wondered who the siren was who could finally domesticate that old jar head. And now I can see the poor soul really never had a chance."

"My, my," Mia murmured appreciatively. "You don't talk like a priest, either."

"I don't get to see many old movies."

In moments Michael had returned, juggling the whiskies for Damon and himself in one hand, something syrupy and fruit laden for Mia in the other. As they tried their drinks he drew her closer to him in a proprietary embrace, absently stroking her bare arm with his fingertips.

"I understand I'm to be indoctrinated," she said, imparting a cautionary sideways glance.

"We call it instruction, but yes. And I assure you, it's painless."

"I would hope so."

"I've kept her in line with tales of the Inquisition," Michael volunteered cheerily.

Mia cleared her throat with comic significance. "I try not to listen," she said evenly, "as my feet get colder and colder." The light in her eyes belied that notion. "But how long do you suppose these lessons of yours will take? Just to give me some idea."

"I'd say the pace will be left up to you. There's plenty of time between now and May—that is, if the great catechist here keeps his nose out of it."

"She's a quick study," Michael countered. "Took her no time at all to learn she couldn't live without me." He looked believably offended when they both burst out laughing.

Perhaps too bluntly, Damon asked, "Are you baptized, Mia?" He was anxious for particulars; Michael's letters had provided none.

"Dear me." She sipped her concoction, considering her answer. "I was christened as an infant. But my people really aren't church goers, never were. I don't know why. It wasn't really discussed, growing up. I can remember being taken to Sunday services only a few times when I was little. Never at Christmas, oddly enough, and only once on Easter."

"What denomination?"

"Lutheran. The church was called Good Shepherd. There was a statue of Jesus with an adorable lamb near the front door, I do remember that." She lowered her eyes self-consciously.

Ever alert to engaging details, Damon noticed then that she appeared to use little makeup, and that she was blessed with long dark lashes and the high cheekbones so prized by women who photograph well.

"So your family was not observant. And you, yourself?"

"In college for a while I dated a boy who was active in Campus Crusade for Christ, but I stayed out of that myself, never attended a rally or went to a meeting. And my roommate for all four years was an unconventional girl, a WASP who dabbled in Zen Buddhism, mainly for the yoga. I would read the tracts she brought in and would argue with her or chant with her, depending on my mood." She frowned slightly. "And that, I'm afraid, is the extent of my background in religion. Except, of course, for having attended Mass occasionally with Michael." Sounding dubious, "It's a little late for Sunday school, isn't it?"

"We'll do it on weekdays," Damon said gently. "No impediments?" This he directed toward his old friend, who began to chuckle.

"What's that?" Mia asked.

"Prior marriage, primarily."

"She saved herself for me," Michael intoned. While his fiancée attempted to stopper his mouth with a chunk of pineapple from her swizzle stick, his laughter took on a fiendish quality. "Come to think of it, maybe you'd better prep her fast, Damey. We might have to apply for a dispensation. They do still have the 'spinster's clause,' don't they?"

"What's that?" Mia asked, coloring.

"Waive the banns and hurry the wedding due to the bride's advanced age."

"Oh, Michael, you're awful. Don't you believe him!"

No fear of that. Damon couldn't have guessed Mia's age—under thirty-five surely, less than thirty perhaps, but impossible to judge in a woman. And irrelevant, he thought, since she and Michael were clearly like youngsters in love.

The club was well attended this evening. Happy Hour was drawing to a close, but in a noisy alcove a wetting-down party was underway. There were several other women present, most of them in uniform, few of them as attractive as Mia, and nearly all of them frequently watching her. In fact, Damon noticed how consistently all eyes seemed drawn to the Marine major and the woman in the red dress, easily the handsomest couple in the room. Michael looked happy, glowing with exuberance and pride in her; and the more animated Mia became, the more fetching she was.

They managed to find an alcove of their own with a candlelit table and comfortable seating. For a swift hour he enjoyed their company immensely, Michael's clumsy jokes and Mia's charming playfulness as she clung to him, alternately shy and alluring. Pretty as a picture.

The ground floor rooms at the BOQ, sparsely furnished with Government Issue, were stuffy and stale smelling that first night. Damon struggled briefly to coax the musty air-conditioner into operation, without success. No matter. He would sleep, regardless. He had eaten little since the cannelloni at lunch; two fingers of Wild Turkey was enough to make him light-headed. And it had been an exceedingly full day, a tiring succession of reunions and first impressions that he couldn't put from his mind.

Pete McLaughlin's candor and advice he'd found somewhat unsettling. Evidently this tour wouldn't be the piece of cake he'd hoped for. But then, he chided himself, who am I kidding? Had he expected a brass-band welcome or a generous operating budget or, for that matter, an eager support staff? Over a decade in the Chaplain Corps should have relieved him of such fantasies. And if there's little joy, as Mac had said, in serving people who don't want you, perhaps there is all the more beauty in it. He would hold that thought, at least, and leave command diplomacy to officers better suited to it. He had no stomach for infighting, none of the shrewd suavity required for psychological games. He was no politician. What he was, first, foremost and forever, was a priest of the Church.

Even if he didn't look like one. Emerging from the shower and catching his muted reflection in the fogged mirror, he remembered Mia's playful comment. He toweled his curly head roughly, his forehead creased with honest bewilderment.

Damon Keith's body was trim and well formed, his patrician face illumined by eyes a deep-sea blue that could pale dramatically in moods of icy detachment. He was in truth a strikingly handsome man, but had never perceived himself so. Earlier that evening it had not occurred to him that some stares from women in the O Club might have been meant for the new chaplain, fascinating in his own right. He looked at his reflection and saw, now as always with alarming clarity, the inner man, imperfect, often shamefully inadequate. And he wondered, as always, if others saw that, too.

God, come to my assistance. Lord, make haste to help me. It was nearly midnight when he had finished the prayers of the evening's divine office and closed his breviary. He knelt to pray personally for Father Pete McLaughlin and for the men who had opposed him here, whatever their reasons. He prayed for Michael and Mia; for the souls of friends now in the care of another priest, his successor at the duty station he'd left; and for his own family. Lastly he prayed for himself, that with the help of God's grace and guidance he might prove worthy of the challenges ahead. Then he lay down in the close darkness a little while, listening. No breeze stirred from the open window, only the murmur of voices outside, male and female, and the rustle of clothing. Lovers taking leave of each other. A car door slammed, headlights intruded momentarily then rolled away, and all was quiet. As usual when he was overtired Damon began a rosary but fell asleep before completing the third decade. He slept deeply but fitfully in the heat. And come morning he would not remember that a lithe ballerina in crimson pirouetted like a flame through his dreams.

5

"Shit heads!"

Sergeant Cisco Diaz blotted perspiration from his brow and upper lip with the rolled sleeve of his camouflage utility uniform, and wearily sank his weight into a pew. All morning long he had been honcho of a combined working party of casuals and brig detainees, tasked with humping *beaucoup* gear and furniture up three flights of stairs to new chaplain spaces in a sweltering converted barracks at The Basic School. He was too damned tired for this aggravation. All morning long, shouting "*Di-di, di-di! Di-di mau!*" at uncomprehending boots and fouled up brig rats! And now this. He stared balefully up at old Noah, the Memorial Chapel janitor, as though he were the problem.

"Are you sure?"

"Sure, I'm sure," Noah bleated. "I seen 'em."

"Which ones?" the sergeant demanded.

"Two of 'em, the little blonde-headed PFC and Ferris."

Shit heads.

"I'm a Baptist, but I know what ain't right. They too lazy to get holy water out the dispenser, is all. They too lazy to walk to the back of the church. I never seen such foolishness before, filling them fonts at the drinking fountain. That ain't right. I know that ain't right."

Cisco stretched his legs and tried to move his heat swollen toes inside his combat boots. It was air-conditioned inside the chapel, at least.

"It ain't right," Noah said again.

"Aw, can it, will you?"

Miffed, the janitor returned to vacuuming the same stretch of burgundy carpeting that had consumed his attention before this fruitless exchange, his mumbling lost in the roaring whine of the sweeper. Up and down along the center aisle, forward and back, stroke after stroke. Old Noah was a wiry, light-skinned colored man. Not a "Negro," nor a "black," no, sir—he was disdainful of such affectations—but just colored, he would tell you; and make no mistake, proud of it. He was as unabashedly old-fashioned in his own way as the gritty Tex-Mex *viejos* Cisco Diaz had grown up with and had so vehemently resented. Those old ones back home were illegals, most of them, meek and falsely polite even to their own kind, forever watching over bent shoulders for The Man. Not that Noah in Cisco's view was weak or an Uncle Tom, exactly. There was just something about him that reminded Cisco of much that he had gladly left behind in his *aldea* near Brownsville, Texas. Maybe it was so simple a something as the fact that Noah was stringy and old and the familiar mocha-brown, and he had no anger. Cisco felt strongly that a man should be capable of a great and righteous anger, holding it in reserve, knowing when and how to loose it. Otherwise, in Cisco's estimation, he was no man.

Rivulets of sweat were trickling cold and clammy inside his cammies, creating an itch, and his new undershirt was cutting into his biceps; Cisco could sit still for only so long. Starting with the vestibule, he began a lone cursory inspection of this church building that was the most onerous of his many burdens. He prowled slowly with the pugnacious gait of the born fighter, whistling absently through his teeth, carefully and thoroughly looking high and low. And all the while reviewing his options.

He could write up Smitty and Ferris for dereliction of duty, with genuine pleasure; they deserved no less. But Chaplain Stannard would likely pull the charges before they got to the company commander, and that would be that.

He was tempted to put to use his knowledge of Ferris's supposed secret stash of pot. It would be easy enough to "discover" a stray roach or a clip stinking with residue among his personals in the barracks. Possession of an illegal substance could be added to his charge sheet. An offense that serious would probably stick, go not merely to office hours but to a court-martial. But then Ferris would be sentenced to brig time, which would leave the work section even more shorthanded and result in longer working hours and canceled leave for everybody, the sergeant included. Besides, Cisco admittedly was not above smoking a little friendly weed, at the right time in the right place—though he was never the habit-head Ferris was, nor stupid enough to do it on base. Turning a man in for what he himself had done on occasion would leave a bad taste. He had his principles.

By the time his inspection reached the rear hallway, his practiced noncom's eye had noted many discrepancies. Unpolished brass, cobwebs overhead in the sanctuary, light bulbs burned out, books and valuables unsecured. Through a back window he could see trash overflowing the dumpster, in violation of safety regs.

In the Catholic sacristy Cisco was surprised to find the vestment drawers ajar, their contents jumbled as though they had been rifled. For an uneasy moment he thought of a break-in, and quit whistling. Nothing other than clothing seemed to be disturbed, though. The chalice closet appeared full. The crates of altar wine were there, the boxes of candles, the ornate chalices, ciboria, and heavy silver candlesticks and crucifix were all in place. He hurried to check the little chapel room where the Blessed Sacrament was reserved in the tabernacle and was relieved to find it apparently untouched, the red sanctuary lamp burning serenely, nothing missing, nothing amiss. The Protestant dressing room and the choir room likewise appeared normal. The safe was secure, and in any case empty at midweek. Only the priests' gear in the sacristy was adrift, and no priest would have left it that way. Somebody boosting Mass vestments? No, that was dumb. It was the shit heads he had working for him.

He peered out across the sanctuary. Noah was still vacuuming, still talking to himself. Cisco rubbed his forehead, his mind abuzz with latent possibilities and difficult choices. Something had to be decided; he felt momentarily depressed with the weight of yet another responsibility. Sighing deeply and leaning against a fluted pillar, he continued to ponder.

The condition of the chapel was unsat overall. The Catholic chaplains in particular would not appreciate the situation, if it was brought to their attention. And whereas Chaplain Mac was easygoing enough, he was on his way out. They were left with Father Roberts, known to be a pain in the ass and a stickler, and the new priest, who was still untried after less than a week onboard.

Maybe the best thing, Cisco reflected, would be to make no official report but to counsel Smitty and Ferris personally as their NCO In Charge. He could threaten to burn them next time if they screwed up again. *When* they screwed up again. *Si*. That way, he would have something to hold over their empty heads for a while. Not a bad idea at all.

He took a few minutes to square away the sacristy, mentally cursing the career monitor whose whim had placed him here. Some faceless jerk-off at Headquarters, Marine Corps, who with the stroke of a pen had reduced a sergeant of Marines to policing a church! His old *amigos* would sneer if they knew the kind of duty Cisco Diaz had pulled in the military. They showed little enough respect already whenever he went home in uniform. The young *Chicanas* were more impressed with the satins of the street gangs than with the dress blues of the Corps. Even his own *Madrecita,* who displayed the blue star of the patriot in her front window, did not know that he was no longer a machine gunner. His mother would no doubt be thrilled if she did know the truth, but she was the only one.

Cisco fingered the faint ache in his right thigh where he had stopped a knife in a brawl at a Saigon bar—his one battle scar—and imagined that it throbbed with all the righteous indignation that he felt. He kicked shut the last vestment cabinet drawer. Damn! He'd been point man of a fire team that chased Charlie through 1,000 meters of thick jungle, not that long ago. He was a Marine, a grunt, and a good one. He belonged in the field.

Noah was becoming more hard of hearing all the time. Cisco began yelling "Yo!" several meters from the old man, and still had to wave a hand in his face to gain his attention. The janitor switched off the sweeper and folded his arms, looking peeved.

"I'm gonna handle this business about the fonts myself," Cisco told him. "Smitty and Ferris will get reprimanded. But let's not get the chaplains all excited, okay?" He flashed a persuasive smile. "The priests, they're touchy about that stuff; their feelings would be hurt." He knew he was really reaching now. "I don't want you telling nobody else, *comprende*?"

Noah mulled this over. Teasing from these boys was tolerable, but he was leery of allowing them the luxury of authority. His eyes narrowed to suspicious slits. "Not even Miss Cassie?"

Cisco was adamant. "Especially not her. I never seen a woman yet that could keep a secret."

Reluctantly, the old man nodded agreement. He could recognize wisdom, even coming from an unlikely source.

"I'll take care of everything," Cisco grinned. "It's cool."

He acted quickly then, before Noah could reconsider and hand him some more guff. Removing the glass cups from the two fonts, he strode with them into the men's head where he stopped short, confronted with yet another problem.

Suppose the old man was mistaken and there was really holy water in these? Suppose it was holy water mixed in with water from the scuttlebutt? Either way, it might be against the rules to dispose of it. If there was one thing Cisco Diaz remembered from his Catholic upbringing, it was that the Church had rules for everything. It might be a sin. They had sins for everything.

He hesitated a moment more, the cups in his hands poised over the urinal. Two decisions within ten minutes was one too many. "Fuck it," he muttered finally, and poured the water out.

Those shit heads were going to pay.

6

She was corrupt, no better than a common whore. Anyone could see that. She demonstrated what she was every time she moved her body, her hips; by the way she showed her firm nipples, so distracting under the thin tee shirt too small for her chest. You could tell just by watching her that she would do anything and would allow any man to do everything. She had seen you observing from the shadows, you were sure of it, and she was pleased with that, and unashamed. You knew without question that with a few soft words of invitation she would have smiled for you, would have worked her seduction for you. She would have gone with you willingly, just as she had gone with the other.

And to be clear, it was not yourself who took her, it was the other. You may have coveted and surely you lusted for her despite best intentions, but it was not you who took her. It was him, the other. It was not your sin.

She was led so easily—far too easily—to that place of isolation, where she was pushed roughly to the ground, onto a pallet of moss and evergreen needles. By moonlight filtered through the canopy of high old trees you recognized in her face the raw distortion of rising panic. It was exciting. In mere moments the other was working capably to inflict what must have been an exquisite pain, confident that she wanted it. And somehow you understood the importance of his need for her to want it.

You wished that they would hold back, make it last. But the other was in control. The other followed his unchecked rage, and you could do nothing about that. Besides, it was a judgment. It was a righteous justice that stole your breath and fragmented your being, that pulled you down, down, down, while your head went floating and your lungs were afire, that made you as powerful as he was now, punishing, thrusting again and again until tortuous release . . . until you knelt gasping, trembling. And she, with the other's hands still strong on her throat, no longer struggled.

The first of the phone calls came before Damon had moved from the Q and within days of publication of the photograph and article in *The Quantico Sentry*. Groggy though he was when the BOQ's Duty NCO roused him, he knew this would not be a hospital call, because he wasn't yet listed on the emergency roster. Instead, his first thought was of Rose. He had grown accustomed to his sister's occasional late night phone calls, her whining, accusatory tone, her timeworn grievances, even her tipsy demands. Guilt had been nibbling at the back of his mind ever since he had chosen to drive straight through to Quantico without even a few hours' detour in Norfolk to see the folks. He steadied himself for a dressing down that was justified and overdue. So it was doubly startling to be standing there by the duty desk in his skivvies listening in disbelief not to her familiar harangue but to a raspy stranger.

"What did you say?"

"Priest," the voice repeated, "confess your own sin."

"Who is this?"

"I . . . know . . . what . . . you . . . did." The words came slowly, deliberate and clear. "Confess your own sin, Judas."

Then it was over. The call was disconnected and he was staring at the telephone receiver as though it was an alien object.

"Anything wrong, sir?" the young corporal on duty asked.

"A crank call," said Damon, replacing the receiver in its cradle. "How did he—who did he ask for?"

"Lieutenant Commander Keith, sir."

"I see." He didn't know how to react, whether to frown or laugh, it was that bizarre.

"Sir, should I make an entry?"

"What?"

"A logbook entry, sir. Should I make one?"

Damon rubbed the back of his neck, suddenly tense. "Yes, I think that would be in order."

The corporal noted the time. "Aye, sir. Good night, Chaplain."

Back in the stifling bedroom, Damon was dismayed at having suspected the usual nuisance call from Rose. What the voice on the telephone had said, upon examination of his conscience, was strangely fitting. The widening gulf between brother and sister was, in Damon's estimation, a sin far greater than most he heard in the confessional. He humbly bore the lion's share of culpability for their estrangement, and it troubled him greatly. He made frequent overtures, he accepted his sister's collect calls and her criticisms with studied good humor, and he prayed. Beyond that, there wasn't much he could do but live with the situation, and with a growing sense of personal failure.

Still fully awake at first light, he rose again to sit at the little writing desk beside his rack and begin a letter.

Dear Rose,

I'm nearly settled in, as far as the job goes. So far so good, but my latent (I hope) talent as an administrator has yet to be tested. Wish I had your ability to do several things at once, and all of them well.

Mike O'Shea is here, and asking about you. Can you believe our Michael is headed for the altar next spring? His fiancée is attractive and seems to have a level head. You'd like her.

The house I'm taking has three bedrooms—two more than I need—and could use a woman's touch. I remember your old apartment on Granby when you and John were newlyweds. Trust me, this place offers that kind of challenge. How about you and Jackie come up for a week or two and lend a hand? Carte blanche at the PX—linens, curtains, whatever you think and my paycheck allows. And there's a family style dinner theater in Woodbridge. I owe you.

If you can't make it yourself—and I hope you can—please consider sending Jack for a few days. I'd love to have some time with my nephew. It's been too long. Think about it, and call me as soon as you can.

Love,

Damey

He evaluated the letter thoughtfully, satisfying himself that its tone was lighthearted and credibly casual, all the while acutely aware of the irony in forced cheeriness with the person once closest to him. He underlined the words "call me," adding his new telephone numbers as a postscript.

As he sealed the envelope, Damon willed himself to envision his sister as she had been in adolescence. Her round face framed with a tightly tied babushka, the cleats on her saddle oxfords clicking march tempo against the sidewalk, she would drag him by the hand on countless hurried errands. It was Rose, nearly eight years his senior, who had marshaled him off to school, who rushed him to Saturday matinees in time for serials before the feature, who hustled him to late Mass and for many an ice cream cone afterward. It was Rose who taught him to whistle, to skate, to tie a boat knot, to dance soft-shoe to "Singing in the Rain." It was she who pulled him round the neighborhood caroling at Christmas, who propelled him door to door on Halloween. It had seemed to him at the time that Rose ran a perpetual race, like Alice's White Rabbit. It was only long after he'd grown enough to match her long strides that he realized she had never failed to make time for him, with a sometimes grudging, almost always maternal affection. That was how he liked to think of Rose, as she used to be, before life soured for her and she blamed him for it.

He addressed the envelope and, recalling those she had sent him at CYO summer camp and later at seminary, he wrote a foolish string of X's and O's in one corner, as Rose had done unfailingly in those days. The opposite corner he inscribed with "T.J.T.M.," his own childhood custom. "To Jesus Through Mary."

It couldn't hurt.

7

The peculiar telephone call was all but forgotten in the clamorous events of the next three days. Damon attended his inaugural command briefing and thus endured his first encounter with McDec's commanding general and the complement of his staff. Chaplain Stannard had prepared him for that fiery baptism with a dearth of information and some dubious advice. "The general will mention Chaplain Capodanno and the Medal of Honor," Stannard predicted mysteriously. "Tell him he was a friend of yours."

"I hardly knew the man," Damon protested.

The captain responded with deliberate care, slowly and distinctly, as though explaining fundamentals to an idiot. "The fact is, you did know him. The two of you weren't unfriendly, were you?"

"No, of course not."

"Then you were friends," Stannard concluded emphatically.

Damon had noticed immediately that the Cap was self-confidence personified, yet every bit as vague as he had been described. His conversation was direct, but his mind usually seemed otherwise focused. Perhaps on the putting green.

He appeared to gather forbearance. "You need to understand something, Keith. Vincent Capodanno did more for the Chaplain Corps by dying under fire than you or I will ever do retiring on twenty. There's a mystique about his kind of heroism. The goodwill that derives from it is invaluable. So is the connection. Invaluable. Believe me, Chaplain," and here he smiled benignly, "Father Vince was a friend of yours."

Damon began to believe it.

The command briefing took place in the general's conference room on the second deck, around a mahogany table nearly as broad and long as the room itself and polished to a mirror shine. Here the cinder block walls were painted pale green and studded with lavishly framed prints of combat art. A deeply padded dark green carpet and custom drapes in Marine Corps red and gold lent an air of executive plush, as did the dozen high-backed brown chairs that had the feel and smell of genuine leather. As the most junior officer present, Damon was placed farthest from the CG and would be called upon last. While he waited his turn he studied the other men grouped around the table.

Lieutenant General George Swaggart presided, seated behind a gleaming silver coffee service that curiously went untouched. He was a comparatively short man, small-boned, lean and taut, with a gray receding hairline. His high forehead dominated his thin facial features, and beneath it his dark eyes roamed restlessly. The fingers of both slight hands, reflected in the waxed mahogany, drummed an incessant, nearly silent tattoo, as though he was telegraphing impatience.

To the general's right sat his chief of staff, the celebrated atheist. This fleshy face was pitted with acne scars and burdened with a permanent frown, the brooding scowl lines cut deep and unforgiving, Damon thought—lacking charity—like a grimace on a graven image. Judging by the iron gray hair and campaign ribbons that dated his career from the Korean War, he was somewhat older than his peers.

There was a commonality of aspect among the others of the general's staff, or perhaps it was merely a shared mood. A gloomy tension hung in the air that boded ill for the newcomer. If there was one easy-going, friendly officer in this group, he was hiding himself well. Michael's boss, the staff judge advocate, seemed no less stern or preoccupied than the provost marshal or the base inspector. Even the air station commander, whose gold flight wings usually signaled a loose élan, impressed on first sight as dour and no-nonsense.

The meeting commenced with a gesture from the general, and one by one the colonels briefed their commander in appalling detail. Many of them held forth with charts, graphs, sheaves of documents. From the comptroller to the head of manpower, from the support staff for supply, motor transport and facilities, to the leaders of the various schools, each department chief spoke with a refined professionalism. Damon was feeling increasingly as much outclassed as outranked. He drew himself ramrod straight in an effort at appropriate military bearing. But from the moment the hapless head of dining services received a subtle ass-chewing on the quality of beef served in the officers' mess, he very nearly held his breath in hopeless anticipation.

"Now the chaplain's report," the chief of staff announced, and to a man all present turned toward the foot of the table, as though their heads were on the same pivot.

"You're Chaplain Mac's relief?" General Swaggart inquired.

"Yes, sir."

"Mackerel snapper?"

"Sir?"

"Roman Catholic?"

"Oh, yes, sir."

"The second in command in the chaplains' shop is always a Catholic," the general attested to the room. He added gratuitously, "Seems to work well that way."

"Yes, sir." Inwardly, Damon was stung by the offhand reference to implied subservience. Some chaplain commands were traditionally Protestant, some Catholic. Quantico was a large base with a proportionately large Catholic population; freeing the two priests to minister to their majority flock by according administration and leadership to a Protestant made good business sense. In theory, at least. It was simple as that.

"I'm not R.C. myself," the general was saying, "but I admire the discipline. Chaplain Mac is a fine man, fine sense of humor."

"Yes, sir." *Mackerel snapper?* That remark was just registering, and its import just now sinking in. It was not the first time during his career that Damon had encountered condescension or prejudice; but coming from the seat of high command, it was decidedly inappropriate. Remembering that helped him regain perspective. He allowed his posture to relax a bit—military bearing be damned—and plunged into what little he had come prepared to say.

"Sir, our greatest need in the coming months will be additional personnel. As you probably know, we operate far under our T.O. as it is. We're losing two enlisted men temporarily to battalion commitments; one has been assigned 30 days of mess duty, and the other will be pulling butts on the rifle range for three weeks. More importantly, one of our permanent personnel is fast approaching his E.A.S. He'll be a civilian before we know it. For training purposes we should have at least one new man onboard before we lose him, but to date no permanent assignments have been made."

General Swaggart inclined his head questioningly toward the spokesman for manpower. That gentleman consulted a manila folder with an air of gravitas. "I believe you're mistaken about that, Father," he said.

Father? Damon noticed now the Italian on the colonel's nametag and momentarily sensed an ally.

"We have made two permanent assignments," Manpower was saying, peering at him over black-rimmed eyeglasses. "A boot private and a corporal who was previously with chaplains—at Lejeune, I believe. Both should be reporting in before the end of this month." The colonel managed a faint smile. "I'm surprised that you weren't privy to that information."

"So am I, sir," Damon acknowledged, coloring. Thank you, Chaplain Stannard. "But what about some temporary assignments? Maybe a couple of casuals awaiting orders or pending discharge? We could make good use of any—"

"That's a battalion level matter," Manpower interrupted crisply. "You should make your personnel request of the battalion commander, through his adjutant."

"I'm sorry, sir, but I thought that your Manpower Department—"

"Battalion level," Manpower repeated, looking away. "Follow the chain of command."

"Very good, sir." Damon felt his color deepening. The colonel had been needlessly curt. "If our staff were brought up to snuff with the T.O., sir," he ventured, "we wouldn't be so troubled with these little crises."

The chief of staff came to life at that, suddenly leaning forward, his scowl growing darker. "The Table of Organization will be reviewed at the beginning of the fiscal year. There may be inequities in some areas, but the chaplains have been functioning admirably for years while claiming to be understaffed."

"Sir, that's unfair."

"It may well be that the chaplains' T.O. should be decreased," the chief added archly. "Many of us believe that religious support should come wholly from the civilian sector, in any event."

Damon caught Manpower's guilty sidelong glance. So much for fellow "mackerel snappers."

There followed a volley of questions that kept the chaplain on the defensive. Did he know that buses for Vacation Bible School were short-cutting through senior officer housing, a restricted area? That residents had complained about the noise and exhaust fumes? He had not known that. He could only make assurances that he would contact the motor pool and talk with the Protestant chaplains, who undoubtedly also were ignorant of the problem. He admitted that he was unaware that work on the chapel's Book of Remembrance, meant to memorialize the names of Vietnam War dead, had long been suspended because the calligrapher could not keep pace with the casualty lists. When could the project be resumed? He could only answer that he would attempt to find out. And so on, and on: He didn't know, he wasn't aware, he would have to check. It was deeply discouraging to make such a dismal first impression.

Finally the general reached for the silver coffee pot, apparently the customary signal that the business portion of the meeting was ended. Chairs were shuffled, gear was gathered, cigarettes were lit. Like a few other officers eschewing cold coffee and making their excuses, Damon began his retreat. But he was not to escape so lightly.

General Swaggart approached him and stood like a barricade between the chaplain and the door. "Captain Stannard tells me you served with Chaplain Capodanno in Vietnam," he began.

Damon's heart sank. Thanks again, Cap. "I knew him slightly, sir, at Chaplains School in Newport, Rhode Island. We served in country at different times."

"Then you weren't close?"

"Not as close as I would have liked," he could answer truthfully. Those seven weeks in Rhode Island had passed quickly and were long ago. He remembered little more of Vince than his crew cut and ready smile, and his expert comedic timing. There had been no hint that amiable Father Capodanno would soon sacrifice himself so valorously in the rice paddies of Quang Tin. He remembered vividly the moment the word came. Four deaths in the '60's had shaken his world: JFK, Vince Capodanno, Bobby Kennedy, Dr. King.

"There's a ship named for him?"

"Yes, commissioned last year." USS Capodanno was a Knox-class frigate, its motto "Duty with Honor." Not a man or woman in the Navy who wasn't mindful of that.

"What do you know about a scholarship fund in his memory?" the general asked.

Still smarting, Damon felt himself flushing. "Very little, sir. I do know that there is one."

"You ought to look into it," Swaggart advised. "The idea interests me. I'd like to know more about it. I should think you would, too."

"Yes, sir."

The general was teetering backward and forward on heels and tiptoes of nervous energy, one arm behind his back. The top of his head was on a level with the tip of the chaplain's nose. Given his height, or lack of it, and the somewhat pompous stance, a caricature of Napoleon leapt to mind all too easily. "To be frank," he was saying, "I have very little patience with conscientious objectors of any stripe. The concept of turning the other cheek, all that; smacks of pacifism." He appeared lost in reverie for a moment, perhaps recalling the roll of battle drums. When the general spoke again he sounded bewildered, wistful, even a trifle envious. "It takes a special quality, all the same, to go into war unarmed, to perform under fire and wounded the way Capodanno was. And *unarmed*." The very word held an obvious fascination. "What would you say that quality is, Chaplain?"

The response came quickly, natural and irresistible. "Faith, sir."

The satisfaction he felt thus taking leave of the general compensated for all the discomfiture before that. On his way downstairs Damon tried to rid himself of his fractious mood. It had been a long time since he had dreamed of the tattered drone of a HU1E drowning out a whispered confession, or woken in the middle of the night convinced the smell of napalm and eucalyptus was a real presence in his room. Mostly now he slept well. Mostly. And often without a thought for those who now slept with the angels.

As he descended the stairs to the main deck he signed the cross and breathed a grateful Hail Mary—for his dear friend, Father Vince.

8

Damon barely had time to brief Chaplain Stannard with an abbreviated version of the staff meeting. His first and ultimately his only counseling appointment for the day, a clearly agitated dependent wife, was already waiting for him. Wearing oversized sunglasses and a long-sleeved dress obviously wrong for the season, she sat hunched over in a corner of the waiting room, twisting a Kleenex to shreds. Her face was turned away toward the window and her chin tucked, as though she was studying her clenched hands and the remains of the tissue in her lap. Even from that angle and at some distance Damon could discern layers of concealing makeup.

He escorted the woman into his office, closed the door, and soon was embroiled in a counseling crisis that would continue full tilt for the next 72 hours, consuming most of his time and all of his energies. Her husband beat her, the petite Mrs. Brady confided. She had reached her breaking point. She was afraid he would kill her eventually, or harm the children. Damon gently asked her to take off the glasses. Setting her mouth in a hard line and lifting her chin, she complied. Her face was a pudding of puffy discoloration, nasty bruises on both cheeks. Her left lower lip was cut and swollen. Overcome with embarrassment or perhaps impelled by some vestige of vanity, she replaced the sunglasses immediately. "He used to hit me only where it wouldn't show," she said faintly, "but that doesn't seem to matter to him anymore."

Damon asked Cassie to hold his calls and closed the door to his office. Martha Brady, in halting monotone, disclosed fevered details that caused him to wince inwardly. It was evident to him from the defeat in her voice that she had recited this story before, all too often.

Her husband was not Catholic, she told him, but they had been married in the church. The first time he had struck her was while she was pregnant with their first child. "It was the war," she said simply. "Vietnam. It changed him." She had considered leaving him when that first incident kept her a night in the hospital, but he begged her not to go and promised it would never happen again. "I wanted to believe, you know? I needed to believe."

Both her sister and her confessor had encouraged forgiveness. She had no access to his money, or money of her own, no marketable skills, no family to turn to. Her parents had barely held their own embattled marriage together before their death in a fire when she was fifteen. Her sister, worlds away in Arizona and well-meaning in advice, was already twice divorced herself and had troubles enough of her own. Besides, she said faintly, "I chose to believe he still loved me, then. I chose to believe it would get better."

But that first time was three children and several injuries ago. And lately all of it was worse. Now his blows didn't stop with her tears or with entreaties from the children, and his rages came more often, with less provocation. She took a deep breath. "Father, I think I should get a divorce." She removed the sunglasses of her own accord at that point, and fixed him with a stare of naked defiance.

Damon had seen that look before. It was meant for the priest-as-jailer. Mrs. Brady knew that he could not in good conscience advocate for divorce if the marriage were valid under Church law. So he chose his words very carefully.

"Perhaps that would be best for all concerned. But you decided to come to me, when you simply could have seen a lawyer. That tells me that you still believe there is another way."

They talked throughout the remainder of the morning. The domestic scenario was not unique but was no less disturbing for its sad familiarity. The husband was a respected "mustang," an officer who had worked his way up from enlisted ranks, a man who had made good use of all the education and advancement benefits that military service offered. His war record had opened yet more doors. His wife had been devoted, his children healthy. On the face of it he should have been a man content in his work, content with his family life. Battering was somehow uglier when the abuser appeared outwardly blessed, and was all the more troubling if the cause was rooted in the sacrifices of his duty.

Damon sent Martha Brady home finally, resigned to his advocacy and fortified with a slim hope. After noon Mass he drove directly to the Education Center in order to confront Captain Brady privately on his own turf. The encounter was disappointing, to say the least. The captain proved to be thoroughly disagreeable, an unctuous egotist who resented the interruption to his workday, who hadn't the decency to show remorse or shame. Or respect for the clergy.

As a priest Damon was well trained in marital counseling, but the love-hate relationship that so many couples seemed to feed on wholly confounded Damon as a man. To love, to live in intimacy with a woman, having become one in sacrament, as one body, one flesh, and then to abuse your other, most beloved self—it made no sense.

Brady refused to visit the chaplain's office. He scoffed at the idea of consulting a psychologist on base, and nixed seeing a civilian doctor elsewhere under cover of anonymity. When finally he realized the chaplain would not drop the matter and could report him to his commanding officer, he agreed with much reluctance to submit to counseling in quarters.

Damon went to the home that evening and returned the next morning and again the following afternoon. He saw husband and wife in sessions together, then separately, then as a couple again. He listened, advised, prayed with them, listened some more. He seemed to be steadily losing ground. How do you turn back the clock? All the little sacrifices, the sharing, the daily recommitment so vital in a Christian marriage had been absent from this relationship. Keeping God present and foremost has to be learned and practiced early on, by both parties. By the end of the third day he could see that he was making little progress and began to doubt his own judgment. The stab of stress in his chest was such that, had he not endured a thorough exit physical exam before leaving Mayport, it might well have caused him alarm.

His great asset, or perhaps his greatest liability, was his own receptive heart. Damon felt poor Martha Brady's anguish and desperation as surely as if he had received the blows himself. He was mindful of and deeply vulnerable to the children's fear and confusion. But he empathized with the captain most acutely, because his was a soul estranged from God. By the third day Damon was drained, mentally and physically. He reviewed his notes on the couple's history, searching for any grounds, however weak, on which to petition the Church's marriage tribunal for an annulment. He pondered it. He prayed on it.

It was after the fourth harrowing session at the Brady quarters that, having returned to his office discouraged and depleted, he found a postcard from Rose in his inbox. It was one of those touristy cards with a color photograph of the Chesapeake Bay Bridge-Tunnel on the back. She must have fired off an answer the same day she had received his letter. Amazing how efficient the postal service could be on occasion. The note, written in her tiny, cramped hand, was short and typically blunt:

Damey,

Glad you like the new post. Store inventory, impossible to get away. School starting early. Aug. 15th = holy day. With you Jackie would spend the last of his vacation in church. Maybe another time. Congratulate Michael for me. Thought he had better sense.

Rose

He was still contemplating that closing comment when Cassie buzzed him. "Call for you on line two."

It was the same raspy voice as that night at the Q. "I know what you did, priest. I know all about it."

"Who is this?"

"Soon everybody will know. I know what you did. Confess your own sin."

Questioned moments later, Cassie was perplexed. "I didn't ask for a name," she said. "He seemed to be in a hurry. Besides, I thought it was someone you knew. In fact—" She stopped, squinting in confusion.

"What?"

"I had the impression I knew him myself, or that it was someone who knew me."

"What do you mean? Did you recognize the voice?"

She frowned, shaking her head. "No, not that. He sounded hoarse. I think he called me by name, though, and it all seemed familiar somehow. Not the voice so much as what he said and the way—" She stopped short again.

"The way what? What did he say?"

"Well, I answered the phone as I always do, 'Staff Chaplain's Office, Mrs. Martin,' and then he said—" her eyes wide open now—"he just said, 'Cassie, let me speak to Father Keith.'"

9

The bloated body lay in an obscene sprawl like a discarded doll, partly hidden by leaves and humus. The staring eyes of clouded blue bulged, and the tongue protruded grotesquely in the manner of strangulation victims. There was a length of some dirtied purple, embossed fabric tied around the neck. The smell of decomposition was palpable from meters away, overwhelming at close range.

Someone had already debriefed and escorted from the immediate area the early morning runner who had first happened upon the remains. The Naval Investigative Service had now arrived in the person of its resident agency leader, with an agent photographer in tow. The boss was sighted immediately, easily recognized by the generous mustache that overcompensated for his shaved head. One of the two young military policemen who had responded to the scene initially was still dry heaving behind a fir tree. "Reiner's here," his partner hissed, and the youngster emerged, pressing the heel of his hand to his nose and mouth.

Grimacing and holding his breath, simultaneously repelled and morbidly riveted, the detective agent with the camera circled the body, snapping several shots in succession. When finally he had to exhale he remarked to no one in particular, "She musta been here days in this heat." He adjusted his lens for a close-up of the head, focusing on the knotted purple cloth. The deep royal color was ornamented with a golden thread and what appeared to be fringe. "What the hell is this," he called, "some kind of scarf?"

Harry Reiner, Quantico NIS boss, ex-Philly cop, recovering alcoholic and former altar boy, stepped forward to take a closer look. "Jesus God," he said after a long moment. It was a confessional stole.

"Do you believe in miracles?" Mia surveyed her new chaplain friend with eyes luminous in amusement. Her attire today was blue-green like the ocean, with a froth of white undergarment barely showing beneath her skirt hem at the knee. Her long legs were crossed demurely at the ankles, a model of decorum. And the informality with which she relaxed on the old brown settee opposite Damon's desk told him she intended to continue chatting trivia. It was nearly eleven, 40 minutes away from his commitment at the chapel. They had already frittered away nearly half the allotted time, and had yet to touch upon the essential principles of dogma. Had any other catechumen so skillfully steered the conversation along a primrose path, Damon rightfully would have been annoyed. But Mia Rodgers was so earnest, so innocent in her wish to get to know him as well as his church, that he could not be stern.

"Christ performed miracles," he answered.

"No, no, I mean you, personally. Do you believe that God actually disrupts the natural order of things from time to time, just to make a noise in the world?"

"I wouldn't say that's what a miracle is, firstly. I think that God works in concert with nature—after all, it's his own creation—and that he gives signs of his power and love rather freely. It's up to us to recognize those signs and accept them, through faith."

"You mean they only happen for believers, like faith healings?"

"I mean that some people will explain away the vision of the Blessed Virgin at Fatima as mass hypnosis, while others will see the hand of God in something as commonplace and natural as the birth of a child." She smiled at that. "True miracles, in the Biblical sense, are beyond explanation and always point the way to Christ."

"And you believe in them?"

"I do."

Mia indulged a slow, self-satisfied sigh. "Sometimes I think Michael and I are a small miracle," she confided. "You see, I wanted for such a long time to belong to someone and to feel needed. I guess I was looking for something, just wasn't sure what. Fulfillment, maybe; some meaning to my life. Once we found each other, well, all that seemed to be answered." She hesitated. "Then again, there are times even now when I wonder whether it will work. Whether we're really right for each other."

Damon looked at her sharply. She was focused inward, not watching for his reaction.

"I do try to be what Michael wants," she continued. "And probably he has enough confidence in the future for both of us." She smiled again as her narrative gained momentum. "I like to think of the first time we made love, how neatly he folded his clothes as he took them off, while mine were strewn all over the room! That pretty much sums up our relationship. Michael always knows what he is doing, every minute. I only know at any given moment what I want." She glanced up at Damon then and flushed a bit. "I'm sorry, I was forgetting myself. I shouldn't have said that."

"No, not at all. That's all right. I want you to be yourself with me. I want you to feel at ease." But the truth was, he was not completely at ease himself. What she had said stirred something like envy, a vague and nameless emotion Mia must have read as embarrassment.

"But I'm not being fair," she said. "I used to be a teacher, so I know what it's like when a pupil keeps changing the subject." She leaned forward, elbows on knees, chin in cupped hands, and regarded him intently. "I'll be good," she promised.

Now Damon found himself asking, "Why did you quit teaching?"

She made a dismissive face, wrinkling her nose. "No guts, I guess. It was Northwest D.C., and the kids were hellions. I had 42 in my ninth-grade

English class. Only three or four were serious students, and even they had limited potential. Not that they weren't smart enough; education just wasn't a priority. I tried awfully hard, but nothing I did seemed to make a difference. Drugs were surfacing there. I still think some of my kids were on something, alcohol or pot or pills, but the guidance counselor wasn't convinced. I had no recourse if she and the principal wouldn't back me up; the school budget didn't include a nurse. In my last semester two teachers were assaulted on the school grounds; one was hospitalized. That shook me." She drew a long breath. "So to sum up, I'm no altruist. I felt I had to get out."

"Understandable. And what are you doing now?"

I'm a court reporter here," she said brightly. "That's how Michael and I met."

"So you work together?"

"Yes. You mean he didn't tell you?"

"I don't recall it."

"Of course." She shook her head. "I should have known. He considers this work here a waste of my education. It's one of the subjects on which we often butt heads. A degree is an asset, not a requirement, in court reporting—which is glorified clerical work, come to that. And I suspect he feels teaching is a more suitable profession for an officer's wife."

"I'd be surprised if he thought that," Damon observed honestly. "More likely, he just wants you to be happy."

"Oh, but I am happy. The cases are interesting, even exciting at times. I'm not bored, and I don't miss teaching at all." She sat back again, smoothing her linen skirt as she did so. "And it pays well. I can afford nicer clothes and treat myself to something expensive once in a while, which is more than I could do on the salary of a teacher without tenure."

Damon thought of Rose's employment history. "My sister is head window dresser for a department store in Norfolk," he found himself volunteering. "'Display artist,' she calls it. Years ago she tried teaching business school, then held some secretarial jobs, but nothing worked out. Too confining, I suppose. Not creative. And I do remember hearing her say when she left her last office behind that the real money was in court stenography. Is it very difficult to learn?"

"Not at all. At least, not my kind. We use the closed microphone method here, the Stenomask."

"Oh, yes, the verbal—I've seen that. I'd forgotten." He had testified once for a promising youngster who'd taken a wrong turn, and had been intrigued by the reporter's recording device, which made her look like she was taking oxygen.

"The results are just as good as with Stenotype, although I grant you, it's not glamorous. If you have an aptitude for it, it's not all that difficult. But it is demanding; repeating everyone's words and getting it right requires intense concentration."

Damon considered Rose's slow Tidewater drawl combined with her near vicious intensity once she had a particular mindset.

Neither of them spoke for a moment. Good. Damon reached for the adult catechism and leafed for the chapter on the sacrament of marriage.

"Why did you become a priest?" Mia asked.

He met her steady gaze again. "Like you," he said, "I was looking for something." He thought hard for a moment, absently rubbing the spine of the book with his thumb. "I feel—comfortable, I think." He tried the word again silently, savoring all it implied. "Comfortable," he repeated with conviction. "I belong in the priesthood."

"But did you always know?" she persisted. "I'm curious because of Michael's time in the seminary. He insists he was serious then about becoming a priest himself."

"Oh, he was. He was."

"Then tell me. Did you always want it? Or was there a time when you wanted to be, I don't know, a fireman or maybe President?"

Damon grinned. "I thought I would be a sailor," he admitted. "My father was in the Navy, so I knew what the life was."

"And you grew up in Norfolk?"

"Yes, where there was always a tin can or a carrier on the horizon, which I thought the most magnificent sight in the world. When I was about nine, my dad took me on a tour of a destroyer in dry dock, probably the biggest thrill of my childhood. I was so excited I wanted to enlist on the spot. He had to break it to me, they don't take cabin boys anymore." He laughed at the memory. "If I had lived in the last century, I would have run away to sea as a child. I'm sure of that."

"But instead you ran to the Church?"

Damon considered his response. "I suppose you could say that. It was a sanctuary in a sense. And I needed something bigger than me to be a part of. That's what drew me to the sea when I was a boy. A naval career is more than just a job; it's a way of life. And even more so, the religious life is much more than a career."

Mia studied him a long moment before speaking again. "I wouldn't want to lose myself in anything to that extent," she said softly.

He couldn't resist chiding her. "It's more like finding yourself." Holding the book aloft, "Shall we get started?"

They endeavored to cover some of the basics in the minutes remaining, and the last of the introductory lesson was assigned as homework. Mia seemed eager to learn, once she'd had a taste of the fundamentals. He caught the scent of her perfume as she was leaving in a flurry of apologies for time wasted, clutching the catechism to her chest like a schoolgirl. The memory of what she had told him about herself and Michael lingered as the door closed behind her. A vision of the two of them in a nude embrace with lacy garments crumpled at her feet drifted, uninvited and unwelcome, across his consciousness, until he drove it from his mind with an abrupt shake of the head. There were times when Damon regretted his priestly celibacy, or to be more accurate, his virginity. Not that he felt any less masculine because of it, but because sex was so much a part of that greater mystery which eluded him. That baffling man-woman phenomenon. The coupling of bodies and psyches that was so natural, yet so foreign to his personal experience. It must be truly wondrous, he mused, to be part of a "small miracle."

Cassie broke his train of thought with the telephone buzzer. "Mrs. Brady is on line two, crying. I think she's calling from the hospital."

He listened to very little that Martha Brady said. All that really mattered was that the captain, God forgive him, had backslid already. "Martha, Martha, listen to me."

"Father, I'm afraid. You don't know how afraid. You don't know what it's like."

"Listen, Martha, please. I want you to call Legal Assistance as soon as we've finished talking. I'll give you the number. Just tell them the truth. They'll keep it confidential, and they'll give you some practical advice. Maybe they can recommend a civilian lawyer who can help you."

"A lawyer?" she echoed faintly.

"That's right. I'll continue to be here for you, you know that. And I'll be here for your husband as well. But what we've been trying to repair can't be fixed. Rebuilt maybe, in time, but not fixed. This can't go on any longer. For your own safety, it's time you found out what your rights are and what options you have."

There was a long silence on the line. Damon heard, or imagined he heard, the Lord's name in a whisper. He waited a moment more for her to speak.

"Martha?"

"Yes, Father," came the immediate response. There was definite strength in her voice now. From the sound of it, Martha Brady wasn't crying any more.

10

Harry Reiner had turned up the volume of his little portable radio on the windowsill just moments before Detective Agent Ed Kaminski, in wrinkled chinos and a short-sleeved plaid shirt, came in with the noon guard mail run. "Try to Remember," one of Harry's favorites, was winding down. He loved that song, even if it did remind him of his ex-wife.

"I don't know how you can stand that old 'easy listening' crap," Kaminski groused. He dropped a large brown guard mail envelope on the desk and stuck his big surly puss in Reiner's face. "You must be the last living fan of Pat Boone."

"It's not Pat Boone, dummy. It's Ed Ames."

"Ed who?"

"Ed Ames. The Ames Brothers? Mingo on 'Daniel Boone'? Tomahawk to the crotch on Johnny Carson?"

Except for the smirk that was a dead giveaway, the detective's fixed stare was deliberately blank.

"Go on, get out of here, Ski."

"I'm gone. I'm gone."

The mail was from the base photo lab. Harry took a minute to clear a space on his desktop so he could spread out its contents. He unwound the string closure, opened the envelope, and pulled out a thick packet of prints, most color, a few black and white. WQVA was playing "Scarlet Ribbons" now, Perry Como. He looked first at the blow-ups of the color shots taken at the homicide scene. All of it was worse somehow when preserved in glossy eight-by-tens. No odor of death, no heat, no flies; just objects and shapes and colors, but graphic enough to gag a maggot. Harry examined the close-up of the dead girl's neck. The stole had been wrapped around it several times and knotted. A sailor's hitch, if he was not mistaken. Threads of gold fringe were tangled in the paler yellow strands of hair. Her scalp was lacerated from the shard of granite that had been her last unyielding pillow, and blood had seeped profusely into the snarl and matted there. Scarlet ribbons.

He switched off the radio and slipped the photos into the case file, then pulled the desk phone nearer and dialed Michael O'Shea's number at Legal. "Ya, Mike," he mumbled when the major picked up. Harry seldom enunciated a clear "hello" on the telephone; his customary opening was a barely civil, indistinct salutation between "yeah" and a grunt that had figured highly on his ex's list of annoying traits. "We got ID on the dead girl," he told Michael. "She was a Marine, PFC Beverly Anderson, Headquarters and Service Battalion. H and S had run her UA on the unit diary since Wednesday, when she was a no-show at morning formation."

"Worst way to terminate an unauthorized absence. How old was she, Harry?"

He opened the file again.

"PFC, must have been a kid."

"Twenty," Harry said. "No, sorry, nineteen. Would have turned twenty in a few more days."

"What do the forensics look like?"

"Well, the clothes and the stole have gone to the FBI lab, and the coroner will do the combings and scrape under the nails, all the usual procedure. Until the lab findings and the autopsy report come back, we really don't have much to go on, other than the confessional stole."

"She was strangled with it, you said?"

"No, judging from the marks on her neck, the stole was an afterthought, or maybe a finishing touch."

"Or a message?"

"Why do you say that?"

"I don't know," Michael said. "It's an odd thing. It must mean something."

"It means we're damn sure going to interview everybody connected with the Chaplains Office, for one thing."

"You think it came from there?"

"We know it did. There was a label sewn into it that identifies it as chapel property. And there's a Marine works there, one Lance Corporal Jimmy Ferris. When H and S inventoried her gear at the barracks, her roommate told the sergeant major that Anderson used to date Ferris, up until the beginning of the summer."

"And that's enough to identify him as a suspect?"

"Maybe not, but he seems like the logical place to start. Like I said, I intend to interview everybody. Chaplains and all."

"Well, go easy."

Harry had to laugh. "What, counselor, you think I ain't got couth? I'm a sensitive guy."

The logical steps that ultimately led to the military apprehension of Jimmy Ferris later that afternoon were routine and totally by the book. He was not at all singled out by virtue of his relationship with the victim; rather, he was approached as casually as was every other individual questioned. In fact, he was interrogated with a perfected nonchalance that, in congratulating himself later, Ed Kaminski would describe as "flawless."

Special Agents Reiner, Kaminski and Parks had descended upon the staff chaplain with the request that all his personnel be made available for private interviews, to begin with himself and the two Catholic chaplains as well as all enlisted, in the Lejeune Hall office spaces. Harry assessed

Chaplain Stannard on the spot as an affable blowhard, agreeable to throwing his subordinates to the lions of NIS without a second thought. He answered the few cursory questions asked of him cheerfully if distractedly, and summoned his staff without hesitation. Harry wondered if the captain appreciated the gravity of the situation. Beyond a murmur of pity over the service record photo of the dead woman Marine, the words "homicide" and "investigation" seemingly didn't register.

Merle Parks was dispatched to Memorial Chapel, where the Protestant chaplains would meet with him at half-hour intervals, one by one. Kaminski would take on the enlisted here in the offices. Harry had decided beforehand that he would question the priests himself, despite the grudging embarrassment and nagging reluctance he privately felt. He had distanced himself from the Roman Catholic Church and its obligations for most of his adulthood, and after his divorce had succeeded in excising it from his mind altogether, with minimum guilt. But the attitudes of half a lifetime could not be dispensed with nor forgotten so easily.

On meeting the priests he stumbled over calling them "Father," hating the telltale color that rose in his cheeks, and settled on addressing them by grade. The older one, the lieutenant commander, seemed to trigger a memory. He reminded Harry of someone, probably some pastor he had encountered back home in Philadelphia. He had about him that same patient, solicitous air that proclaimed "grace," for want of a better word. The other, however, this Lieutenant Roberts, physically looked more like a preppy magazine model than a priest or a military officer. His demeanor conveyed that he likely was as much out of touch in his own way as Chaplain Stannard seemed to be. Harry had an unfortunate habit of sizing up new people in seconds, another characteristic that had irritated his ex. It had grown out of the demands of the job, and sometimes it paid off. His immediate take on young Roberts was that he viewed things temporal through other-worldly detachment, most likely rooted in arrogance. Harry definitely had come across some priests like that in Philly, he remembered irritably, and he hadn't liked them, either. He decided to question Lieutenant Roberts first.

The young chaplain was by turns flushed, then ghostly pale, then flushed again, as Harry sketched the loose facts of the investigation and began inquiries to fill in the blanks. By the time the full import of his questions had sunk in, Roberts was livid. "Surely you can't think that—"

"I don't think anything at this stage, Lieutenant. I'm trying to gather as much information as I can. That's all. You weren't aware that any of the chapel vestments were missing?"

"I don't use them," Roberts said loftily. "I have my own. My confessional stole was made for me by my aunt."

Harry raised an eyebrow.

"As an ordination gift."

"And who is the responsible officer for gear of that sort?"

"I'm signed for it, if that's what you mean, but we do an inventory only once a year."

"And does Lieutenant Commander Keith use the chapel vestments?"

"I wouldn't know. I suppose he does."

"Okay. And did you know the victim, Private First Class Beverly Anderson?"

"The name doesn't ring any bells." Roberts began flipping through his appointment book. "Was she Catholic? I wouldn't have seen her unless she was a Catholic."

"As a matter of fact, she was, according to her service record."

"Well, I don't think so."

Once again Harry pulled out the black and white snapshot of the girl in uniform, from her service record book. "About five-four, blue eyes?"

"I don't recognize her," Roberts said, studying the photo. "Sorry. There are so many who come to Mass."

And you really don't make eye contact, I bet, Harry thought. "Okay, Lieutenant. Your whereabouts over this past week?"

Father Roberts stiffened perceptibly. "I left for Baltimore on Tuesday evening and officiated there at a wedding on Saturday. My cousin's wedding. I was back to assist with Masses here on Sunday."

"Okay."

"All of which can be verified."

"I'm sure it can, Lieutenant." Harry was enjoying the priest's discomfiture. He rewarded him with his most unctuous smile. "Would you be good enough to supply me with names, addresses, telephone numbers if you know them?"

In contrast, he was favorably impressed by the forbearance with which the older priest listened to what case information he was free to disclose. All the questions put to him were answered without argument, hesitation or quibbling. His movements during the period from the time the girl was last seen until the approximate time of death were easily accounted for and could be corroborated, except for the late night hours when he was, naturally, alone. Harry noted that the apparent theft of the sacramental stole concerned Lieutenant Commander Keith nearly as much as its ultimate use; but as to how or when it had been taken, he hadn't a clue. He had heard confessions at Memorial Chapel on the two Saturdays since arriving here, and each time had used one of the stoles kept in the sacristy. He had never noticed their number.

"And this Chaplain McLaughlin that you relieved," Harry asked, "he detached here on 30 July on orders to Great Lakes?"

"That's right. But he may not have checked in yet. He intended to make a retreat first." When Harry remained silent, writing in his notebook, the chaplain began an explanation. "A religious retreat. We go away, usually in isolation, to meditate and pray."

"I think I can grasp the concept," Harry growled, but checked the urge to say more in the same vein, as he continued to scribble his version of shorthand. It would do no good to antagonize these people, and this man in particular did not seem deserving of sarcasm. He would make an effort to curb his tongue. "Do you know what retreat house?" he asked evenly.

"No. I don't even know if he was going to a retreat house." The chaplain smiled. "I've made some of my best retreats on a lake with a fly rod."

Harry's gaze met Damon's with a glimmer of increased respect. "I can grasp that concept even better," he said.

Observing that Kaminski was making adequate progress on his own with interviews of the enlisted men, Harry decided he would next ask a few questions of the secretary, Mrs. Martin. It was from her that he learned exactly where the priests' vestments were kept, how many of each type was supposedly on hand, what they were worth, and how each item was cataloged. Cassie showed him a list of chapel volunteers. There were the women of the altar society who regularly had access to the garments in order to keep them presentable, as well as the deacons, Eucharistic ministers, lectors, ushers, organists and choir members, all of whom had been allowed free access to the rooms in the rear of the chapel at various times. Aside from that, she added finally, to her knowledge Father Mac had been in the habit of leaving a stole inside one of the confessionals at the front of the church, for convenience.

While Harry used her telephone to call Memorial Chapel, Cassie examined the victim's SRB photo. "I know I met Jimmy Ferris's girlfriend at the office picnic at Lunga Reservoir last spring," she was telling him as he dialed, "and I know she was here in the office right around Easter. But if you asked me to describe her, or even tell you her name off the top of my head, I couldn't do it." The women Marines, the WM's, always looked so different in civilian clothes, with both their hair and their guard down.

She knit her brow mightily, staring at the snapshot, commanding a memory into focus. The day the boys stripped palms in Father Mac's office. The whole heads of palm had been delivered late, that Friday before Palm Sunday, and all the Marines and she herself had worked feverishly to get them done in time. Stripping long, full strands for the Catholics; stripping, cutting, folding and stapling hundreds of little crosses for the Protestants. The girl, this "Bev," had stopped by in civvies to see Ferris and had stayed to pitch in, standing ankle deep in palm fronds, peeling and giggling. It was Bev who found a worm in a head of palm and squealed. That much Cassie could recall of her, and no more. She felt sadness and an irrational shame, having taken so little notice of the girl.

"She was murdered, you say?"

Harry nodded.

"Where did it happen?"

He put his hand over the mouthpiece of the telephone receiver. "The body was found in the woods, on the knoll above the corner of Barnette and Neville Road. Next to the officer housing, near Q-Town."

"Waller Hill, where the old officers' club used to be?"

He nodded again and began to speak into the telephone. "Ya, Parks, we need to dust those back rooms. Do you have your kit with you?"

Cassie stared still harder at the photo, trying again to recognize in the sober expression of the prim Marine the girl she had seen, without makeup, in jeans and a ponytail. The poor kid. "How was she killed?" she asked, but Harry waved her off, turning away, his voice lowered.

"Okay, okay," he said. "I know you've got your hands full. I'll be over there in five."

Father Keith had come up behind Cassie to peer over her shoulder at the photograph. He put an arm about her momentarily in a companionable gesture of sympathy, and somehow that made her feel even worse.

Cisco Diaz watched the questioning of Lance Corporal Ferris with keen interest and very little empathy. His own interview had concluded quickly. He'd known the girl, sure, seen her around, he'd told the agent, but he never messed with her or laid her. He left that class of poontang up to the shit heads. His kind of woman didn't join the Marines.

From the reception desk outside the waiting room's open door there was an unobstructed view of Ferris and Agent Kaminski, although he could not hear what was being said. Ferris was seated next to the coffee mess, on the chair Cisco had occupied minutes before. His beady little ferret eyes did nothing to betray what he might have been feeling, other than maybe get tighter and smaller. As always, Ferris wore resentment of authority like armor. He was shaking his head from side to side in obvious denial after denial. What he could not know was that Cisco had told Agent Kaminski that he'd seen Beverly with him at The Sentry Box on Tuesday night. The reason he remembered was because it surprised him to see them together. They had broken up; Ferris had been bad-mouthing her for a while. And he'd seen them having an argument. The NIS agent had perked up at that news, come to attention like a *perro dogo* offered a bone. He had dismissed the sergeant shortly after that disclosure, directing him to advise his superiors that he was to visit the agency later that day to provide a written statement.

Cisco had not wanted to implicate anyone, but he had to tell the truth, didn't he? Ferris was now staring determinedly at the floor. Agent Kaminski pulled a small laminated card from his back pocket. Straining to hear, Cisco made out a word or two and realized Ferris was being advised of his rights. The lance corporal's head jerked up finally like somebody had pulled a string. It looked like, for the first time in Cisco's memory, those beady little eyes had gone wide.

Shortly thereafter, Noah made one of his infrequent afternoon forays into Lejeune Hall. He had come directly from his own NIS interview at the chapel and was somewhat invigorated, buoyed by the unaccustomed pleasure of speaking to willing ears. Thanks to his own hearing problem, the precise reason for all the questions and polite attention to his opinions had escaped him entirely. His mind remained set upon retribution for the holy water crime, among others.

"Miss Cassie," he began, "them NIS people got black powder all over the Catholic rooms, and it ain't coming out the carpet. I knew it was going to be a mess. As soon as I seen that stuff just like soot and these folks not caring where it fell, I says, that ain't coming out with the vacuum."

"All right, Noah," Cassie said absently. She and Sergeant Diaz had been hovering at the reception desk, ostensibly sorting mail but surreptitiously watching the NIS agent with Lance Corporal Ferris in the next room. Kaminski was chewing gum now, leaning into the doorjamb with folded arms, elaborately casual, gesticulating and apparently conveying a proposal of some sort. The lance corporal took his time, looking out the window, staring at the floor. He glared up at the detective and shrugged his shoulders.

"I don't know but what a shampooer might take it out," Noah went on resolutely, "but I bet you a dollar it don't."

"A dollar," Cassie echoed.

Turning in the direction of her gaze, Noah saw his least favorite miscreant and a burly white man emerge from the waiting room.

Agent Kaminski smiled benevolently at Sergeant Diaz. "Lance Corporal Ferris here has decided to accompany me to my office and give me a statement."

Ferris was escorted down the hall with the agent's custodial grip tight on his arm.

Noah gave Cisco a knowing look. "It done hit the fan now," he said triumphantly.

11

The events of this long day weighed like an anchor, burdening Damon with sadness to the depths of his soul. A young woman was dead, a chaplain assistant was suspect, and a sacramental stole had been debased as an instrument of murder. Murder, the ultimate sacrilege.

He had asked Father Roberts to accompany the casualty assistance officer to the dead girl's home, to break the news to her parents and help them plan her funeral. Three hours by staff car, they estimated, to a small town in the Amish countryside of central Pennsylvania. It would be Mark Roberts' first time. In his ignorance he was eager to go, once he had recovered from the perceived insult of interrogation, anxious to be of service. Hoping to be of use.

Better you than me, Damon couldn't help thinking. Casualty calls. He had pulled more than enough of that duty during Vietnam, enough to know that you never approached the front door of a house of bereavement with eagerness, not after your first time. There were no lessons in seminary or at Chaplains School to prepare you for what lay on the other side of that door. He had physically supported next of kin who collapsed upon him in their grief. He had been hit and cursed and spat upon. Each loss was the same, a precious soul and child of God, but each reaction to loss was different. People expect us to be good custodians, he reflected grimly. Even in wartime, they entrust their sons, their daughters, their lovers and husbands to our foster care, to the great uniformed family whose honor is wrapped in the flag. And they don't bargain for losing their loved ones to friendly fire or training accidents, to hazing or suicide. Certainly not to murder. Better you than me, he thought again.

It had been weeks already, but he had yet to decipher the walking enigma that was his chaplain subordinate, his brother priest. Damon had glimpsed among Roberts' personal papers an indication that his nickname was "Robbie," but nothing about the man's distant manner encouraged any familiarity. He made a stiff-necked first impression, just as Mac had implied he would. He was obviously on another, clearly pedantic, wavelength, and was unmistakably earnest. It was that very earnestness, Damon reasoned, which made Roberts vulnerable to criticism. He had witnessed as much already.

There was an unfortunate paradox at work here. Young people were particularly drawn to Father Roberts through what might be called his charisma—his musical talent and the sure magnet of his own youthfulness and good looks. Unfortunately they were at the same time turned off by his aloof other-worldliness and an intractable attitude toward sin. Roberts was the type of zealot who would have followed Christ into the temple, routing the dove sellers and moneychangers, and for that the people would have championed him. But in that scenario, because of his nature he could then not help but berate the people for suffering the ancient customs, and with the rebuke their support would be lost. Life is a great mystery, by no means simple even for the simplest of souls. Things are not always either black or white. For someone like Father Roberts, that truth could be learned only through personal experience, by touching the frayed edges of others' frail existences. This first casualty call might be one such opportunity.

Damon looked again at his appointment calendar, rearranged to a fare-thee-well, crisscrossed with postponements, cancellations and write-ins in red ink. It was a daunting schedule, by any man's standard. He would of necessity take on Father Roberts' commitments until the casualty assistance duties were finished. He also wanted to work in a brig visit as soon as possible, to see what could be done for Lance Corporal Ferris. As he understood it, the Marine had been confined as a flight risk, even though he was not yet formally charged.

Earlier in the afternoon he had telephoned Michael for an update and an explanation of all that was happening, in layman's terms.

"Apparently he made some sort of admission," Michael had told him. "The kid said he didn't want a lawyer, and then he must have told NIS what they were waiting to hear. They briefed his CO, and the CO wanted him locked up."

"Can we get him a lawyer?"

"He'll be assigned a defense counsel, requested or not; that's standard operating procedure. Somebody will be out there to the brig to see him within 72 hours."

"Can't you talk to him?"

"I'm a prosecutor, Damey."

"Oh, right."

Damon knew virtually nothing of Lance Corporal Jimmy Ferris. There had been time to learn his name and his dubious reputation, little more. He had been told that Ferris was from West Virginia, and at first glance it appeared that the hardscrabble life of Appalachia had leeched itself into his very bones. He was undersized, with a scrawniness about him that the Corps had honed into hardness. But for better or for worse, he had been with the chaplains for more than a year; there existed the sense that Ferris was "one of our own." The nagging fear that he could be presumed guilty and abandoned when he most needed a friend was worrisome. The Cap had floundered in discomfiture when informed of the arrest, then closed himself in his office. Perhaps Chaplain Stannard was not deserving of it, but Damon envisioned a disavowal in the making, one worthy of Pilate himself.

The chaplains' office was long secured, quiet as a tomb. It was nearing the dinner hour, almost dusk. Mia Rodgers was to have come in this afternoon for instruction. When he contacted her to postpone her lesson, she had kindly offered him a meal this evening, and he had accepted.

He set his appointment calendar aside, checked his wristwatch, and peered out the window. The sun was going to rest in the hazy hills beyond the chapel, tinting the world pink and gold. The color guard was standing by on the courtyard outside the front entrance of Lejeune Hall, prepared to retire colors. A bugler was poised near the flagstaff there, ready to sound the haunting strain that unfailingly reminded Damon of his childhood and the theme from the old radio and TV show, "Death Valley Days." It was beautiful, and on an evening such as this, as mournful as funeral "Taps."

Damon reclined in his chair to listen and watch the colors ceremony. Four young Marines, one of them a woman, stepping in unison, crisply correct, folding Old Glory into perfect points of red, white and blue. Honor wrapped in the flag. They are all entrusted to us, he mused once more, all of them, the heroes, the victims, our fallen comrades, the Vincent Capodannos and the Beverly Andersons. So many casualty calls, so many funeral details, far too many to count. *"Eternal rest grant unto them, O Lord, and let perpetual light shine upon them. May they rest in peace."*

At the reception desk in the darkened outer office, the telephone rang jarring coda to the bugle's faded notes. He pushed the button by the blinking light at his own desk.

The scratchy voice was muffled, the tone incredulous. "Why? Why haven't you told them what you did, priest? Confession is good for the soul."

Damon slammed the receiver down. He had meant to report the crank calls to the military police. They were coming more frequently now and were increasingly unnerving. He had meant to. Today just didn't seem to be the right time.

12

"You're a naughty girl, Colette."

It was obvious that the serenely self-possessed Mademoiselle Colette did not agree. Nonetheless, she abandoned her plan to spring from dinette chair to countertop, circling instead and settling gracefully onto the chair's tufted cushion to wash one dainty paw.

"Get down from there!" Mia swatted at the chair legs with a dishtowel, causing the cat to leap to the floor where, unruffled and unrepentant, she continued washing.

Mia was slicing beef sirloin as thin as she could, for stir-fry. She had already cut vegetables into neat piles, the broccoli and carrots heaped together, the onion, celery and mushrooms apart, to be stirred in after the beef browned. When the doorbell rang she overturned a clean bowl onto the carving board to cover the meat, just in case the cat got ideas.

But contrary Colette, predictably unpredictable, raced through the front door just as Mia opened it, so fast she was little more than an orange blur.

"Who was your friend?"

Damon was still in uniform, a bottle of rosé tucked under his arm. It crossed her mind that Michael, who had endured shouted obscenities from strangers upon his return from Vietnam, still wore civvies to and from work. He was rarely seen off the military base in uniform. And that

Michael was probably correct about Chaplain Keith; she might never see this priest in a Roman collar.

"That was my neighbor's cat, if anyone can own a cat. We sort of share her, actually, or she shares us."

"You've got to admire the independence of felines." He was looking over her shoulder. "Michael not here yet?"

"Not coming." She couldn't help that her lips compressed in a show of disapproval. "It's just you and me, I'm afraid. He had work to do, witnesses to prep or something." She was both annoyed and disappointed, and consequently a bit self-conscious. "I should get used to that, I suppose."

Damon thought it best not to comment, nor to waste an unseemly thought on what some people might perceive as an awkward situation. He followed her into the kitchen, murmuring to himself, barely aloud, that perhaps Michael had gone out to the brig after all.

Mia had heard him. "Oh, I doubt that. He's not a defense attorney, you know. He'll be prosecuting Lance Corporal Ferris, so he'll have to leave him alone. No choice there."

Damon was crestfallen. "You know about that business, then?"

"Of course I do. You must have called Michael right before he called me to let me know he'll be working tonight. Besides, Lejeune Hall isn't that big. It's hard to miss military police and NIS all over the place all day long." Her voice softened with concern and kindness. "And Cassie told me. I am sorry."

He thanked her. "Cassie's one in a million. Do you know her well?"

"I should say so. She was my first friend at Quantico. In fact, earlier today I was thinking of one of the first times we ate lunch together, at the Greek place down by the water. I'd wanted to go to the Globe and Laurel, I'd heard so much about it, but was shocked to learn they didn't serve 'unescorted females.' I was already in a bad mood because a local working girl named Joy had ignored one of our subpoenas, apparently left town. She stiffed Uncle Sam for the advanced witness fees and made us lose a contested court-martial." Mia reddened a bit. "I'd never met a prostitute or taken one's testimony, so I suppose I was also a little miffed that my curiosity wouldn't be satisfied. Anyway, I remember saying to Cassie, 'Do you think her first name is really Joy?' and Cass said, 'Why not? My middle name is Faith.' And then she rolled her eyes."

They both laughed. "That's our Cassie. During my first tour of duty at Quantico, Public Affairs was between your legal offices and ours. Their little adjunct recording studio for WQVA was next to the stairwell, with a 'silence' sign and a light bulb over the door. Cassie loved telling people she worked at the dead end of the hall, just past the red light district."

He was at her elbow now, watching her mince garlic and ginger root. Mia never cared for company in the kitchen while she was busy, no matter how pleasant the company. It tended to make her nervous. She was already disconcerted, given Michael's abrupt change in plans; she would indeed be an "unescorted female" tonight. Hoping to keep her guest occupied and to gain some breathing space, she suggested that Damon set the table in the dining room. "You'll find everything we need in the hutch there. I'm going to use an electric wok. I'll bring it to the table in a few minutes, and you can help stir fry, if you want." Damon moved obligingly to the cupboard she had pointed out. "I hope you like Chinese," she added.

He called out, "I like anything and everything. And Chinese is a treat."

Mia stole repeated glances into the next rooms while she finished preparations in the kitchen. The chaplain was arranging the place settings properly, hesitating only over placement of the chopsticks she liked to include, for fun. He found a corkscrew and decanted the wine expertly. She glimpsed him loosening his tie and shirt collar when he was finished, and trying the couch for comfort. The sight of Damon looking about appreciatively made her smile. She loved her rambling old house.

This was the first home Mia had not rented or shared with someone, so she had been free to make it wholly her own. The house was small enough to be affordable, but big enough for two. Or three, or even four. Its turn of the century charm and many architectural challenges had stirred her imagination. From the cozy bay window seats in the bedrooms to the corner fireplace in the parlor to the Victorian moldings, bits of leaded glass and converted gaslights everywhere, it bespoke a simpler, more romantic era. She had dressed the rooms downstairs formally in muted shades of blue-green and gray, accented with an airy yellow delicate as sunshine. The upstairs was decked out in the bright colors of Laura Ashley posies, braided rugs, stained glass lamps and antique quilts. She had sunk most of her savings into exterior repairs, new heat and air, and updating the bath; and there were countless hours of her own hard work in the paint and wallpaper, as well as in the refinished floors. She fervently hoped that Michael would want to live here after they were married, rather than insist on base housing for the proximity to his office or to save money. Even the best of base housing felt institutional; and the Officers' Wives Club—the pecking order, the endless white-glove receptions and formal teas—would be harder for her to dodge, living on base. This was one of the many things, important things, they had yet to discuss seriously. She found herself frowning again, but only for a moment. She saw that Damon had moved to the bookcase crowded with favorite volumes and knick-knacks and had found the pink conch she kept atop it. He was holding the shell to his ear, listening to the sound of the sea.

"This is some good chow," he told her later. He was no stranger to chopsticks, employing them well; he had polished off a third helping of ginger beef in no time.

"I'm glad you're enjoying it. According to Michael the best choice tonight would have been Italian, but I'm out of pasta, and this was easy to throw together."

Damon grinned. "He told you that because whenever a group of priests gather for dinner, it's invariably spaghetti. And every one of us thinks he has the best recipe for sauce."

"So do you?"

"Absolutely! Mine came from the wife of a friend of a cousin of the papal nuncio. The secret's in the Chianti, added last."

"Lots of it?"

He winked. "Exactly."

Damon was feeling good, better than he had all day. The best he had felt, in fact, since returning to Quantico. The food and wine had dispelled his tension and fatigue, and the company had made him feel—well, *good.* He wanted to help Mia clear the table, but she steered him to the parlor, insisting that he relax while she made coffee. Her manner reminded him of the way his mother had always catered to The Chief. As a young boy he had resented that for her sake, but he had come to realize that she served his father out of love and a need to be needed. It was nice to be spoiled by a pretty woman. His old friend was a lucky man.

Because Michael hadn't joined them, over dinner Damon had considered broaching the matter of Mia's missed appointment, but had decided to check the impulse. He was pleasantly surprised, then, when she brought it up herself.

"I've read ahead in the lessons," she admitted. "I told you that my family and I were never church goers. But I've always prayed, all my life. Even when I wasn't quite sure who God was, or if he cared to listen, I was talking to him. I was shy, and we moved a lot. Always new people, new schools. God, or my idea of him, steadied me through many a scary situation in strange surroundings. So I've decided it's appropriate that I have some education in religion now. It's been a long time coming."

She set down a tray laden with coffee and freshly baked lemon squares, and from the lower shelf of the coffee table pulled two library books. "This book says a little about each saint's life," she told him, "and this big one is on the subject of angels." She curled up on the couch next to him with the second book opened on the seat cushion between them. "The artwork is exceptional." She showed him stunning color plates of masterpieces by

Botticelli, da Forli and David. "The text goes into great detail about seraphim and cherubim and archangels, all that." She wrinkled her nose, one of the many nonverbal commentaries he was learning to recognize as spice in her conversation.

"But?"

"But it doesn't address the subject of guardian angels," she said solemnly. "That's what I most wanted to read about."

He studied her face and saw only a sweet sincerity there.

"While I was that shy little girl, my father told me I had a guardian angel who would always be near and keep me safe. You see, he knew he was going to die soon, and he wanted me to be brave. And I understood that." Her voice had gotten smaller, wistful. "I was only eight years old, but I was grown up enough to know why he told me what my mother later called 'a pretty story.'" She met Damon's gaze, which was still intent on her face, and her smile faltered. "I believed it. I always have. I feel there has been someone, or something." She closed her eyes momentarily, searching for words. "Like a safety net, a mental security blanket. As a child I pictured a presence, a strong but gentle spirit guiding me, protecting me from harm. If I were afraid of anything at all, I'd concentrate on him. My angel." She finished softly, "I ran to him, in my imagination, and he folded me inside his wings."

"And now?"

She inhaled deeply. "And now, for the most part, I think he's still on the job." Slightly flushed, she gestured toward the wine bottle they had nearly emptied. "And I think I may have had too much of that."

She was fascinating to watch, the way her moods were like light and shadow on her face. There was much of the child about her still, he thought, a rare simplicity of spirit that was touching, and oddly compelling.

"Did your mother remarry?"

"No. Never even dated. Never even thought about it, that I know of. Not that she would ever have told me." She was suddenly amused. "Okay, Psych 101. 'Aha,' you're thinking, 'no father figure throughout puberty. Undoubtedly affected her attitude toward men.'"

He denied it. "I was thinking," Damon said, "of similarities, of Michael's being without a mother since birth, and the early loss of your father."

Mia reflected a moment. "You're right, that's something Michael and I have in common. Probably had he lived I would have remained closer to my father than to my mother. I do love her," she added hastily, "but my father had a gift for fantasy and so much warmth. More spontaneity, too; he wasn't afraid to show his feelings. I would have gotten more mothering, in a sense, more nurturing, from my dad. Of course, in fairness to my mom, once he was gone I tended to idealize his memory."

"Your angel?"

She smiled. "Perhaps."

Her frankness emboldened him to part with a confidence. "I haven't been very close to my father since I was old enough to think for myself," Damon said. He recounted for her his family's diverse reactions when, at the age of seventeen, he had informed them of his vocation. His sister outwardly seemed pleased—he had since learned otherwise. His mother rejoiced, privately and publicly, to a degree that embarrassed him. But his father withheld approval and, never a demonstrative man, became more distant than ever before. The Chief sat him down for an unprecedented man-to-man, "the worry—no," Damon corrected himself, "the distaste coming through loud and clear." That speech was locked forever in his memory, vivid as though he had heard it only yesterday. *Are you sure, Damey*? asked over and over. "He didn't think much of our parish priest, Father Mahoney." Damon said. "Dad was fond of criticizing the old man. He said he lived in an ivory tower, a dream world of prayer books and rosary beads and useless outdated rules; that Mahoney's idea of suffering was having only one brandy after dinner. And there may have been some truth in that," Damon conceded. "I've known better role models. But my father said—I remember it distinctly—he told me, 'Praying isn't real work, not man's work.' He asked me if I ever shook hands with Mahoney. I hadn't. He said, 'His hands are as soft as a woman's. Is that what you want in life?'"

Damon had spread his palms before him as he spoke, recalling the disappointment, the hurt and confusion he had felt. Mia took one of his hands in both of hers and held it lightly, wordlessly.

"We never really understood each other," he told her, "but I respect him. And I've hoped for as much in return."

"Surely you have that." Her voice was soothing, her gray eyes luminous.

Very conscious of the intimacy, Damon withdrew his hand from hers. He picked up the first of the two library books and scanned the table of contents. All the old saints of tradition were profiled; the copyright and imprimatur dated the book prior to Vatican II. "I'll bet there's a colorful section on Saint Patrick in here," he said lightly, flipping through the pages.

"Oh, yes." She was animated again, all smiles. "Michael's patron saint. I read about him first, of course. Michael has the most unusual medal that was made in Ireland. All intricate silver handwork, and it has a lovely green stone in it, jade or maybe aventurine. He wears it all the time, and—" She stopped in astonishment as Damon opened his shirt and displayed its twin. When he told her the story of Michael's departure from the seminary she listened intently, her expression unfathomable. They sat in thoughtful silence for a long moment, until Mia asked mischievously, "And who is your patron saint, Damey?"

Damon smiled broadly and opened the book to the page he had thumbed, in anticipation of just such a question. "Saint Brendan the Voyager, Patron of Sailors."

"I thought as much."

He shrugged sheepishly, coloring slightly.

They devoted a scant but fruitful twenty minutes to reviewing her lesson over coffee and dessert, until a chiming clock reminded them both of the hour. Mia had docket call early the next morning, and the first of Damon's appointments was slated for eight o'clock. She wrapped some of the little cakes for him and beamed with appreciation when, at the door, he bent to her ear and whispered, "I believe in guardian angels, too."

The night air was pleasant, warm but less humid than it had been in the day, and smelling of freshly cut grass. Damon's car was parked in a pool of light from the lone street lamp on Mia's cul-de-sac. As she watched him walk toward it there was something, a furtive movement or the insinuation of one, which stirred behind her neighbor's hedges; and for a moment Mia sensed that someone hidden from view was observing them. She turned on her porch light and saw only Colette. The cat was closing fast on Damon, intent on wrapping his legs lovingly. He stooped to rub Colette's ears, and before he entered the car he waved.

"Well, that's a new one," Mia called from the door. "She usually doesn't take to strangers, especially men." That cat barely tolerates Michael, was what she was really thinking.

When the car's engine roared to life, Colette made a beeline for the house, grazing the ankles of her sometime-mistress on the way in. Mia stood in the open doorway, arms folded, until the Chevy's taillights disappeared round a distant corner. She was delighted that the evening had gone well, so much better than she had expected. So pleasurable, in fact, that it seemed almost disloyal to Michael to have enjoyed it so completely in his absence. As she pondered that bit of twisted feminine logic, a dog barked nearby. Slowly the sensation that someone was watching crept back upon her, and she shivered with it.

Closing the door abruptly, she turned to see Colette's hard green eyes fixed on her. The unblinking, all-knowing, inscrutable cat stare reserved for humans who dare to have secrets.

"Well, what are you looking at, you fickle thing?"

13

You damn well couldn't keep a secret at Quantico. That much was a given.

Harry Reiner shoved the medical examiner's report into the burgeoning file on the Beverly Anderson homicide, feeling increasingly like a disillusioned old man. In the few hours since the Report of Autopsy had been delivered to him under seal, certain details and confidences contained in it seemed to have become common knowledge among the denizens of the law enforcement services. From NIS the facts—often intact but more likely bent or fragmented yet still recognizable—as if by osmosis would be assimilated with impressive speed throughout the Criminal Investigation Division of the Provost Marshal's Office; and from CID and PMO they would leak in the form of rumors, hot and cold, from base Mainside to Q-Town and back again. By the end of the week every living soul aboard Quantico would have heard that the Anderson girl died three months pregnant. And over the weekend the kibitzers and gossip mongers from Fredericksburg to Woodbridge would have her ex-boyfriend neatly indicted, tried and convicted in the court of public opinion.

Ordinarily Harry accepted this phenomenon as part and parcel of the job, just one more indicator of a jaded and imperfect world; but this morning there was something unusually grating about it. Ed Kaminski had invaded his office, carrying his "#1 Stud" coffee mug. He sidled close to look over Harry's shoulder and with characteristic sleaze in his tone commented, "So Ferris off'd two for the price of one, the lying little bastard."

Harry bit his tongue for a moment. Kaminski was a good cop, but much enamored of the salacious and always prone to take the path of least resistance in an investigation. Any collar was a good collar, in Ski's book, and an easy collar was like found money. Pure gold. His boss's withering look didn't faze him, nor would his sarcasm: "I suppose you'll be wanting to add your observations to the M.E.'s." Mistaking restraint for invitation, Kaminski reversed the one extra chair in the office—straight backed, notoriously and purposely uncomfortable, meant to discourage—and straddled it, resting his chin on the chair back. He appropriated the case file from Harry's desk and proceeded to devour specifics from the autopsy report, lingering with appreciative grunts over such delicacies as "small tear without hemorrhaging noted anteriorly inside vagina, possibly consistent with postmortem intercourse."

"Damn!" Kaminski sucked an audible gulp of coffee and slapped the mug carelessly onto Harry's desk, slopping java sludge over a note pad. "Petechial hemorrhaging indicates victim was strangled, allowed to regain consciousness, and strangled again," he read aloud. He looked up, befuddled. "What the hell is that, some kinda pervert thing, or just inefficiency? Little bastard!"

"I don't know." Harry blotted the note pad with a wad of tissues from his bottom desk drawer.

"Don't know what?" But Kaminski understood what was coming.

"We may have the wrong man."

That possibility was dismissed with an impatient flip of the hand. "What, another one of your gut feelings?"

"There's . . . not . . . enough," Harry said slowly in "read my lips" fashion. "And what there is, is circumstantial."

"That's crap. And you know there's nothing wrong with circumstantial evidence. The fact of the matter is, they argued in The Sentry Box. Witnesses corroborate that, and the argument places him near the scene. Hell, he admits that he felt like hitting her, that he followed her outside.

According to this"—thumping the file folder—"his blood type is consistent with the kid she was carrying. That fact, plus the fight they had, establishes a motive."

"Suggests a motive."

"Whatever. He did it."

"I don't know."

Kaminski emitted an exaggerated sigh. He knew that he walked a fine line here with his superior. Reiner was Special Agent in Charge of this resident agency even before Kaminski joined the service, and with his priors first as a beat cop and then as a detective in Philadelphia, he definitely had the edge in field experience. But he was cautious to an exasperating degree.

Harry leaned forward in his swivel chair, propping his feet on that open bottom desk drawer. He rested his elbows on his knees and his chin on his folded hands, ready for verbal combat. "What about the confessional stole?" he asked. "What does that mean? And why would he use it, knowing it would be one more factor implicating him? That stole looks like premeditation, but there's no indication Ferris knew he'd run into Beverly that night. In fact, everyone questioned so far backs up his story that he was surprised to see her show up."

Kaminski riffled through the folder again, hunting an opening for a change of subject. "How about prints?" he muttered. "I missed that."

"There was a latent partial, probably a thumb, on her belt. Not enough to ID."

"Did they wash her?" More shuffling of pages. "Yeah," he answered himself, "here it is. 'Body was both treated with cyanoacrylate fumes and dusted with metallic powder for latent prints. No prints were developed.'"

Betty, Harry's secretary, stuck her head round the doorjamb, took in the scene and suppressed an impulse to laugh at the sight of Ed Kaminski on the "visitor's chair." "There's somebody here to see you, Harry. Father Keith."

Reiner sat bolt upright, shot the desk drawer closed, and hastily straightened the mess on his desktop. He rose when the priest entered the room, a reflex courtesy. Kaminski obligingly left, closing the door behind him, but not before shooting Harry a quizzical, wiseacre look behind the chaplain's back.

Damon sat in the chair the special agent had vacated, after turning it around properly. He looked a little embarrassed. "I don't know where to begin."

"Try the beginning."

He pulled a deep breath and frowned, as though bracing to tell something unpleasant. "I've been getting these phone calls," he said.

"What kind of phone calls?"

"Strange. Harassing. Disturbing."

Harry folded his arms across his chest. "Sounds like a problem for the telephone company."

"There's more to it," Damon said. "The caller keeps telling me over and over that he knows what I did. He says I should confess that I'm guilty."

"Guilty of what?"

"I don't know."

"And you don't know who the caller is?"

"I haven't the foggiest."

Harry ruminated for a moment, wondering why the chaplain had come to him. Suddenly it became clear. "When did you start getting these calls?"

Tensing, Damon ran a hand through his curly hair and rubbed the back of his neck. "The wee hours of last Wednesday morning," he said. He halted the absent-minded gesture and clasped his hands in his lap. "The fact that PFC Anderson was last seen alive on Tuesday is not lost on me, Mr. Reiner. But I swear to you, I know nothing about that."

Harry believed him, but he made no response.

"There have been maybe half a dozen of the calls since then. It started at the BOQ and the office, but now I've received them at home, too. He knows where to find me. And he knows who my secretary is; he called Cassie by name the first time he phoned the office."

Harry considered this. "But you don't recognize the voice?"

"No. It's rough, raspy. In an effort to disguise, I imagine."

"What exactly does he say, again?"

Damon pursed his lips. "It's usually something like, 'I know what you did, priest. Confess your sin.'"

Harry uncrossed his arms and made a note on the dry portion of the coffee stained pad. "He says 'sin'?"

"Yes. 'Confess your sin,' sometimes 'confess your guilt.' He says soon everyone will know what I did." Damon managed a nervous smile. "Including me, I hope."

There was a tap on the door, followed by Betty's head poked in again, Kaminski nosing behind her. "It's time," she said.

Harry took a set of keys from his middle desk drawer and tossed them overhand to the other agent. "Will you excuse us for a few minutes, Chaplain?"

Kaminski unlocked a wardrobe in the next room and hefted out a small portable TV that he brought into Special Agent Reiner's office. While he attached the TV set to antenna wires near the window, a number of people drifted into the office and several more congregated at the door. Damon surrendered his seat to Betty, but Harry motioned to him that he should stay. As soon as the East Room of The White House appeared on the television screen he realized what they were about to witness. One of those moments that would define an era. "History," Damon observed aloud.

"Yeah, he's history," Ed Kaminski observed. "Now Old Tricky is one for the books."

Nixon's military aide, Jack Brennan, lit up the TV screen in Marine Corps dress whites. "Ladies and gentlemen," he announced soberly, "the President of the United States of America." As the Marine Band played "Hail to The Chief," Richard Nixon walked on camera, greeted by applause, applause that seemed to go on for several minutes while members of his family joined him.

Harry signed the chaplain an invitation to move next to him, behind the desk. "Getting back to your problem," he said in confidential tones, "I want to record the calls from now on, with your cooperation."

"Of course."

"And if you can keep him on the line long enough, maybe we can get a trace."

"I can try," Damon said.

"Go along with him," Harry advised. "Do whatever it takes to keep him talking, without making him suspicious."

They turned their attention to the television. President Nixon had begun the resignation speech he had promised the nation the day before. He looked older than ever, tired and strained and teary eyed. "My mother was a saint," he was saying. Someone in the corner where Ed Kaminski stood sounded the raspberry.

"One thing more," Harry whispered. "I'd like to put a man inside the Chaplains Office, undercover. Not because of what you've told me, but because from our interrogation of Ferris and some others, it sounds like there's drug use, maybe dealing, among your troops."

Damon nodded; bad news, but no real surprise.

"You can square that with Chaplain Stannard?"

"It shouldn't be a problem. We're pretty much desperate for any kind of help. We were shorthanded to begin with, and now with Lance Corporal Ferris in the brig, there's a severe need."

Nixon was winding down. "Always remember," he said, "others may hate you—but those who hate you don't win, unless you hate them, and then you destroy yourself."

The little group dispersed in silence moments after the TV was turned off.

Harry was looking intently at his visitor. "You know, it's funny," he said, "I can't shake the feeling that I've met you before."

"That's entirely possible," Damon said. "This is my second tour at Quantico. I was here in '67, '68."

"Did you have any dealings with NIS?"

"Ye-es," Damon said uncertainly. "We had a break-in at the chapel, as I recall, some money stolen."

"Anything else?"

The chaplain hesitated, then nodded. "I remember being interviewed about a chaplain's assistant we had for a while. He was a former seminarian who had some emotional problems. I thought I could help him, but I couldn't. Didn't, at any rate," he said sadly.

"Any possibility that he . . . " Harry inclined his head toward the telephone.

"Oh, no, I don't think so. He's long gone; medically discharged, if I'm not mistaken."

Harry continued to eye the chaplain thoughtfully. "That must be it," he said finally. "That scenario sounds vaguely familiar."

Damon had noticed the label on the homicide case file. "Is it true that PFC Anderson was expecting a child?" he asked.

The grapevine again, news by osmosis. "According to the medical examiner, it is," Harry said, "but how did you know?"

"Father Roberts, casualty assistance. Her parents weren't certain, but they suspected."

Damon had gone to the office very early that morning, long before his accustomed time and well before the troops arrived to open up, and had been surprised to discover Father Roberts already there, playing his guitar softly in his darkened room. Caught somewhat off balance, Roberts had loosened up a little, and consequently they'd had what amounted to their first real conversation on a personal level.

The casualty call in Pennsylvania had been a bitter disappointment. Roberts described a middle-income neighborhood and a townhouse busy with bric-a-brac but devoid of the religious objects commonly found in a Catholic home. A middle-aged couple apparently devoid of the charity common to Christian hearts. "She was their only child," he told Damon, "the woman's natural daughter, adopted by the husband when she was a few years old. At first I thought they only seemed callous to the news because of remarkable self-control. But the longer we were with them, the more I was convinced that they just didn't care. They obviously had other priorities."

Damon had suggested that people deal with pain in varying ways, but Roberts was adamant and insisted that the casualty officer had formed the same impression. They had both noticed there were no pictures of Beverly anywhere, not even the near obligatory boot camp graduation portrait, although there were several framed photos of the parents and other persons displayed prominently. "They wanted to know if she was pregnant, and you would have thought they were speculating about a dog in heat." Father Roberts' eyes were puffy, his sensitive features weighted with sleep deprivation and an obvious disillusionment. He had looked and sounded as though he was about to cry. "No spiritual life there, at least none that I could see," he said passionately, "and Lord knows I was looking for it. No thought for the sacraments. The mother kept harping on how she'd been against the enlistment. Neither of them seemed interested in making arrangements for the funeral Mass. The stepfather didn't ask when her body will be released to a mortuary, only wanted to know how soon he can pick up her car. Can you believe it?"

Damon could. And Father Roberts would, in time. Casualty calls. They were almost always somehow different from expectations. That's what made them so hard.

"And what were their suspicions, exactly?" Harry Reiner was asking.

"Apparently she had called her mother, asking for money, and refused to say why she needed it."

"Did they mention Ferris at all, or do you know?"

Damon shook his head. "Not that I'm aware of." He told Harry about Father Roberts' impressions and of the memorial service planned for the next day. "The parents aren't coming," he said, "and since Beverly was fairly new here, Father Roberts is concerned that not many people will show up. I tried to assure him that her battalion and her work section would be well represented; that's SOP."

"I'll have Agent Kaminski attend, just to observe," Harry said. "He might pick up on something useful." He wrote again on the notepad. He also made a mental note to contact an NIS agent at the Philly Navy Yard who owned him a favor. Someone should pay the grieving parents another visit.

"And will we see you there?"

Harry held up both hands in a warding off gesture. "No need. Anyway, I'm allergic to churches."

Damon glanced about self-consciously, and nodded his understanding. He felt much the same way about police stations.

When he emerged from the NIS building onto sun baked Barnette Avenue, Damon felt scarcely better than when he'd gone in. There would be assistance now with the crank calls, and that was good; but the police believed the calls were somehow related to their murder case—he'd seen that plainly in Harry Reiner's face—and that was bad. It was a thought that Damon had avoided, had dared not acknowledge.

And until today he had allowed neither curiosity nor concern to draw him to view the crime scene. But now he detoured from the route back to his office, driving the extra half-mile to the traffic light where yellow police barricade tape could be glimpsed high on the hill above the intersection. He turned onto Neville Road, then onto the dogleg of a narrow side street lined with tidy white clapboard officer housing, steering the Chevy finally up into the one-way loop that wound to an overlook at the crest of the hill. The few houses here were dankly shaded, ivy covered, nestled against the steep rise like sedate dowagers in a choir loft, their yards little more than a series of slate steps and pathways descending among aged rock gardens.

Below the overlook the terrain fell away in terraces graced park-like with long-needle pines and fine old hardwoods, a serene and leafy sanctuary above the hot concrete and traffic. And it was there, where stately Waller Hall had long stood like a white ghost, on the most remote terrace, beneath the tallest cluster of aristocratic trees, that the obscenity had taken place. An irregular circle perhaps 20 feet in diameter was outlined there in yellow tape.

From this vantage point atop the hill Damon could see that a small splash of other, paler colors lay inside the circle. It was a bouquet of flowers. He stared at this incongruence until a horn sounded behind him. He must tell Father Roberts about the flowers, he thought, as he moved on, turning the Chevy toward Lejeune Hall. Some compassionate soul was mourning PFC Anderson, and Father would want to know that.

Naked save for slippers, Harry Reiner padded down the dark hall from the bathroom, felt for the door to his catch-all closet, and flipped on the overhead light inside. He had a hunch that he'd wanted to act on all day. There was a box on the top shelf that held a mélange of investigative miscellany that he had squirreled away over the years. Photographs, forensic reports, news clippings, bits and pieces of case files, the oddments that had piqued his interest or flicked his funny bone throughout his career. Whereas Ed Kaminski savored the "juice," the cases with sexy angles,

Harry loved the oddball incidents, the quirky complaints, the unsung yet memorable investigations; the red flags that alerted his orderly mind to the challenge of future possibilities.

He rummaged only a moment before he found it. An incident report from 1968, a complaint of harassment filed by one Cassandra Martin, civilian secretary at the Chaplains' Office, against a Marine named Winslow, who had proven to be a Section Eight candidate. He scanned the "results of interview" summaries on Cassie and Lieutenant Damon Keith. The harassment had been verbal and had sexual overtones. The good chaplain had been "too lenient/kind," according to Harry's scribbled margin notes, reluctant to send the ex-seminarian to the shrink. Winslow's command ultimately had referred him to Bethesda Naval Hospital for a psych eval anyway, and subsequently he was discharged as unfit. Something about the incident had caused Harry to save the file. Perhaps fortuitously.

"Harry!"

The fair Marilyn, his current lady, was calling to him from the bedroom, where light from the television screen flickered. Her voice even when it was not raised was shrill, too sharp at the edges—in notable contrast to her body, which was all supple and seductively contoured. She was too young for him, he supposed.

"Harry, you're missing it!"

Too young, too loud, but God, how he enjoyed the girl. He closed his eyes; his body was responding to her summons, shrill or not.

"You're missing Carson's monologue," she was calling to him. "He's doing Nixon."

14

His skin was peeling away, detaching itself, translucent and dead, layer after layer. It shuddered away from him like soiled gauze, leaving his nerve endings exposed, raw and vulnerable to the countless ice-fire shocks that bombarded from every side.

Nothing was as it should be. All was false, haywire, topsy-turvy. Everything was spoiled, ruined, fouled beyond redemption. They all were corrupt, all of them; it was much, much worse than he had suspected. He had no choice now. He would continue to warn and he would continue to watch, and he would wait. But they would have to learn that his patience was not endless.

And with the scalding chill of each new shock, his skin was dropping away.

Michael O'Shea fogged the lenses of his eyeglasses with his breath and polished them in his handkerchief. Before replacing the wire rims on the bridge of his nose, he squinted at his adversary, Vic McManus, who had just stepped to the podium to make a sentencing summation. The moment defense counsel opened his mouth, however, as though by magic the roar of gas-powered hedge clippers erupted outside the courtroom windows. He shot Michael a poisonous look, as if the prosecution had orchestrated the nuisance.

McManus struggled to be heard, making the dubious case for his client's good character, until the military judge—himself a master of killing looks—held up a hand to stop him and addressed the prosecutor icily: "Mister Trial Counsel, if you please?"

Michael scribbled a note that he passed to the Marine bailiff for delivery to the yardman, and within minutes the noise outside subsided. The noise inside was invited to start again, from the beginning.

McManus's spiel progressed from the few mitigating factors in his client's circumstance to the stigma associated with a bad conduct discharge, which included the loss of VA benefits and a supposed bar to government employment. It was his standard, cliché-ridden sentencing argument, tattered and worn but still serviceable before a military judge relatively new to the bench. Mia's face behind the Stenomask was unreadable, but beneath her table a jiggling foot betrayed her impatience.

Surreptitiously Michael eased his file on the Anderson homicide out from under the pile of papers pertinent to the present case. He would not request to make a closing argument this morning; if offered the opportunity to do so, he would decline. His work here was done. This Marine's record of priors read like a catalog of military offenses; nothing his counsel could say would save him from being sentenced to discharge. His court-martial had been simple, a UA guilty plea "dive," open and shut from the start, unlike the case Michael was studying in stolen moments.

With the Anderson-Ferris folder opened to a point about halfway through the NIS report, he neatly concealed the names written on the tab of the folder with the side of his hand. The subterfuge reminded him of the comics he had hidden inside textbooks in parochial school. His work in this court-martial might be virtually finished, but it still would not do for the military judge to catch the trial counsel reading documents from another case during argument. Michael glanced up at the bench. His honor appeared to be mesmerized by defense counsel's rhetoric, but more likely was mentally composing a shopping list for the commissary; it was, after all, payday.

Michael was well aware that Harry Reiner had a "bad feeling" about the Anderson murder investigation thus far. Reiner was about as scrupulous as Agent Kaminski was overzealous, but his hunches had paid off before. Admittedly, the case against Lance Corporal Ferris was weak. Nonetheless, there was a convincing case to be made. Jimmy Ferris had had the opportunity. It took little imagination to conclude that he also had a motive.

And if the prosecution case was weak, Michael thought, the defense case was anemic. Ferris was stonewalling Captain Dawson, his appointed defense counsel. The kid had already made that initial, ill-fated statement to NIS—the statement that Kaminski, the hot dog, called a confession—and that much had landed him not just in the brig but in maximum lockdown. Most likely the lance corporal had reasoned that further talk to anyone in authority would only make his situation worse. It was a touchy spot for an attorney to find himself in; his hands were effectively tied. And young Charlie Dawson, for all his enthusiasm, was comparatively inexperienced.

With a modicum of sympathy Michael looked from today's accused, sullen and resigned, to Vic McManus, still talking. Having paid his own dues as a defense counsel before being assigned the responsibilities of prosecution, he well knew that it was difficult enough to represent a client who's cooperative, especially when he's guilty. And his own gut feeling about Lance Corporal Ferris was just that. Guilty as sin.

He had interviewed a number of prospective witnesses within the past few days, people who had been at The Sentry Box that night, people who had known Anderson and Ferris as a couple. The picture they painted collectively was one of an intense, on-again, off-again relationship, its volatility inflamed by mutual jealousy. Michael was himself no stranger to the power of desire, but his logical mind could not understand that degree of obsessive passion. He equated it with immaturity, irresponsibility, even lack of intelligence. Add to that mix a combination of drugs and alcohol, and therein lay the recipe for violence certainly, potentially even for murder.

McManus finally sat down. The military judge announced that he would deliberate over the noon hour. All parties to the trial were free to go to lunch. Michael shuffled the Anderson file back into his briefcase. He wouldn't be going anywhere; he never ate on court days. He could spend some time with Mia, though, get her reaction to this case, her assessment of his performance in court today, maybe a wager on the sentence. He liked to solicit her opinions because he could always count on her objectivity. Or he liked to think that he could. But when he looked around for her, Mia had already disappeared.

"Is Father Keith here?"

With moistened forefinger Cassie Martin was capturing the poppy seeds and crumbs that had fallen from her Keiser roll to the paper napkin spread out on her desk. *Pat, pat, pat.* She answered Mia without looking up. Her mouth full of bread, she managed to eject the word "Chapel" and to jerk her head in that general direction. For the third week in a row she had taken responsibility for phone watch, and her mood had worsened with each succeeding day. The military, she reminded herself daily, were entitled to a full ninety-minute break midday, whereas she as a civilian on a time clock had a scant half hour for lunch, catch as catch can. She had already savaged most of her sandwich between phone calls and unscheduled visitors, and the rush had left her still hungry and uncharacteristically morose.

The waiting room was filling up with walk-ins. There was a giddy young couple—the girl alarmingly pregnant—wishing an interview to make initial wedding arrangements. The notion of marriage had at the eleventh hour struck the two of them like a thunderbolt, Cassie presumed darkly, and compulsive giggling was their coping mechanism. There was a Will and Baumer salesman who hoped to waylay the Cap and score a candle order. There was a toddler on the floor, gleefully ripping pages from magazines. His mother, engrossed in an intact back issue of *Good Housekeeping*, was doing nothing whatsoever to restrain him.

"What's the matter, Cass?"

Cassie shook her head, still bent to her task. *Pat, pat, pat.* She licked the seeds from her finger. It really wasn't fair to be stuck with phone watch every day. It wasn't fair to be stuck with a middle-aged metabolism, either, or the appetite of a teenager. *Pat, pat, lick.* A teenaged sumo wrestler.

"Are you all by yourself again?"

She lifted her gaze to Mia finally with a weariness that said it all. Mia was wearing Cassie's favorite summer dress of hers, a flowery jersey that clung to her trim figure just right, and she looked great, even with the funny imprint of that mask she used in court still circling her nose and mouth. "The phone's been ringing off the hook," Cassie said, "and people keep coming in without appointments—I don't mean you, of course, you're no trouble." She threw a scowl toward the little magazine editor on the floor of the next room. "But it's been hectic. I'm just having a bad day, I guess."

Mia pulled a half dozen Hershey Kisses from one of her deep pockets and laid them on Cassie's desk. "Bad day present," she said.

Mollified, Cassie talked as she peeled the silver paper and popped a chocolate bud into her mouth. "Father Keith is saying noon Mass, and after he grabs lunch, he was planning to go to the brig to see Lance Corporal Ferris. We had the memorial service for Bev Anderson yesterday, you know."

Mia knew. "What do you think of him, Cassie?" she asked suddenly. "You've never told me."

"Well, he's not the most likeable person, God knows, but I never would have thought Ferris was capable of—"

"No, no, not Ferris. *Damon.* Father Keith."

Was it her imagination, or was Mia blushing? Cassie didn't have to think twice about her answer. "Why, Father Keith is probably the most caring chaplain I've known. He's a good man."

Mia was nodding vigorously. "He's a very good priest, isn't he?"

"Yes, I expect he is."

"I never thought I would like learning about Catholicism, you know. I had no interest in that at all, really, except for pleasing Michael."

"I remember," Cassie said. "So Father Keith makes it interesting?"

"In a way. He's an interesting person, and it's his whole life. That's intriguing, you know?"

"Intriguing," Cassie parroted; without meaning to, she sounded skeptical.

"Well, it makes me curious. Makes me want to know more about it."

Some inadvertent signal, the rattle of foil paper or the scent of chocolate, had brought the small boy to his feet. He peered at them from the waiting room door, his senses alert to the fact that he was missing something. Cassie hastily unwrapped the last Hershey's Kiss and, shameless, crammed it into her mouth. She took some paper and colored markers from her desk and with a shred of real misgiving handed them to the child. "Here, sonny, go sit down and draw us a picture." To Mia she said, "I just remembered, Father Keith has something here for you."

She retrieved a paperback from his office. It was Billy Graham's *Angels: God's Secret Agents.* "He had me track this down in the Protestant lending library," she said.

Mia opened the book to a page marked with a cardboard scrap and read aloud the lines from the Bible which someone had underlined in pencil: "For he shall give his angels charge over thee, to keep thee in all thy ways. They shall bear thee up . . . lest thou dash thy foot against a stone."

No mistake, Mia was blushing now. Cassie made a mental note of it so that at the opportune moment she could tease her favorite chaplain about his continued effect on women. That old Keith charm, she was pleased to conclude, must be working overtime.

No sooner had Mia Rodgers left than an apparition appeared in the outer doorway, a lanky, ebony skinned vision in a canary yellow cutaway coat, white shirred tuxedo shirt and white trousers, sporting layers of gold—obvious, genuine gold—round the neck. "I'm looking for the NCOIC," it said. "I'm your newbie and I got a check-in sheet here." The well-manicured hand that proffered the dog-eared paper wore several heavy gold rings.

Cassie took the sheet and read in disbelief. "You're checking in wearing civilian clothes?"

"I'm still on leave, Mama. Just making good use of my time."

"I'm not your mama."

The vision grinned. "O' course not, fine young lady like you. You prob'ly too young to be anybody's mama."

Cassie ignored the snow job and studied the check-in sheet more closely. "I can sign this for you, Lance Corporal Johnson."

"Willie," he said. "You can call me Willie. Some folks call me Willie the Swoop."

"Is that right?"

"'Cause I swoop to the Big Apple every weekend."

"New York?"

"Center of the Universe." He was still smiling. Even one of his teeth was gold.

"Well, you know you'll be working most weekends here, don't you?"

The grin didn't fade. "We all got sacrifices to make, Lil' Sister."

"I'm not your—" Her eyes fell upon some numbers on the paper she was about to sign. "When does your leave end, anyway?"

"Tonight, Lil' Sister."

The grin froze as Cassie ran a fingernail over a flake of Whiteout. "I don't think so," she said. The telephone console lit up again. "So Willie, how are you at answering the phone?"

He was speedy, if nothing else. He rattled, "Chap'l-Offiz-Lans-Corp'l-Johnson-speakin'-sir," at a remarkable, unintelligible rate. His brow wrinkled as he listened to the caller, who had to be speaking an alien tongue. "Holy Day?" he sputtered, "Obligation?"

Cassie pointed to the Mass schedule for the Feast of the Assumption, posted on the wall above the desk. As Willie haltingly read from it she poured two cups of coffee and closed the door on the waiting room. Her day had taken an unexpected turn for the better.

In a van parked a half block away, NIS Agent Merle Parks chuckled and removed his cumbersome headset. He sipped some of his own stale coffee from a Thermos, making a face and wondering why he bothered. Then, taking up the clipboard and yellow legal pad he used as a log, he noted the time of day and beside that wrote one word: Swoop.

15

"I'm a sworn officer of the court!" Mia protested, as firmly as she could. She was at a decided disadvantage, trying to talk. She wanted to make herself heard, but her voice wouldn't rise above a croak, weak and quavering. She was trudging through a deep ditch in soupy mire, cold mud that was glue sucking at her shoes. The effort took all of her strength, and try as she might she made little headway.

Michael gazed on her kindly from higher ground where, warm, dry and relaxed, he monitored her progress. "You're a typist," he called softly, as though soothing a petulant child. "You talk and you type, and you are paid well for that." He smiled at her. "No need to fuss. You have yourself a rest when you get there, and don't wait dinner for me." She felt sudden hunger at those words, a hurtful emptiness in her belly. Both her shoes were off now, gone, swallowed up by the muck that was pulling like quicksand at her feet. She looked up. The cat was on the rim of the ditch, wearing a black and white Roman collar. It was reaching its paw for her, trying to save her, but God help her, its claws were extended.

She woke breathing hard, and a little sweaty. Her bedside lamp was still on. It was four in the morning. The angels paperback from the Chaplains Office had fallen to the floor; her page was lost. She went to the bathroom and drank some cold water, and looked at herself hard in the mirror. No insight there. She crawled back into bed, turned off the light, and pulled the extra pillow over her head.

16

A late afternoon rain was falling intermittently, the soft, soaking kind of midsummer shower that was the answered prayer of farmers, gardeners and groundskeepers. The sternly manicured lawn fronting Quantico's Correctional Facility was well watered by mechanical means when nature was not this cooperative. It consistently wore a lush green, its soft texture and deep hue the perfect complement to the pale brown brick of the complex.

As he dodged raindrops on a trot from the parking lot, Damon thought again that whoever had designed this bright new place had overcompensated for the brutal starkness of the old one. The former brig, vacant now, resembled a warehouse, a stout cube of naked red masonry with iron barred windows and a barbed wire perimeter fence. "The stalag." This newer facility was built of pastel block, clean and sleek, all high tech and high beams. From the molded plastic McDonald's ambiance of its dining hall to the scrupulously ecumenical motif of its little chapel's stained glass window—Bill Stannard's pride and joy—much of this innovative creation seemed contrived, taxed with masquerading as something other than what it really was, a medium security federal prison.

Once inside, Damon shook the rain from his head cover and signed in with the young Marine sergeant on duty on the outer quarterdeck. The sergeant announced the chaplain by intercom to the control center and gave him the coded key to a small safe repository. Damon removed his necktie and belt and placed them, along with his damp cover, his keys, his wallet and all the contents of his pockets, inside the safety box. He locked the box and returned the key to the duty desk. Moving along through a heavy compression door to the grille gate that separated the outer from the inner quarterdeck, he waited until, cued by an unseen hand, the steel bars slid open so that he could step through.

When the gate clanged shut behind him with that curiously hollow, echoing reverberation that never failed to chill him, a quotation from one of his favorite classics played and replayed at the back of his mind:

"Good of the chaplain to enter Lone Bay
And down on his marrow-bones here and pray
For the likes just o' me."

The chapel was situated off to the left immediately beyond the grille gate. It was simple reflex to glance inside. The room was empty, as expected; today wasn't Friday. The sixth day of the week was the one reserved for command visits, for Protestant Bible study, for Catholic confessions and Mass; and in theory, for Jewish Sabbath, although it seemed Jews rarely needed incarceration. To facilitate those ends the minimum custody prisoners were kept on the grounds on Fridays.

There was a gloomy character to all prison chapels, in Damon's opinion. Like meditation rooms in hospitals, they were burdened with a permanent atmosphere of desperate melancholy. This one was no exception, despite the daylight that streamed, whatever the weather, through the window's abstract shapes of colored glass, and despite the reassuring promise of the upright piano kept tuned and polished but rarely heard.

On first impression he had liked this little chapel, and usually he felt heartened by the restful light blue of the cinderblock walls, brightened here and there with the earnest if artificial cheeriness of felt appliqué banners. But today, with images of the memorial Mass for Beverly Anderson and that yellow taped hillside perimeter still fresh in his memory, images that collided with facts he had newly learned about Jimmy Ferris, all that forced cheeriness was oppressive.

According to Michael, Jimmy's unwed mother was killed in an auto accident in Wheeling when Jimmy was eight years old. His maternal grandmother relinquished his care to social services, and he languished in the foster care system throughout childhood, bouncing like an unlucky pinball from one underprivileged home to another. He aged out of the system at eighteen with a juvenile record for assorted misdemeanors that was expunged by a judge in exchange for enlistment in the Corps. Not an auspicious beginning for a military career, or for life.

The guard at the console inside the glassed-in control center was an Air Force enlisted man, someone Damon had not seen before. He bent to speak to him via the pass-through slot. "Lance Corporal Ferris?"

"He's in max, Cell Block 2," the airman said. Checking his closed circuit TV monitor, he added affably, "Just so you know, Padre, he ain't wanting to see you."

The only window in the maximum custody cell was on the cellblock corridor. It existed solely for the convenience of the guards, but through it Ferris clearly had observed the chaplain approaching. That was evident in the deliberate insolence with which he had turned his back. His posture was a pose, but the tension and frustration it communicated was genuine. He was seated on his rack, forearms resting on his knees, hands dangling. His head was hanging, his thin shoulders rounded. The shapeless blue prison uniform bagged on him.

Cellblock 2 was reminiscent of the old brig. Paint wasn't wasted here. Ferris's rack was no more than a cement slab outfitted with a rolled mattress, three inches thick. In cases of proven troublemakers the mattress would be replaced with another that was yet thinner, or it could be eliminated altogether. There was a stainless steel combination basin and toilet unit bolted to the floor next to the rack, and to one side of that was likewise secured a battered metal school desk, sans books or writing materials.

Damon stood in the cramped space between the solid steel door to the corridor and the locked bars that defined the front of the lance corporal's living area. A closed circuit TV camera was mounted on the inner wall above the chaplain's head. Like the caged red light bulb that aided the watchers' night vision, it was trained 24 hours a day on the prisoner inside the cell.

"I didn't ask for you," Ferris announced without turning around, before the chaplain could speak. "I don't feel like talking, I don't like being stared at, and I sure as hell don't want nobody praying over me."

"Understood," Damon said. Drawing a breath, "But I do feel like talking. There are things that need to be said here, so you'll just have to indulge me." He grasped the steel bars with both hands and waited until Ferris turned slightly toward him. "We haven't had time to get used to each other, you and me. If we had, you'd know something about me. You'd know that I like to talk to a captive audience; it comes with the territory. And the more I'm ignored, the more I'll find to say."

Ferris made no comment but permitted himself a furtive glance at his visitor, a quick sizing-up. From that angle Damon realized with a start that what he'd overheard this young man called, "the ferret," and had dismissed as inventive and unkind gossip, was rooted in some truth. His face was elongated and sharp featured, the chin receding. His pupils seemed small and glassy, like the antique jet beads Grandmother Keith used to wear at her neck. His wiry body would probably never run to fat; he had the feral look of a man who lived on his nerves.

"I've been told that you won't cooperate with your lawyer," Damon began again. "I may not know much about the law, except for God's law, but it doesn't take much legal savvy to see that by doing that, you're making a big mistake."

Again the head jerked in the chaplain's direction, and the small eyes darted, full of resentment.

Making a concerted effort to temper his words with some of the compassion he sincerely felt, Damon lowered his voice. "Look, I don't know you at all, Lance Corporal. But the people who think that they do know you—Smitty, Cassie Martin, Sergeant Diaz—they don't believe you could have committed this crime. They think there's been a terrible misunderstanding."

Ferris did not glance his way again. He was rhythmically clenching the muscles at his jaw line, probably grinding his teeth.

"And maybe they're right," Damon said. "Certainly I would like to think so." He paused for a moment in hopes his words would take effect. Dropping his voice to just above a whisper he added, "Only you know what is in your heart. Even if you are guilty, you still have the right to a defense. Giving up serves no purpose."

Suddenly the public address system barked: "Attention in the brig. All prisoners in secured areas. Stand by for a count." Prisoner Ferris pulled himself to his feet at that announcement and locked his body at the corner of his rack, facing the cell door as required. Standing thus at attention, he was forced to face his visitor but still would not focus his eyes on him. He appeared to be fully in control of his feelings, his closed expression set like stone. Damon decided to try another tack.

Speaking deliberately and kindly he said, "I didn't know the dead girl, of course. Bev, was it? I saw her photograph, though. She was very pretty. And I tried to find out a little about her. The most important fact I could learn was that she was going to have a child. Or at least that she was pregnant; whether she was going to have the baby or abort it seemed to be undecided as yet, according to her roommate." An emotion of some sort washed across the lance corporal's features. "That's a hard thing for an unmarried girl to go through," Damon continued, "especially a Catholic. And I don't think her parents would have been supportive, either way. Beverly must have been very troubled."

Ferris made eye contact finally, with something like loathing. The intensity of his stare was unsettling, and Damon was momentarily rattled by it. As he always did in every counseling situation, he was struggling to empathize, to imagine himself in the other fellow's shoes. He could comprehend grief, humiliation, panic; he could relate to the guilt that could well be driving this young man. But he was at a loss to account for the hostility.

Ferris had said something under his breath.

"Pardon?"

"We did it in the church," he said clearly.

"You did what in the church?"

"We did it in the chapel, me and her; on the couch in the choir room. We had sex there." Ferris smiled crookedly. "She said she didn't care if God saw."

If the lance corporal intended to shock or provoke the priest, he would be disappointed. Damon gripped the metal bars more tightly. "And why was that?" he asked quietly. "Was that because she loved you?"

All the control so rigidly mastered faltered as Ferris's eyes brimmed with telltale wetness. He swallowed several times and licked his lips, torn between the desire to keep his cool and a sudden, urgent need to make himself understood. When finally he did speak, it was with such vehemence that his entire body shook.

"Maybe I don't know if I did it or not, okay? I just don't know. I was too high on—on stuff to remember what all happened." He swallowed and breathed deeply several times, gathering his reserve again. He glared up momentarily at the closed circuit TV camera. "I do remember that I wished her dead when she told me about the kid. I remember that, all right. I didn't see how it could be mine."

Damon let go of the steel bars; his fingers were cramping, and they felt like ice. There it was again. Men and women. Love and hate, incongruous, entwined. His thoughts fled to the Bradys, and then to that hillside, its natural beauty spoiled by the unnatural acts committed there, the harsh necessity of "do not cross" police tape contrasted with the noble sentiment which had bypassed that barricade with flowers.

"Attention in the brig. Secure count."

Ferris slumped onto the rack and, taut as a coiled spring, resumed staring at the floor, his back again to the chaplain. His revelations were over.

Damon prayed silently, groping for Jesus, his Brother. The constant challenge was to find Christ in everyone, to be Christ for everyone. The Ferrises and the Captain Bradys of his world did not make the task easy, but he believed there was good in every man, waiting to be tapped. God made each of us, and He did not make us evil. When he had finished praying he said aloud, "Whatever you did or didn't do, Lance Corporal, please remember that we're here for you, we want to help. *I* want to help." He waited, but there was no response.

As he collected his things minutes later and signed out of the brig, the familiar quotation from Melville leapt crazily to mind once more. *"Good o' the chaplain to come to Lone Bay . . ."* Whatever else he may be, Damon reflected grimly, Lance Corporal Jimmy Ferris was no Billy Budd.

Outside the building the air was fresh and good; he filled his lungs with a cleansing breath. It was raining much harder now, and the temperature had dropped noticeably. Although he ran to the Chevy as if the devil himself was in pursuit, Damon could not help but get soaking wet.

17

With two discreetly placed fingers, Meredith Smith hitched up the strapless underwire bra beneath her sundress, then flicked out the ruffle of pink gingham that had wilted across her bosom. These critical adjustments completed to her satisfaction, she held a deep breath and examined her reflection in the Plexiglas that covered the announcement board in the vestibule of Memorial Chapel. She frowned. It was the best she could do, without padding.

She had not yet looked inside the church to discover which of the priests was hearing confessions today, one of the two chaplains or one of the civilian weekend helpers from Georgetown University. But with her mother waiting outside for her, it wouldn't matter. She would have to take her chances and be done with it. Peering around the narthex doorway, she counted the repentant souls slouched along the wall. Three before her turn, and no one she recognized from Quantico High. Exhaling with relief, she walked quickly to the end of the line. With fingers crossed for luck she turned, lifting her eyes to the nameplate above the confessor's door. Father Keith. Her heart sank.

Most of the kids she knew would take anybody at all over Father Roberts, he was so solemn and uptight, but Meredith preferred him. There was nobody cuter outside of the movies. And if you have to whisper dreaded secrets to a man in the dark, she had reasoned of late, it may as well be to someone drop-dead gorgeous. Besides, she thought smugly, Father Roberts was only uptight because he was young and sexually frustrated. They had discussed it at Marcie's party last week, she and Marcie and Toni Bates and Karen, and that had been the consensus of opinion. Sexual repression was responsible for fully half the world's troubles. It was a well-documented fact. Probably greed was what accounted for the other half, she reflected ruefully, twisting the ring on her finger. Probably so.

She glanced about her as she waited. There were only a couple people inside the church, other than the queue of penitents. One was a man in gym clothes who was huddled in the far corner of the last pew, and one was a pregnant woman with a rosary, who was seated on the aisle nearest the statue of the Holy Mother. It was interesting to speculate about strangers. Sometimes she and Marcie would sit on a bench down by the docks, feeding the gulls and making up stories about the passers-by. The man in the corner was troubled with something very serious, she thought, and was working up courage to confess. And he might feel self-conscious, wearing shorts in church; he was hiding his face with his hands. The woman with the beads was praying for her baby, of course. Or maybe she was praying for herself, because she was scared, or because she really didn't want the baby at all.

Meredith didn't pray as often any more as she supposed she ought, and when she did pray in public she was very conscious of how she looked doing it. Since she had left Catholic school behind in eighth grade well over a year ago, more and more often her thoughts wandered at Mass. Usually she found herself thinking about boys, or whether she'd make junior varsity cheerleader next semester or only the pompon squad; or worse, about the weekend homework she hadn't yet done. She wondered if God understood her stresses and concerns, His never having been a teenage girl on a military base. Life must have been simpler in Palestine. Well, up until the Crucifixion, anyway.

Her turn at the confessional came all too soon. She knelt down, careful to pull her full skirt aside so that it would not be caught beneath her knees and wrinkle, and hastily she crossed herself. "Bless me, Father, for I have sinned. It's been one—no, almost two months since my last confession."

"Yes?"

The void of silence to be filled with remorseful sincerity loomed cavernous in the dark. Meredith began as she had always begun, reciting a mechanical and half-hearted enumeration of minor failings, before reaching the precipice of her Most Serious Sin and Whole Reason for Coming.

"Is there anything else?"

"I—I did a selfish thing and lied about it and hurt my best friend," she said all in a rush, her voice coming out louder than she had intended.

"Tell me about it."

"Well, before school was out for the summer my girlfriend told me about an initial pin she saw at the PX that she'd just fallen in love with. It was 14 caret gold, very expensive; she was going to try hinting about it to her parents. You know, so they would get it for her birthday." She stopped short, fearing she was saying too much.

"Go on." Father Keith's voice was kindly, encouraging. It made her recall that he also was rather handsome, for an older man.

"When I saw it, I wanted it, too. Our first name initials are the same, you see. And it has a sapphire stone in it that matches my birthstone ring, so it was even more perfect for me. And since my father is a lieutenant colonel and hers is only a gunnery sergeant, her parents might not even have been able to afford—"

The shadow behind the screen cleared his throat, and now she was certain she had said too much.

"I bought it with my own money," Meredith continued, beginning to feel miserable again, "and I forgot about it. Until I wore it to her birthday party and saw the look on her face. It was like she just found out about Santa Claus or like I stole her present from her. I lied and said my aunt gave it to me." She paused to steady herself. "I don't think she believed me," she added, her voice faltering. "For these and for all my sins, I am most heartily sorry."

The silence at first was worrisome, but when Father began to speak, the depth of his patience was obvious.

"There's a saying that the truest mirror any of us has is the face of a friend," he said. "I think you have learned something from this experience, something about values and about yourself. Am I right?"

"Yes, Father."

"God gave us one another so that we might become closer to Him, through the love required for the daily give and take in relationships." He paused a moment, as though to let that thought sink in. "And Jesus gave us the greatest tool for relationships in the Golden Rule, did he not?"

"Yes, Father."

"For your penance I want you, first, to examine your conscience, remembering that when we care about someone, we put that person's happiness before our own. Can you do that?"

"Yes."

"The second part of your penance is not as easy. I want you to perform some act of generosity for your friend, and to at least consider being brave enough to tell her the truth. If you make it clear to her that you are owning up because you value her friendship, she will forgive you."

"You think?"

"Yes, I do. And maybe once that is done, the two of you could share the pin, take turns wearing it."

Maybe, she agreed silently, remembering Marcie's white angora sweater, which she might in turn borrow. "Sharing, that would be an act of generosity, wouldn't it?"

"That's right."

Having made a proper Act of Contrition and received absolution, Meredith proceeded to the altar rail. There, in addition to the three Hail Marys called for, she would pray the Hail Holy Queen and The Memorare, prayers doubly righteous to her mind, in that they had not been officially prescribed. And as she did so, she made a firm new resolve that she would concentrate on what she was doing rather than how she looked doing it. All the same, though, she thought, allowing one last moment of wistful vanity as she bowed her head, all the same, it was too bad veils had gone out of style.

In the cubicle Damon was smiling to himself. He supposed he had to have been that young and heedless once, although he doubted it. He stood up for a moment to stretch and to ease the stiffness in his knees, yet another proof that middle age would soon get the better of him. Hearing confessions could be an arduous duty during Advent or Lent and was a sure killer right before Easter, but today was a slow day, an ordinary Saturday in Ordinary Time; not many penitents. He picked up the *Catholic Digest* and returned to the article he'd been reading on Marian devotions.

Only a rustle behind the screen disclosed the presence of another person. Damon put his magazine aside again and made the sign of the cross. "God bless you," he said. "Are you ready to begin?"

A gruff whisper: "I have many things to tell you."

"Has it been some time since your last confession?"

"An eternity," the whisperer answered. "'Vengeance is mine; I will repay, saith the Lord.'"

The Bible verse took Damon aback. It couldn't have been less appropriate. "The Sacrament of Penance is not about vengeance," he exclaimed. "It's about forgiveness. It's about healing."

"We can't heal her," the voice behind the screen whispered. "She's dead."

Even as those cryptic words hung in the air, a dreadful realization crept upon Damon, beginning as a thread of fear in his gut, climbing to his collar where the hair of his neck was surely standing on end. It was the caller.

"What do you mean? What are the sins you wish to confess?"

"The sins are yours. I know what you did. Betrayal! Corruption! And you call yourself Melchisedech!"

"I don't understand. Tell me what you think I did. Tell me who you are."

"You call yourself Melchisedech. You are Judas!"

"And who are you?"

"I am the hand of God sent to smite the ungodly, the imposter-priest, the harlot." The voice had lapsed into natural tones, intimate, strangely familiar. "She *was* a harlot, you know, unclean, corrupt. She would have gone on tempting men, seducing, spreading sin and wantonness; she couldn't help herself. She had to be stopped."

"You killed her?"

"I stopped her"—now the voice sounded incredibly gleeful—"and they have blamed one of her lovers, one of your helpers." The croaking whisper was affected once more. "Will you betray me yet again?"

Damon's mind was reeling. The anonymous caller was Beverly Anderson's murderer, and was here, only inches away—a madman surely, and someone who knew him, someone whom he must know. It was confounding, too much to be taken in all at once. With the rustle of fabric again, the creak of a hinge, he was aware of movement on the opposite side of the confessional. The man was rising. He was leaving.

Suddenly short of breath, Damon felt a painful tightening in his chest. The confessional walls seemed to tighten upon him as well, as he was transported emotionally to the unsure days of early priesthood, choking on a rising wave of claustrophobia. There was no time to think, hardly time to react.

He fumbled at the latch of the cubicle door and burst through it, looking hurriedly about. There was no one. Hearing the thud of the heavy front door he ran for it, nearly knocking over a young girl in a pink dress on the steps outside. He saw a knot of women and children on the sidewalk, three parked cars, a family van. Frantic, he rounded the east corner of the chapel, scanning the lawn, the roadway, searching the horizon. Nothing. He forced several deep, ragged breaths in an effort to calm himself, to ease the pain in his chest. More and more vehicles were beginning to turn into the horseshoe drive, early arrivals for Saturday folk Mass, and the parishioners already here were staring at him in curiosity. His mouth dry, his pulse still pounding, he retraced his steps, picking up the confessional stole which had fallen from his shoulders.

Inside again, he checked the penitent's side of the confessional. No one. It was then that he glimpsed through the etched and frosted memorial windows a figure in running shorts, loping away from the rear of the church. Of course. The man had hidden himself—in the other confessional or behind the narthex wall, most likely—and had exited from the back, while Damon in his confusion had run to the front of the building.

Going quickly to the nearest window, Damon peered through a clear portion of glass. But even before he looked, he had guessed. The figure he had observed was already too far away to be overtaken and too far away to be recognized, save by his gait; but Damon knew the identity of that man instantly, intuitively, by the way he carried himself. He was as certain as if he had seen his face.

"You look as though you've seen a ghost." The sound of Mia Rodgers both startled and warmed him. He had pretty much expected to see her and Michael at this Mass. His friend had always loved the contemporary liturgical music, and preferred Saturday afternoon, so he could sleep in on Sunday.

"A ghost? No, nothing like that," he said lightly. Glancing past her, he saw that Michael had already taken a front row seat. He usually maneuvered near the guitarists, so he could shoot the breeze with them as they tuned up.

"I wanted to thank you for the book you loaned me," Mia said. "I've very nearly finished it." She was smiling up at him uncertainly. "Are you all right?"

It was like her to notice that he was shaken; more specifically, he thought, it was like her to care.

"I'm fine," he said, but he must have sounded unconvincing, for she nodded as though he had dismissed her, and gently touched his arm in an overture of comfort.

"These windows are beautiful, aren't they?" was her parting comment.

He watched as she went to join Michael. She genuflected with an uncommon grace, as though she had been bowing to God all her life. The act called to mind a dream. He seldom remembered his dreams upon waking, but last night had been different. He and Michael were struggling in heat amid bursts of fiery light and the wrenching cries of wounded. In the dreamscape he was then shifted to a neutral place, neither hostile nor friendly, but cool and very beautiful. Michael was no longer with him, but he knew that Mia was there. He caught her scent and could sense her near him as he searched for her. And all the while Vince Capodanno, covered in blood, was sadly shaking his head.

Damon was beginning to harbor a tender feeling toward Mia, and on the whole that made him uneasy. Physical attraction to a woman, any woman, was one thing, natural and unavoidable. Spontaneous affection for an appealing personality was also just part of being human. Something entirely different was the combination of those emotions. That experience was new to him, or so long buried in memories of his youth as to seem new. He was used to exercising all the recommended ploys for avoiding carnal thoughts or temptations—averting one's eyes, calling upon *lectio divina* for focus, intense, frequent prayer. But these people were his friends. He felt changed now when he saw Mia and Michael together, a reaction different from the sincere happiness he had felt for them the evening he had first seen them as a couple. He could not—would not—call it jealousy, but there was an alien element of pain and resentment that pulled at his heart.

Having caught Michael's eye, he returned his nod of greeting with a sense of betrayal. Betrayal. Was that not what the voice in the confessional had said?

Damon gazed at the window through which he had glimpsed his tormentor running away. This one was the Civil War commemorative. The Scripture etched in its lower panes beneath a vignette of the Monitor and Merrimac was from Proverbs: "A brother offended is harder to be won than a strong city." He sighed deeply as he went to the sacristy to prepare for Mass. He had much to think and pray about.

18

The coffee was too strong even by Marine Corps standards. The doughnut box had been left open since 0630; the doughnuts tasted day-old stale. The late morning sun beaming through the jury room's broken window blind caught Michael in the eyes, no matter how he positioned his chair to avoid it. Was there an unwritten rule that Monday docket call had to be a purgatory for the unfortunate bastard responsible to wrest order from chaos? He squinted at this week's gathering of legal clerks, court reporters, attorney colleagues—yammering wisecrackers all—and raised his voice above the tumult in an attempt, as he was wont to say, to "move it along."

"Okay, people. Benson. Those charges have been preferred. Who's his counsel?"

Maryann Phillips, their newest judge advocate and most junior lieutenant, spoke up, her diffidence all the sweeter for the smear of doughnut jelly on her mouth. "I'm assigned to that one, sir, but I just received the package yesterday. I haven't met with the accused yet."

"Then he has a treat in store," called an appreciative voice from the other end of the table.

"Thank you, thank you," she acknowledged; a modest grin.

"Benson, is that the barracks larceny?" someone asked.

"No, that one's Bennett. Benson is forgery; bad checks, a lot of them," Vic McManus said.

"Another paper case?" muttered Mia from her corner. "I hate paper cases." Reams of evidence to be photocopied, endless numbers to be transcribed, proofread, and proofed again.

"But you'll like this one, Mia," McManus called over his shoulder, forgetting for the moment which side he was on. "Hearts and flowers comedy. Benson 'finds' a checkbook," he said, making air quotes, "goes on a spending spree to impress a girl, picks out gold jewelry, lingerie, Godiva candy, the works. But he goes to a PX salesclerk who knows the very Marine whose account he's ripping off. Plus he makes some of the checks out to himself!"

"Now, there's a world-class brain," muttered the trial counsel assigned to prosecute the case. "Ah, the mind of the hardened criminal. How I do love a challenge."

"Yeah, Miss Rodgers," called a review clerk, "they can't all be messmen gone wrong."

"What do you mean?" asked Maryann.

"Mia's favorite charge sheet. Some Joe Shmuck on mess duty, 'willfully wilting lettuce in the officers' mess.'"

"How do you do that?"

"By running hot water on it."

"Was he convicted?"

"Is there military justice?" two wise-asses chimed in unison.

"Okay, okay," Michael said. "Benson's not locked up. We're looking at three weeks from today to docket this one. That should give both sides enough time. What do you say, defense counsel? Guilty plea, trial before judge alone?"

"I can't commit to anything until I've talked to my client, sir." Lieutenant Phillips had just discovered the errant scattering of confectioner's sugar on the front of her uniform blouse and was diligently brushing at it, making it worse.

"Maybe he'll buy you something pretty, Maryann," someone teased.

"A bib would be nice," she offered good-naturedly.

"Okay," Michael allowed, grudgingly making the notation on the court calendar. "We'll carry it on the docket as a contested case for now, and leave the forum open as a jury trial." He narrowed his eyes against the sun and attempted a stern look at her above his eyeglasses. "I want to be notified the minute that changes, all right?"

"Yes, sir."

"Okay, the Swanson case is set for a week from Thursday. No witness availability problems on that one?"

"We're ready to roll."

"Good. What about Bennett?"

"He's willing to deal," McManus reported. "He'll plead to willful appropriation if the government drops the assault charge along with the larceny. The proposal is with the convening authority now, and it's almost a hundred percent certain to be approved. Bennett still wants a jury for sentencing. We're all set for Friday."

"My victim wants to testify real bad," Vic's opposing trial counsel observed. "The deal's going to break his heart."

McManus shrugged. "You can still parade your cast of characters in aggravation on sentencing," he said complacently. "They might buy the unfortunate Mr. Bennett a little more brig time."

"All right, Bennett's special court-martial on Friday," Michael confirmed, raising his voice again. "We've already talked about Byrne, Kennedy and Williams," he added, gaining momentum. "That brings us to Ferris."

"Speaking of the criminal mind, there's a genius for you."

"What's he doing over there in max, re-inventing the wheel?"

"Yeah, the Ferris wheel."

"Our Charlie's getting an inferiority complex."

Charlie Dawson, Lance Corporal Ferris's defense counsel, smiled wanly. "He still won't talk to me, sir," he said. "His brig counselor says the control center watch reported that he opened up a little to Chaplain Keith a while ago." Michael and Mia exchanged glances at the mention of Damon. "But I checked it out, and the watch didn't overhear anything that would amount to a defense. I have Ferris scheduled for a psych eval at Bethesda Naval Hospital tomorrow, but I don't expect much. The kid's competent. He's just stubborn."

"Face it, sir," offered one of the clerks, "you got a loser there. Why would he cop to it if he didn't do it?"

"Yeah, and what about a polygraph?" someone else was asking simultaneously, talking over the other. "Would he submit to a lie detector test?"

"The government don't need it," the first clerk retorted. "They got enough. Ferris the Ferret is as good as cooked."

"That will do!" Michael chided.

Captain Dawson shook his head. "I decide nothing until I see the report of the psychiatric board. We may waive the pretrial investigation, and we may be willing to plea bargain. At this point, I just don't know."

Michael announced that he would pencil in the pretrial investigation for week after next, contingent upon the psychiatric board's report. He didn't give voice to what he was thinking, that so far Charlie Dawson had very little to bargain with.

Damon sat alone in his office with the door closed, his unseeing eyes fixed on the telephone. He had been undisturbed for nearly an hour, a respite from customary routine so rare as to be considered a blessing. Normally he had little opportunity to lose himself in thought, so lose himself he had, completely.

He was positive now that the person who had been plaguing him with phone calls was Gary Winslow. He had thought that when he glimpsed the man hurrying away from Memorial Chapel on Saturday evening. Winslow had always displayed a very distinctive carriage; not truly bowlegged, but a stride with his legs far apart, as though an invisible object spread them. It was a gait Damon had observed in men used to straddling horses, although Winslow so far as he knew had never been a rider. The characteristic was simply a part of his physical makeup, as distinguishing as a birthmark. It was that trait which Damon had recognized in the figure retreating from the chapel grounds, and it had been enough to trigger a memory. Since that electrifying moment his memories had become increasingly vivid, had crystallized to the point that he was now unshakably certain not only of the identity of the caller, but of his motivation as well.

He had first encountered Gary Winslow when Winslow was a child of six or seven, although he really did not remember it. Years later Winslow described to him how he had cheered for Damon Keith, wide receiver, through his long run to the decisive touchdown in an otherwise forgettable outing by Our Lady against Norfolk Western High, and how he had met his hero after the game. The introductory meeting Damon did recall took place much later, during a visit to his parents a few summers after ordination.

Winslow had approached him outside the Keith family home, identified himself as a former classmate's cousin, and had walked with Damon to Mass. Along the way he talked about the vocation he had discerned and his desire to attend St. John Vianney Seminary. His grades were not exceptional, he'd admitted candidly, but they were consistently respectable. Perhaps most convincing was his claim of a flair for public speaking; drama and debate were his chief interests, after religion.

Gary Winslow made an indelible impression on the young Father Keith during that stroll to church. He spoke passionately about his faith and convictions on issues of morality, interspersing compelling original thought with Bible verses he had committed to memory. Touched by the intensity of the young man's sincere determination, and flattered by his unabashed admiration, Damon ultimately gave him a letter of recommendation for the vocations director at St. John's.

With increasing interest, then, he followed Winslow's erratic progress during his first five years in seminary. By most reports he held his own, advancing admirably through the theology maze, stumbling through the quagmire of social sciences, until sometime in the sixth year of studies, when all indications were that life had somehow gone haywire for Gary Winslow. His infrequent communications to Damon became more and more puzzling. There were embarrassed accounts of Winslow's bizarre behavior from Damon's acquaintances on the sem's teaching staff. As his grades followed his conduct on an unacceptable downhill slide, it became inevitable that the seminary would finally let him go; and just as inevitably, he was reclassified 1-A by Selective Service.

When word reached Damon at Quantico during his first tour there that his former protégé was not simply enduring Marine Corps boot camp at Parris Island but would emerge with a meritorious promotion to private first class, he made what he considered at the time to be a wise administrative move, rather than an overture of charity. He asked his senior priest to exert influence to divert the PFC's first orders assignment from Infantry Training School to the Quantico Chaplains Office. That was how Gary Winslow came under the protective wing of his would-be counselor, mentor and friend. And that series of events began the most regrettable episode of Damon's priesthood.

The confident young man who in the early going had assimilated well to the insular, tightly structured world of the seminary, who had thrived on the yet more rigid controls of boot camp, foundered dismally when confronted with the relative freedoms of daily life in a stateside military. Of course some adjustment difficulties were to be expected. As a junior enlisted man, the seminary dropout was older than his peers and superior to them in education, while his social skills and worldly experiences were markedly inferior. But PFC Winslow's troubles went far deeper than the obvious. The questions of morality that had concerned and agitated him, even as a youngster, had acquired new significance in young adulthood and had assumed a grotesque shape. He was both obsessed with sexuality and repulsed by it; he saw lewdness and thus temptation to sin everywhere. And poor Cassie Martin had borne the brunt of his abuse.

No matter to Winslow that Cassie was newly married, as decorous a young woman and as decent a soul as the chaplains could hope to employ. Everything she wore, every word she spoke, every move she made, he perceived as provocative and vile. He set about making her daily existence wretched, her persecution his unholy crusade. He stalked her; he criticized her persistently; he embarrassed her before visitors to the office.

To her credit, Cassie brought the matter in confidence to Father Keith before she resorted to making an official complaint. But there was little Damon could do. He tried talking with Winslow but couldn't reach him. He tried assigning tasks which would keep him away from the office most of the day, only to hear that Cassie was haunted with invective and Biblical admonitions by telephone, or that he was lurking in the parking lot to accost her at quitting time. Damon attempted more formal counseling, but rational discussion was impossible, and threats of disciplinary action fell on deaf ears.

What authority could the military have, after all, over someone who believed himself empowered by God? Gary Winslow demonstrated day after day, week after week, that he was becoming more severely disturbed. By the time Cassie reported him to the military police for trailing her home, his company commander had already requested a psychiatric evaluation. And this, Damon recalled with some irony, was at a time when, given the political climate, peculiar behavior patterns were commonly suspect and often ignored. With war protest at its height in 1968, "conscientious objector" was the catchphrase of choice for discharge seekers, and "mental disease or defect" emerged in the most unlikely psyches.

Coincidentally, immediately before his referral to Bethesda Naval Hospital for evaluation—a journey that became for Gary Winslow a one-way trip back to civilian life—he had come to his friend Father Keith in confession, unburdening himself of hideous imaginings, or sins that Damon prayed were imagined. Had Damon been permitted to divulge the content of that frightful confession, he could have attested that in his layman's opinion, Gary Winslow was indeed psychotic. And that, he reasoned, could well be the "betrayal" Winslow blamed him for. He had confessed to his priest in one instant and in the next had found himself confined to a psychiatric ward, being processed for discharge.

Damon had felt despondent, even guilty, for a long time over his unwitting role in bringing Winslow's illness to the point of crisis. He should never have interfered and brought him here. His efforts at keeping in touch after the medical discharge had failed when letters to Winslow's home address of record came back unopened. He had always tried to keep the lad close in prayer, but that clearly had not been enough. Where had Winslow been in the intervening years? Why was he here? Why now, and why poor Beverly Anderson?

Cassie tapped on his door and opened it enough to lean in. "Call for you," she said, holding up two fingers to signify which button he should push. She worked her eyebrows mysteriously, and disappeared. He reached for the receiver with a tingle of apprehension. But the agitated voice on the other end was not Winslow's.

"What are you doing back there in Marine World, Damey Boy-o, plotting an insurrection?"

"Mac!"

"The feds tracked me down on leave to grill me about my comings and goings, about Jimmy Ferris and his girlfriend, Mass vestments—what in the name of all that's holy is going on?"

"They didn't tell you what it was about?"

"NIS tell? You must be kidding! They're in the dis-information business, Boy-o. They didn't tell me a thing. All they did was ask questions, ad nauseam."

Damon thought of the tap on the phone. It was strange, knowing that your conversations were monitored.

"The Anderson girl was murdered, Mac."

"Holy Mother of God!"

"I'm sorry. You knew her, then?"

"I did. I did that. I thought it was something to do with a theft at the chapel, or with marijuana, knowing Jimmy Ferris. Well, that's—that's a tragedy, for certain."

"They have him in the brig for this."

"Ferris?" Father Mac sounded surprised. "He didn't do it, surely."

"I don't think so myself, but it doesn't look good for him. What can you tell me about him, and about her?"

There was a silence on the line. Damon could visualize Father screwing his broad brow in thought. "Hard to say what he is like," Mac said finally, "other than weak. Or what he could be if he wasn't always fooling with the drugs. He's not a bad kid, but a kid still and wanting everything now, this minute. He's defiant, resentful of authority; doesn't belong in the military."

"And Beverly?"

"A bit of a Magdalene, that one, and not in a good way. She came to me for counseling a couple of times. Pretty girl, God rest her, and brighter than most, but looking for answers—for approval—that I just couldn't give her. Looking for someone to 'love her back,' as she put it, to give more than take. But she kept looking in the wrong places."

"Jimmy Ferris?"

"Him, and before him others. From what she told me—never meant as a confession, now, never apologies; she'd come to church from time to time but never take communion—I gathered she'd had friends or family back home who were in the life, and that she may have even tried that herself for a while, or considered it."

"In the life?"

"Sorry," Mac said, "it's my years with a halfway house in Hell's Kitchen, before the Navy. By 'In the life' I mean turning tricks; prostitution."

It was Damon's turn to knit his brow. "She was expecting a child," he said.

"Dear God."

Damon's thoughts were jumping from one riddle to another. "Ferris was high on something the night she was murdered, angry about the pregnancy. He doesn't remember killing her, yet he seems willing to accept the blame."

"That doesn't sound like Jimmy."

"I think he loved her."

"Told you about their escapade in the church, did he?"

Damon was more conscious than ever of the hidden listener on his line. He felt he was exposing a confidence, sharing secrets that NIS need not know. Deftly he brought the conversation to an end, begging off with the excuse of an appointment; but not before getting Mac's number so he could call him back from an untapped phone.

19

There's more," Damon told Pete McLaughlin moments later, "and for this I ask you to share in the seal of confession."

"Go ahead," Mac said. "I'm listening."

"I think the man who did kill Beverly Anderson came to me in the confessional on Saturday."

Mac's breath whistled as he exhaled. "You say you think so. Did this person confess doing murder?"

"No. There was an admission, but there was no confession of sin, only the rambling of a sick mind. And there's no remorse. He knows that someone else is blamed for what he did, and he's happy about it. The only reason he came to me was to torment me with the knowledge of it."

"You know him, then?"

"I'm sure I do. I didn't really see him, just a glimpse from the back, at a distance. But I know who it was. I feel it in my gut."

"Well?"

Damon fought to subdue the threat of tears by blinking hard. "An ex-seminarian, a young man I tried to help a few years ago when I brought him here as a chaplain's assistant. He was put out of the Corps with a medical discharge, a psyçhiatric case." He swallowed the lump in his throat. "I failed him, Mac. He trusted me, and I let him slip through the cracks into God knows what oblivion."

"Damon—"

"No, it's true. The boy cast me in the role of his spiritual father, and I should have been there for him. I was intrigued so long as he made good grades in Greek and wrote entertaining letters. When he washed out of the sem, that would have been it, from my perspective. But he ended up at Parris Island and did well there, and that interested me again. Once he reported to me for duty, though, and I saw how messed up he really was, I didn't try hard enough to save him. I put him into a situation where he was bound to fail—I should have seen that—and when he did fall apart, I wrote him off."

"But what could you have done for him, realistically?"

"I don't know. Once he was a civilian again, there were steps I could have taken to locate him, to keep in touch." Here his voice broke. "I could have prayed harder for him and more often."

"Just whose confession is it you're sealing me to?"

Damon had to smile faintly at McLaughlin's perceptiveness. "Mac, I honestly don't know what to do. Ferris is sitting over there in the brig willing to be tried for murder—for *murder,* Mac—because he was too doped up to remember what he did or didn't do that night. And here I sit on information that could set him free, or at the very least could point the authorities in the right direction."

"You have no choice. You don't need me to tell you that. Whether the man was competent or not, you can't speak of anything you learned from him in confession."

"This was hardly a confession."

"That doesn't matter. You know that." Mac paused. "And consider this. You admit you're going largely on a gut feeling. You might be wrong."

Damon thought again of the eeriness of that voice from the darkness; "Judas," it had whispered. He wasn't wrong.

"Damon?"

"Yes."

"Remember the examples our instructors gave us in seminary? The poisoned altar wine, that's a classic."

"I remember."

"The confessor can't cry out to save the Mass celebrant, but he can sprint to the altar and knock the chalice from his hands. I think that's why subconsciously I'm most comfortable wearing Nikes under my cassock." Mac paused again. "The point is, a priest can't speak of what he learns in the confessional, Boy-o. But he can act."

There was little else to say. They each promised to keep in touch. After he replaced the telephone receiver Damon looked about him, taking in the details of the room for the first time. He had told himself that he would walk down the hall to the legal department looking for the first available phone, but in truth he had come directly to this empty room, had stopped at her door. Not at Michael's door, but at Mia's. He had not entered her office before, but he had seen her behind this desk, sitting in this brown chair, before this window. There were African violets on her windowsill, where the familiar view of the parade deck and the chapel mirrored his own. There were two photographs on her desk, one of her mother, by the look of the pensive woman with gray hair and gray eyes so like hers, and one of Michael and Mia in evening dress, a memento from a Marine Corps Ball.

Why did it make him ache so, this unreasoned need? For it was a need; that was truth, much as he should deny it. He needed now to be near her, near anything that was hers or was of her. He needed not merely closeness, but her closeness. He wanted to talk with her, to tell her of his hurt and uncertainty, to hear her ease him with a word.

She had shown up at noon Mass one weekday after their dinner together. Her sudden appearance had surprised and shaken him somewhat, but she had ultimately charmed him with her air of rapt discovery. The liturgical prayers that were rote and tradition to him, as natural as drawn breath, were still fresh and new to her. She had returned often on weekdays when he was celebrant, until he now watched for her at noon and missed her when she did not come. It was dangerous, this emotional attachment to a woman. And more than that, it was shameful, in that this woman was soon to be his best friend's wife.

Damon stared momentarily at the photograph of Michael and Mia, she in a satiny ball gown, low cut and green, he in his dress blues. Best friend. He had hardly given it thought before, but certainly Michael was that, even though they'd had little contact over recent years. There was no one Damon felt closer to, no fellow priest or Protestant chaplain, no seminary classmate, no family member. No one. The priesthood had its emotional and spiritual rewards, but in all honesty it was a lonely existence. Companionship was rare, and faithful old ties were precious. He and Michael O'Shea shared much in common, and he was ever grateful for that.

The smiling pair in the photograph stared back at him, teasing. *Some things cannot not be shared*, they seemed to say. He took one last look around him before he quit the room, knowing as he did so that the picture of that happy couple would follow him, a persistent reproach. Some things could not be shared.

The new lance corporal, Willie, was draped on the threshold of the Chaplains Office suite and appeared to be waiting for him. He cut a dapper figure in his impeccably tailored uniform, almost a poster Marine, were it not for his bearing, which was as laid back as a snake's in the sun. "NIS calling for you, sir. Mr. Harry Reiner." Willie the Swoop pointed not one, but three long fingers burdened with chunky gold toward the telephone receiver laid on the reception desk.

"I'll take it in my office," Damon said; and once back there, he listened for Willie to replace the receiver before he spoke.

"Ya, Chaplain," Agent Reiner acknowledged. "You haven't had any more of those crank calls since we started surveillance." It sounded as much like an accusation as a statement of fact.

"You're right, I haven't."

"That's the way it goes," Reiner observed, adopting a friendlier tone.

"I guess."

The agent paused, cleared his throat falsely. "Ahem. I, ah, have some information here I thought I'd share with you."

"Yes?"

"Remember I said you seemed familiar to me, that we'd met before; and you mentioned the interview back in '68?"

"Yes, I remember that."

"Well, I had a hunch, you might say, and I looked up some old files and refreshed my memory on Gary Winslow."

Damon felt a flutter in the pit of his stomach.

"Yes?"

"So I still had a hunch, so I made a few phone calls and contacted a few people—"

Damon was holding his breath.

"Bottom line, Chaplain," Harry Reiner said, not unkindly, "is that Gary Winslow is a patient at Eastern State Hospital in Williamsburg, and has been since 1969. I talked to a gal named Patti in their medical records department. It was more what she didn't say than what she did, but he looks to be a permanent fixture there for some time to come." He ahem'd again. "Just thought I would let you know."

"Thank you. I appreciate—" But Damon could not finish; he was dumfounded, and worse. The lump in his throat was back, along with a stunning, sickening thought. "Do you have a tap on Father McLaughlin's phone?"

"Now, Chaplain, what makes you ask that?" The question was clearly rhetorical, since Agent Reiner did not wait for a reply but unceremoniously hung up.

Damon sank to his chair and stared blankly out his window at the chapel spire for what seemed like an eternity before, still unseeing in his melancholy, he crossed himself and asked his God's pardon. Then he began a fervent prayer for Gary Winslow.

20

"I've created a monster!" Michael was holding Mia at arm's length in open astonishment, examining her as he would a stranger. She shrugged herself free and pulled the silk chrysanthemum kimono closed over her naked breasts.

"Don't make a joke of it," she said. "Do you think this is easy for me?"

"Frankly, I don't know what to think." Her new attitude had ambushed him. He felt wounded, exposed, as though he should reach for something to hide his own nakedness. He sat down on the bed and smoothed the rumpled sheets beside him. "Sit," he invited, patting the mattress. "Talk to me."

She sat, clutching silken folds to her chest, but she did not speak.

"You're angry because I changed my mind about seeing a movie," he guessed. "Chinatown" was playing at the base theater. She had talked of little else at work today. "Is that it?"

"No, no, that's not it," she said peevishly. "Or maybe that is a part of it. A symptom. Our relationship is just one cancelled plan after another. We never seem to do anything together, except this." She jerked a bare toe toward underwear—hers—on the carpet. "And even this is—is at your convenience." She looked at him with undisguised resentment. "When you need sex, Michael, and when your needs fit your schedule, that's when you find time for me."

"That's not fair! You know what my job is, Mia. You know how hard I work. How can you fault me for that?"

"I don't."

"You do if you're accusing me of not making time for you." He pulled a tendril of hair out of her face and stroked it gently behind her ear. His fingertip traced the outline of her cheek and neck, then moved tenderly downward to her breasts. "Is it such a crime to want us to be like old married folk?"

"That's just the point," she said, stopping the progress of his hand with her own. She squeezed his fingers tightly before letting them go. "In a Christian marriage nobody is taken for granted."

"Jesus, Mary and Joseph," he muttered, getting to his feet again. He shook his head in disbelief. "My own little Frankenstein."

Mia was not amused. "I just think it would be better if we stopped for now, if we concentrated on other—"

"Has Damey put you up to this?"

"Don't be ridiculous!" she bristled, instantly defensive. "Can't I have a serious thought of my own?"

"Not on this subject."

"Well, you wanted me to study your religion," Mia said pointedly. "I have, and I want to do this right."

"There it is." To Michael's way of thinking, she was behaving like a petulant child. "Maybe we should move up the wedding date."

"No." She answered sharply, and much too quickly for his taste.

Michael paced barefoot, silently counseling himself to count to ten. For all that he was Irish and a redhead, he prided himself on his ability to keep his temper. He did this by looking for the logic and the humor in a situation. He knew women, knew them well. God knows, he had grown up with enough of them. There was a time, not so very long ago, when Mia probably would have agreed simply to live together, if he had asked her for that. Perhaps he had moved too quickly, rushed her needlessly or pressed her too hard for consent to a church wedding. His church, his terms. But that was because he believed in it, ultimately, and because he loved her. There was the logic of it. And as for the humor . . .

"We have the trip to Norfolk coming up," Mia was reminding him. "I don't know your sisters, but from all you've told me about them, surely you can see that it will be best if we stay in separate rooms, separate homes if need be. Not just for appearances but out of respect. And I really think it would just be best all round if we—what?" He was standing over her, grinning broadly, and that brought her up short.

"Fine," he said. He patted the top of her head, child that she was, and he laughed as he headed for the shower.

"What's funny?"

He turned at the doorway, still grinning. "Can't help but notice, Mary Virginia me sweet, you waited to spring this on me until *after* we made love."

"I told you," she murmured, so softly he could barely hear, "this won't be easy for me, either." And from that distance, without his eyeglasses, he couldn't see the guarded sadness in her face.

21

Jimmy Ferris had found a way to get over. That was how he thought of it, as getting over on his jailers. For weeks now they had observed his every move, monitored his every sound. He couldn't scratch or fart, much less bawl, without amusing an attentive audience. But he'd found a way to have a secret, a furtive momentary snatch at privacy; and that, in his mind, was getting over.

His method was part Yoga, part P.T., part stone stubborn will, and all his own ingenious invention. He would strain at push-ups until his body trembled, then do some of the breathing exercises he'd learned from a buddy in the squad bay; then sit-ups until his gut protested, followed with more breathing, and finally, with his imagination focused, he'd hold his breath until he nearly passed out. Just at the point the roaring began in his ears, before his vision started to shut down, there would be that giddy, dizzying, fairy-headed feeling that was almost like orgasm. Yeah, almost like that. He would time it so that with that last held breath he could move quickly to the expanded corner opposite the head, with its drain and showerhead. And there under the lukewarm water, away from the constant suicide watch, where no eyes, no camera lens was on him for three, four minutes tops, if he'd gotten his head right, he could manage. He could take care of himself.

Sometimes.

Getting his mind right was the hard part. Psyching himself to achieve an erection so he could proceed precisely when he was ready, alone and unobserved, that was hard. Psyching himself sexually without thinking of her, that was even harder—but it was essential. If he thought about Bev at all, it was over.

Not every day did he put himself through this bizarre evolution of self-abuse, not even every week, but only on the odd day now and again when he was desperate to feel something, anything, any sensation with which he could prove to himself he was still alive, still hanging on. And it was after those moments of brute intensity and hasty release that bits and pieces of that horrible night began to creep back into his consciousness.

He remembered the watcher now. There had been just enough moonlight under the trees to see something, a shape, and there were the ragged, heaving breaths that mimicked his own. He remembered the watcher now. He understood now, in theory at least, where the confessional stole had come from.

And in a weird and twisted way only he could appreciate, the fear of remembering more just added to the excitement of getting over.

22

Cassie had been working on a staffed letter for the general's signature on command stationery, with four tissue carbons. Even a piece of paper had to follow the chain of command, up the line for approval or for edits, then back down again if changes were suggested, to be redone, sometimes more than once or twice. And anything intended for the general's eyes, much less his signature, had to be perfect; no erasures, no White-out. What she wouldn't give for one of those fancy new word processors they had in the Public Affairs Office, or for their very own Xerox machine! Unfortunately the chaplains' budget was light years away from producing such miracles. Heaving a sigh, she pulled the finished product from her IBM Selectric and placed it in a file folder, attaching the appropriate cover note for the Chief of Staff. She would deliver it to his secretary personally, at 1300.

Relieved of phone watch for a change, and having already downed a tuna salad on white from home, Cassie grabbed a couple dollars from her purse and hustled for the back door off Lejeune Hall's so-called quarterdeck—a lobby, in civilian parlance—in search of something sweet and better than the vending machine offerings in the basement. Chubs had already pulled his roach coach up in the nearest reserved parking area and unfolded his rig like a Japanese puzzle box. He had a long line forming.

She almost changed her mind when she saw that Jamie Hutchins was queuing up. "Bollocks!" she muttered, under her breath. Having read a number of British mystery novels lately, she had been pleased to discover that on the odd occasion when her halo slipped, she could get away with a "bloody" this or that, or even a "bugger," without exciting the chaplains' attention.

She would have recognized Jamie from the rear by the rumpled polyester jacket slung over one arm and the shine in the seat of his pants, had his grating voice not carried. He had latched onto Mia, whose body language was all discomfiture, torso listing backward, stance poised for flight.

"Mee!" Cassie knew that if she caught Mia's attention her friend would relinquish her place in line to join her. To her dismay Jamie followed, only too pleased to bring up the rear and have two, count 'em, two, charming ladies to regale.

"Mrs. Martin, isn't it?"

"Yes," Cassie said weakly.

"I never forget a face, and rarely a name."

The old ambulance chaser was at least fifty-five or sixty by now, Cassie reckoned, and might be considered somewhat distinguished looking, in the proper clothes. With his mouth shut.

"I was just catching up with Miss Rodgers here. Terrible case load they've got down there in Legal, just terrible."

Mia turned slightly so that Cassie could see her pained expression and rolling eyes, which was lost on Jamison Hutchins, Esq.

"With this murder of the WM now, they'll be in over their heads for sure."

"Oh, I don't think so," Cassie bristled, feeling defensive on behalf of her friends. Mia set her jaw and stared ahead.

"Oh, yeah, they'll be needing assistance. That's definitely in the cards. I may be taking a couple cases off their hands, lighten the load, so to speak, but they'll still have a difficult road ahead. Hard case to prosecute. And the whole thing must be a blow to the chaplains, right? One of their own. This Ferris, you know him, of course?"

"I really don't want to talk about it."

Jamie didn't miss a beat. "Well, it's not like they have the right man in custody," he scoffed. "Prime suspect, I give you that, but the actual murderer?" A slight breeze lifted tufts of his baby fine blonde-gray hair, reminding her of a dandelion gone to seed. "Have you ever known NIS to make a good arrest so fast? I mean, when the guilty party didn't walk into PMO and give himself up out of the kindness of his heart." Jamie grinned in appreciation of his own witticism. "Keystone Koppers!"

The line was moving, but not before an officer about to be waited on turned to glare pointedly in their direction, clearly annoyed.

"I'm sure I don't know what you mean," Cassie said.

"A poor reference, my dear. Before your time."

"No, I know what Keystone Kops are. Were. I just don't agree that NIS is anything like that."

"I've had many dealings with them, Mrs. Martin." Now it was he who was rolling his eyes.

"Well, I've worked at Quantico several years now, and I hear things. To the best of my knowledge, the NIS agents are quite professional," Cassie countered. "And the judge advocates we have here are more than capable." She sensed Mia's amusement out the corner of her eye. "And as for Lance Corporal Ferris, naturally I would like to believe someone else is responsible, but—"

Chubs to her rescue, jangling the coin dispenser at his belt. "You're up, Cass. What'll it be?"

"Do you have any pie?" she asked brightly. "I could really go for a piece of pie today."

"The wife baked a lemon meringue this morning," Chubs said, reaching into the refrigerated chest where he kept his specials.

Mia stepped up, money in hand. "Make that two slices, please, and I'll get it." She flashed Cassie a smile. "My treat."

"Lemon meringue sounds delightful," Jamie said, as the girls turned away with their desserts.

"I'm sorry, sir, that was the last." Cassie looked back in time to see Chubs slowly folding his arms over his paunch. If memory served, he had retired from the Marine Corps as a gunny, with an MOS in law enforcement. "What else can I do you for?"

Making their escape, they could hear Mr. Hutchins settling for an Eskimo Pie, chips and a cola, and instructing on the appropriate way to stock a lunch wagon.

23

It was strange how things happened sometimes, how unplanned incidents fell into place to form a plan; how people despite their best intentions were thrown together. Amazing, really, that disparate lives could so easily be brought parallel, to coincide or even merge in a shared experience. Life-altering events often blossomed from seeming insignificance. In hindsight it was easy, Damon reflected, to perceive the hand of God and His mysteries in all of them, all the small happenings, all the little coincidences. While you were living them it was possible only to observe a magical thread running through affairs already past, a tenuous connecting strand that wove through all that had gone before, a link that could lead to as yet undreamed of small adventures, each one of which would one day be recognized as part of a pattern, a greater design. *God writes straight with crooked lines.* If we could see into the future, he mused, we would be too joyous—or too frightened—to accept our roles in the here and now.

He was considering all this as he stole yet another glance at Mia seated next to him in the Chevy, also apparently abstracted in thought. Her profile was like an artwork, a study of anxiety in luminous shades of gold. They were passing through the tunnel beneath Hampton Roads. Although it was quite late and they had ridden for nearly three hours, and much of that in darkness, the interior of the car was bathed now in the yellow, eerily artificial light reflected off the tiles of the tunnel walls.

The radio crackled static and white noise. He switched it off. She looked at him then, smiling weakly. She was no more ready than he was, he suspected, to face the appointments ahead of them, he at his father's bedside at Portsmouth Naval Hospital, and she with the prospective in-laws she had never met.

It had all happened so quickly, unexpectedly. A phone call had jarred him awake in the middle of the night, and this time it really had been Rose, not tipsy and angry but tired and trying hard not to sound scared. A stroke, she said, a mild one, but serious enough to warrant emergency leave. Then there had been the embarrassed awkwardness of Michael's request and the initial hesitancy in his own acquiescence, all pushed aside in the flush of hurried preparations. He'd had to clear space for Mia on the Chevy's front passenger seat, littered as it always was with scribbled homily notes, forgotten reminders, directions to parishioners' homes; with his empty Thermos and half eaten bags of "pogy bait," with old dry cleaning slips and yellow While You Were Out phone message slips. And he'd had to rearrange his own bags in the back seat, to make room for hers. The trunk was already full, what with the ice chest that traveled everywhere with him in the summertime and the collection of wrapped and labeled packages containing the odd gift or quaint souvenir found here and there, for members of his family.

Because it was a woman—because it was Mia—he'd driven to the base car wash before picking her up, and had vacuumed the front seat and washed the car. And because it was Mia, he was acutely aware that not so very long ago the sight of an unmarried woman, or any young woman for that matter, alone in a car with a priest would have meant certain scandal and probable censure. But this was innocent, he told himself, a simple favor granted, and therefore a good thing. It was one of those unremarkable yet magical happenstances that brought people together. It was part of God's plan.

And for Mia, it was no less strange or unsettling to be riding alone with Damon. From the moment he had taken his seat behind the wheel and closed the door, an unprecedented intimacy had descended upon them.

He was attired in a perfectly tailored uniform, fresh by the look of its smart creases; and as always, he filled it extremely well. She had not sat this close to him before, not even the night they had shared dinner at home. She was close enough now to catch a scent reminiscent of her father's Old Spice, close enough that his hand brushed hers when he felt for toll coins on the console. She had been uneasy at first, miffed and somewhat shamed that Michael should dump her on Father Damon like this at the last minute, when he was already burdened with a family crisis. But Damon's graciousness had dispelled her misgivings, if not all her worry. He seemed a trifle bashful tonight, but at the same time in control—of the evening, their progress, their growing friendship.

They were emerging from the artificial light of the tunnel now, back to darkness relieved by lit signage. "Not much farther, is it?" she asked, although she knew the answer.

"Ten minutes at most," he said. She was frowning and had sucked in her lower lip. "What is it?"

"You'll think I'm awful."

"You know better than that."

"I was wishing I didn't have to go there," she told him. "Not tonight. Not by myself."

Damon kept his eyes on the road ahead of them.

"I'm not expected, really, until the baby shower for Colleen on Sunday afternoon. Michael told me to call Maureen and let her know you were dropping me off tonight, since he has to work. But I didn't do it. I mean," adding hastily, "I did call, but I didn't mention you or that I was coming ahead."

He didn't have to look at her to know that she was nervous, that she had folded her arms, a defensive posture against—what? It was neither his place nor his inclination to reprove her. His mind was already racing ahead with possibilities.

"I thought I could get a motel room once I got here," she was saying in response to his unspoken question, "kind of take things at my own pace."

"Mia, Virginia Beach is a resort town, and this is a weekend." There was reproof of a sort in his tone, whether he intended it or not. "It's nearly ten. Without a reservation . . ." They rode in silence the next few miles, until he decisively slapped the flat of his hand against the steering wheel and flipped on the right-turn signal. As they moved onto the exit ramp for Ocean View he felt her watching him, wondering. "We can call a few places from my sister's," he said. "You'll want something close to Maureen's." As they rounded the ramp under the orange glow of street lamps, he glanced at her. She had unclasped her arms.

"I was hoping I might meet your sister," she said.

Damon, never sure what to expect from that quarter, only nodded.

Rose lived in a modest two-story detached house on a narrow lot, its rough gray siding trimmed in black. It huddled in the middle of the block in a neighborhood within city limits but miles away from the beach and downtown, and worlds away from the newer city sections of high-rise apartments, pastel condos and waterfront mansions. Tonight it was well illuminated everywhere, lights on upstairs, downstairs, at the front stoop. Even the alleyway that led to the patch of concrete that was their back yard was lit. Damon could see a bag of clothespins hanging there from a double clothesline, and the rim of Jackie's basketball hoop. He recognized Rose's Dodge hatchback parked at the curb; and unless he was mistaken, the sedan behind it would be his mother's.

There was no mistake. His mother's arms found him before he was fully through the storm door, and in the crush of that embrace it was impossible to tell where the wet of her cheeks left off and his own tears began. "Damey, Damey, my little Damey," she was murmuring between kisses, "my sweet, sweet boy." Rose was the blur in the background, the lumpish presence in a lavender housecoat moving haltingly toward him as he held out his hand to draw her close. He hugged the two of them until Rose pulled away, calling to her son. Jackie had already appeared behind her, half a foot taller than last time and gangly as a weed. Damon blinked his vision clear and felt a momentary stab of heartache. His loved ones were aging, were changing more than he could realize. With each reunion he saw it, and with every absence he resigned himself to all that he was missing.

Finally noticing the stranger outside on the front steps, his mother stiffened perceptibly and began to dab her eyes and blow her nose. "Who's this, Damey? Is someone with you?"

His introduction of Mia Rodgers and his explanation of her circumstances were not enough for his mother, who had suffered a number of shocks to her equilibrium of late. She parroted, "Michael O'Shea's fiancée? You're Michael's girl?" It was Rose, surprisingly, who greeted Mia with a warmth Damon envied, kissing her cheek welcome and guiding her to the kitchen with an arm about her waist. As the others followed, over Mia's shoulder Rose glared at her brother to signify that, explanations and hospitality aside, there was something peculiar here.

The kitchen was the largest room in the house, yet undeniably cozy. School mug shots and crayon drawings on the fridge; chickens and roosters everywhere, in ceramics above the maple cabinets, on the curtains, in the towels and potholders dangling jauntily by the stove. Rose set the little Formica topped table swiftly with coffee cups and spoons, dessert plates and forks and paper napkins. She put a platter of bakery streusel and what appeared to be homemade cookies before them and poured coffee that smelled freshly brewed. "Would you like a sandwich, either of you?" she asked. "I have lunchmeat, some Muenster, and that Jewish rye from Goldstein's you like, Damey."

He grinned, "I could eat."

"These cookies will be lovely," Mia said. She had assumed that Damon's sister would resemble him at least a little, but Rose was wholly different, dark eyed and thick featured and already graying. Lines were deeply etched around her mouth and across her forehead. Like the furrow at the bridge of her nose, they betrayed a tendency to frown much and smile little. Her brother got the looks in the family, Mia thought, and immediately felt ashamed at her lack of charity.

Rose's boy was physically something like his uncle, or perhaps like his father. Certainly at first impression there was nothing of his mother about him. While they ate and drank coffee Jackie busied himself with instant hot chocolate loaded with mini marshmallows, happily stirring, spilling and slurping until his mother's stern stare drove his curly head lower in his chair. He looked like a Protestant's image of a Catholic altar boy, Mia thought, at once angelic and mischievous. He'd be a heart breaker by the time his voice changed.

The need to find Mia a place to stay was nearly forgotten as the conversation centered on Damon's father and the small stroke that had taken them all by surprise.

"He's a strong man, your father. The doctor said this could have done for the average man his age, but he's a fighter. They need to keep him a few days for observation. And that's the only reason they're keeping him," Damon's mother stated emphatically, "for observation." She was a small woman, a handsome woman; Damon had her blue eyes.

"He's had a CT scan already," Rose said softly, watching her mother closely, "and they have him on an intravenous anti-coagulant."

"It's aspirin!" Mrs. Keith shot her daughter a wounded look. "He's been taking two aspirins a day since that time he had the double vision."

"No, Ma," Rose corrected. "The aspirins were to thin his blood, but this is a different thing." To Damey she said, "He's out of danger, but he may need physiotherapy." Their mother was tight lipped, shaking her head.

"The Chief's gonna talk funny and smile like this," Jackie demonstrated soberly, grimacing to one side of his face. "Lenny Sutphin said his grandfather had a stroke, and he drools on the side he can't smile with."

"Like Lenny Sutphin is a world authority," Rose snapped. "Don't make fun. Finish your cocoa and go to bed."

"It's Friday night!"

"It's late."

Jackie rolled his big blue eyes and smiled appealingly at Mia, as if to say, "See what I have to put up with." He'd be a real heart breaker, all right.

Damon finished his coffee and reached for a refill. "I'd like to see The Chief tonight."

"It's past visiting hours," Rose said. "We just got back from there a little while ago. He's *all right.*"

"If a son wants to see his father, they should let him in," their mother pronounced.

Damon tugged at his left collar device, the Chaplain Corps cross. "If a priest wants to see a patient," he said, "they will let him in."

"Fine." Rose set down her coffee abruptly and noisily. She went to the sink and began to run water in the dishpan.

Mia caught Damon's eye and silently mouthed "phone."

"Jack, would you run get the Yellow Pages for me?" Damon asked.

Rose's back stiffened. "Jackie's on his way to bed, Damey. Aren't you, Jack?"

"Aw, Mom!"

"Go."

Jackie said his goodnights and slouched toward the door, catching a wink from the pretty visitor before he disappeared.

Rose turned toward them and stood drying her hands a moment, gazing thoughtfully from her brother to Mia and back again. "If the telephone directory is to look up motels, there's no need. Miss Rodgers is welcome to stay here in the guest room."

Mia began to protest, but Rose was adamant. "Nonsense," she said sweetly. "It's no trouble at all. Ma can sleep with me if she's a mind to—"

"I'm going home," Mrs. Keith said emphatically. "Your father might try to call me."

"—and Damon," Rose's tone turning frosty, "can use the fold-out bed in the parlor."

Damey was watching his sister with amazement. She never failed to surprise him, one way or another.

Rose added succinctly, "After he gets back from the hospital."

The old man looked small in the bed and exceedingly vulnerable. So fragile, in fact, that his son had the fleeting sensation he was looking at a stranger. Purplish marks above and below the plastic tubing taped to his arm attested to many failed attempts to locate a cooperative vein. That battle done, he was deep in a medicated sleep now, slack jawed and breathing shallowly. Traces of dried spittle had collected at one corner of his mouth.

The other occupied beds on the ward were few in number and were yards away. "Chief," Damon called out in a normal tone. That elicited no response. Somewhat louder, "Dad?" Nothing more than the flutter of an eyelid. Damon laid his hand over the old man's and leaned in closer. "Daddy," he said softly. The eyes flew open then, and in a moment focused on him. Damon curled his hand round his father's fingers, smiled at him and waited for his mind to clear.

"Damey. You come all the way from Mayport, Damey?"

"From Quantico, Chief. You remember. I'm back at Quantico now."

The chief nodded, wetting his lips with his tongue. Damon poured water from the bedside carafe, supported his father's head and held the cup to his lips. As he slowly drank the mental cobwebs seemingly melted away. "I knew that," he said when he had finished. "I knew that." He looked long and appraisingly at his son. "You look good."

"So do you," Damon lied.

"Your mother call you?"

"Rose."

"Well, she shouldn't have. I'm all right."

"I can see that. But you wouldn't begrudge me a couple days away from duty, would you, Chief?"

"You been there a couple months already and didn't see fit to visit."

"You're absolutely right," Damon agreed, smiling again. "But maybe I needed a really good excuse to get away."

A silence ensued reminiscent of those common between them in the days following Damon's decision for the priesthood.

"So how's the church business?" his father said at last. "You saving souls?"

"Right and left."

"And solving problems, you fellas with all the answers?"

"Not me."

"Well, don't tell your mother that. She thinks there's nothing her boy can't fix."

"Mothers are like that."

"She used to think that about me, you know. But no more."

Silence. Damon had never known how to talk to his father, not really. So much shared, yet so little in common. The Chief was a good man, Damon knew, faithful to the laws of the Church, but hardly spiritual. Physical prowess had always defined his self-worth and shaped his opinions of other men, his son included. The day Damon finally bested his father at arm wrestling was the day he earned his respect; and the day he entered the seminary nearly a year later was when he all but lost it.

"You weren't praying over me, were you?" The Chief's gaze was faltering. He was fighting to stay awake.

"Maybe I was," Damon answered, falling easily into the old litany, knowing what was next.

"Let me see your hands," The Chief demanded.

Damon held out both hands for his father, who felt of the fleshy parts of his palms like a butcher grading meat.

"Not as soft yet as a baby's ass," he announced weakly, "but getting mighty like a woman's."

Damon pulled his hands away. He hated that teasing ritual, never quite knew what to say.

"But you wouldn't know about that," his father finished.

Another silence, emptier and more desolate than before.

"I need to make a head call," the old man said suddenly. "I can't use that thing," indicating the bedpan. Damon glanced down the ward at the brightly lit nurse's station, where a corpsman sat reading. "No, no," the Chief growled, "you help me. I just need a boost."

And so Damon helped his father sit up, feeling his aged boniness where there had always been muscle; and he slid his father's feet into woolly scuffs, and supported him as he stood. He guided the intravenous trolley while the old man shuffled to the nearest stall with a commode, and he waited at the door. When he helped The Chief settle back into the bed, he saw the old man's eyes were wet.

The Chief pulled his son down closer to him and whispered near his ear, "I'm sorry."

"I know."

"You can pray for me if you want."

"I do. I always do."

"You can give me Last Rites if you want."

Damon nearly laughed. "Dad, you're not dying. I can anoint you tomorrow, if you like; it's a healing sacrament. But I can give you the Sacrament of Reconciliation now, if you need to confess. What is it that you want?"

"I want to sleep," The Chief said.

Damon stretched out across an empty bed and watched his father drift back into the depths of drug-induced slumber, praying all the while with all his heart. When it was safe to do so, he blessed him and kissed his sleeping face.

24

The next morning Damon and Mia took separate yet parallel paths, each on a personal mission of discovery. Damon initially returned to the hospital for a round of waiting and watching with his mother. Mia accompanied his sister to her department store. It was Saturday, and Rose was to work a half day.

The decision to accept Rose's invitation to visit her workplace was spur of the moment, born of a desire to postpone the inevitable meeting with Michael's sisters. In the manner of the ordinary yet life-altering events Damon had privately pondered only hours before, it would prove to be a providential choice for Mia, one that she would marvel at in retrospect but would not regret.

The department store was a venerable old establishment of sandstone and polished granite that filled an entire city block in Norfolk's "revitalized" downtown. It had been renovated the previous year and was just glitzy enough to hold its own against newer rivals that drew crowds to the trendy suburban malls. Watching her approve an elaborately animated window display of her own design and hearing her direct a small, efficient staff, Mia perceived a transformation in Rose. Removed from her kitchen and the proximity of family, she no longer looked the part of somewhat dowdy older sister. The change was subtle and difficult to analyze, because outwardly she appeared the same. The tailored royal blue she wore today was little more flattering than the soft violet robe of the night before. Today's make-up was really not different, simply a tad brighter. Yet in these surroundings, valued and obviously respected in this professional role, Rose was extremely attractive. Still not precisely pretty, Mia decided honestly, but a vital and handsome, vivacious woman.

After her work was finished Rose took Mia to the third floor "Tea Room," a charming oasis of chintz and deep plush carpet, just around the corner from the bridal salon. They lingered over shrimp salad and blackberry crepes, finding out more about each other in a leisurely hour than two men bent on forging an alliance would have learned in a week.

"I salute you!" Rose raised her nearly empty iced tea tumbler. "Taking on two institutions at once, marriage and the Church of Rome, that's gutsy."

"Oh, I don't know," Mia laughed.

"Well, I do. Believe me, I do. The two of them together almost killed me, even though I had thought at the time that I was invincible." She swirled the contents of the tall glass and tapped it to loosen frozen chunks at bottom. "You tend to do that when you're young. Think you can stand anything, I mean." Rose gave her a faint smile. "I'm a little surprised that my brother the father entrusted you to me today." Her tone became sardonic. "Maybe he thinks your introduction to the faith could do with a devil's advocate."

"Now you're confusing me."

The smile dissolved into a frown. "I haven't been on the best of terms with the Vatican and all it stands for, for quite a long time." She studied the nuggets of ice in the glass and was still for a moment. "Jackie is and forever will be my only child." She looked at Mia closely, trying to gauge the extent to which she might trust, and hope to be understood. "I married his father rather late in life. Considerably older, I'd judge, than you are now. Not for lack of suitors," she added significantly. "My first love, my first innocent and perfect love, was for a young man who decided at the eleventh hour that his true calling was to the priesthood."

Mia felt a trip in her heartbeat.

"It's not a pleasant thing to be someone's idea of a sacrifice," Rose said, "or to hear your dream of married life referred to as a temptation. It took years to put that experience behind me." She was still searching Mia's face for empathy.

"But you did, obviously. You married someone else."

Rose weighed her answer while chewing a piece of ice. "Yes, I did. And there was as much happiness as I had any right to, in the beginning," she said. "But I went into the marriage for all the wrong reasons. The man I should have married—my second grand passion—was far too different to pass muster in my parents' house. And I was very much the obedient daughter in those days."

"Different how?"

"He was Jewish; Jewish and a New Yorker, to boot. We met at business school, which was one of my many attempts to get my life on track. He taught there." She closed her eyes momentarily and fairly glowed with the memory. "You know how sometimes you can meet someone new and it's like recognizing an old friend, someone you instinctively connect with?"

Mia nodded.

"We belonged together. We fit. And we both knew it. We both wanted it."

"What happened?"

"The Catholic Church. The Gospel according to The Chief—he's religious when he feels threatened—and as filtered through my mother, who has no equal when it comes to instilling guilt. Even Damey played a part. I suppose it was his job to. Now, there was a devil's advocate." She scowled again, staring harder at the last stubborn bit of ice in the glass. "Collectively, they made me feel I would lose my soul if I married outside the faith," she said.

"So I put him off, my Benjamin. I was too cowardly to make an honest break, but he knew. When he finally tired of waiting for me, he went back to New York, and I went back to Mass—after making a good confession, of course. In time I married Jack Kelly, a Catholic fellow from the neighborhood I'd known since high school, and eight years later I found out how you really lose your soul."

Mia waited.

"Divorce," Rose explained dryly. "I don't recommend it."

"I'm sorry."

"Or I should say, I don't recommend it for anyone whose so-called support system consists only of practicing Catholics. I don't regret divorcing Jack. It's my marriage in the Church that I wish I could undo. 'In the eyes of God,' as my mother likes to remind me, I'm still married. Jack remarried long ago and is happily growing old with his new wife and kids. But if I even consider attempting a relationship, I'm in a state of sin." She smacked the bottom of her tumbler against the table and shimmied the last of the ice into her mouth. "Needless to say, whether I'm seeing someone or not—and currently and for a long time now I'm not—that's pretty much my permanent state of residence."

"But don't the same rules apply to your ex-husband?"

"Sure they do, but Jack never took religion all that seriously. He hasn't had the Keiths, father, son and holy terror, breathing down his neck." Rose paused to calm herself, conscious that she was becoming too loud.

"I do the best I can by Jackie," she continued, "without being a complete hypocrite. I won't enroll him in parochial school, but I see that he goes to church. He'll be confirmed next year." Pain and pride competed in her eyes.

Mia gulped the last of her own tea, unsure what to say.

Rose patted her hand maternally. "Come on," she said, her mood suddenly livening. "Let's check out the bridal salon."

Mia began to murmur protest.

"Or is everything already ordered?"

Forced to remember her reason for visiting Norfolk, Mia colored with embarrassment. "To tell the truth, I haven't planned anything."

It was true. Since accepting Michael's proposal her only move forward was the catechism, and even that had been initiated by her fiancé. She shrugged. "I guess I'm not the hope chest and *Bride's* magazine type." That was also quite true. In all the years since college, finding a husband had hardly been an objective, much less a priority. She had worked intensely, traveled a little. Her few romantic encounters had been completely haphazard, serendipity. Nearly everyone she knew was married, or had been, so she had always supposed that it would one day also happen for her, that she would stumble into a fated, perfect-fit match such as Rose had described, and everything else would fall into place. Of late there had been not so much a sense of urgency as a subtle, nagging awareness of incompletion, a heaviness of heart that was lifted when she met and became intimate with Michael O'Shea.

"The trappings of a formal wedding, all that," she told Rose, "all the details, I haven't thought—other than, I guess I should wear something simple in ivory, rather than pure white . . ."

"I get a thirty percent employee discount," Rose announced, and her commanding air of finality settled the matter.

Perhaps three-quarters of an hour later—which seemed a leaden lifetime to Mia—she was alone, standing in stocking feet on a chiseled Aubusson at the center of a spacious fitting room mirrored on three sides. Nearly a dozen gauzy, sequined and pearl studded possibilities had narrowed finally to a probable selection, one of understated elegance. She was staring at her triplicate reflection in disbelief, and to her dismay she was crying.

The bride in the mirror was a storybook creature, a romantic vision that could easily have inspired tears of joy. What trickled down Mia's cheeks, however, was hot and angry. This wasn't happiness, she sighed; this was frustration, pure and simple. She leaned in closer to her blurred image and involuntarily began another of those useless silent discussions with herself, the kind of taking-stock inner dialog that almost always spiraled into indecision.

Why doesn't this feel right? I'm in love. We *are* in love, aren't we? The bride stared back at her, serenely impassive. Mia backed away from the mirror and, digging her toes into the carpet, lifted herself taller, turning this way and that. Even under this harsh fluorescent lighting the creamy satin shimmered as it flowed, as though it returned the glow of blessed candles. She took a deep breath that strained against the bodice.

All that's been missing from my life is that special someone to share it, she told herself, someone who would appreciate me and always be there for me, and I for him; someone who would need me. She peered hard at her reflection again, so close to the glass that she could have rested her forehead against it. Isn't it time? Don't I deserve a happy ending?

Of course you deserve love, the ashen eyes in the mirror answered.

"Then why do I feel so lost?" she murmured aloud. "And why does all this look like a masquerade?"

Because you're not sure anymore.

"Did you say something? How are you doing in there?" Rose had waited patiently outside, and only to be disappointed.

"It isn't quite right," Mia lied, her voice faltering. She reached for her purse and a tissue, and hurriedly blotted away tears and dissolving mascara. That's the trouble, she realized. Marriage should be a happy beginning, not an ending. And I'm more confused now than ever. I'm just not sure anymore.

Her fingers flew, scrabbling clumsily at tiny satin covered buttons. The gown was more than right, it was perfect; it was beautiful. And she could not get out of it fast enough.

Across the wide Virginia Tidewater peninsula, Damon had stationed himself near a wall of smoke filmed windows in the patients' lounge at

Portsmouth Naval Hospital. The view of the Elizabeth River and of Hampton Roads beyond was seductive. His mother he had left on the ward. She was more than content to hover over The Chief, tenderly pressing him periodically to take a bit of pudding or to finish his juice. Something in the looks that passed between those two had made Damon see not simply father and mother but husband and wife, so that he had thought to allow them a measure of privacy.

A visit with some of the other patients was in order now, if he could leave the view of the waterway that drew him like a siren song. Ostensibly he had been listening to an elderly man beside him talk graphically about his prostate; but in truth Damon's mind was drifting out to sea. The old gent was a retired submariner and lapsed Catholic; he had homed on this Navy chaplain like a sub on sonar. Unfortunately, the more Damon attempted to appear attentive, the more his gaze floated to the sight of those ships on the horizon, heirs to vessels he had watched tirelessly as a boy. Probably the old man sensed the chaplain's inattention; his parting shot, as he lumbered away in the direction of a TV, was a baleful reminder that prostate trouble is common to the priesthood.

There was just enough smog in the air to render the ships' silhouettes in the distance ghostly, indeterminate. But identifying them by size and shape had always been an easy game. There was a destroyer tender out there, a carrier of the America class, an LST, and a commercial tanker, and a stout tug that was little more than a dark smudge against the skyline.

"Excuse me, sir." A young corpsman in baggy blue scrubs, with a telephone in his hands and a directory under his arm, was standing at his elbow, in the space just vacated. "Are you the one wanted a phone?"

The corpsman showed him where the nearest phone jack was, in a corner next to a pedestal table and vinyl padded barrel chair. This was something he had resolved to do at his earliest opportunity, the moment he realized he was coming home. Sighing, Damon seated himself with his back to the temptation of the windows. He opened the Chesapeake and

Potomac Telephone Company directory to the E's. There were no fewer than 26 entries for Eastern State Hospital in Williamsburg. He ran his finger down the column of fine print, hesitating at "Chaplain" but stopping at "Medical Records Director."

The cheery, high-pitched voice was polite but firm. "I'm sorry, sir, we have a confidentiality issue here. We don't disclose that information."

"Well, surely please you can just confirm for me that he is a patient."

"No, sir. That information is confidential."

"Perhaps if I cleared it with the—the administrative office?"

"No, sir, the answer would be the same. Unless the patient or the patient's family has authorized it, we simply don't disclose patient information."

"So he is a patient, then?"

"Sir." Cheeriness was giving way to irritation.

"Father; it's Father, please. I'm a priest. Mr. Winslow knows me, would remember me, I'm sure."

"I'm sorry, Father. I'm really not at liberty to make an exception."

"I see."

"What I can do, however, is take your name and number, and *if* there is such a patient, and *if* the patient, his family, and his doctor agree, you may be permitted to see him."

"That's kind of you. I'm in the area this time only through tomorrow evening, but any step closer will be a step in the right direction."

The matter of the harassing calls and the strange "confession" was a quandary that had cost him sleep many a night. Damon was still convinced that the answers lay with Gary Winslow, illogical though that explanation might be. He supplied Rose's home address and phone numbers, as well as his own telephone numbers at Quantico. But an inner voice told him there would be no phone call, no invitation; not this weekend, most probably not ever. And for now, for this most unusual weekend at least, he felt relief rather than disappointment.

25

"You can't go home again." He'd read that somewhere. But it wasn't true. He had gone home, many times. It just wasn't the same, is all. And "You can't turn back the clock," they say that, too. Also more than a lie. What they should say is, "The moving finger writes, and having writ" . . . retribution. No turning back. "Fugit irreparabile tempus."

His thoughts were like foam on a whirlpool, eddying irretrievably toward an insistent funnel into darkness. So many ideas had already made that swirling descent, and their loss to the depths was piercing sharp. The more he thought, the more his head hurt, and he could not stop his thinking. But his thoughts this time would not be delivered up for dissection, nor would he admit to their pain. The pain in particular would be his secret. Like the phone numbers on the message paper he'd slipped inside a pocket of the old woolen sweater he wore here year round like a uniform, or a hair shirt. "Carpe diem." The doctor didn't need those phone numbers.

With all of them together again at Rose's on Saturday evening, Damon remembered the gifts from Florida in the Chevy's trunk. A book on sunken treasure and a piece of coral for his parents, a silk scarf and gold sand dollar bracelet for Rose, a yoyo and a fishing pole for Jack. Damon had offered to take them all out to dinner, but Rose wouldn't hear of it. She laid a lace cloth on the dining room table and set it with her good china and crystal. She fixed baked pork chops layered with sliced potatoes, onions and sage, the way their mother used to, and served buttery mashed squash on the side. There were beaten biscuits light as clouds, and cucumbers in hot vinegar as well as fresh corn on the cob and Tidewater tomatoes from the farmer's market. For dessert Rose had resurrected yet another Keith family comfort food, old-fashioned bread pudding full of cinnamon and rum-plumped raisins, generously topped with whipped cream from an aerosol can. It was a meal comprised of happy memories, and it was wonderful.

If it occurred to any of them that Mia's rightful place was with another family only a few minutes' drive away, they gave no sign of it. Hospitality had already yielded to familiarity. It seemed natural and right that she should be here, seated to Damon's left, laughing, talking easily of court cases, of favorite movies and recipes. Mrs. Keith had drawn Mia into her confidence, sharing stories about The Chief and herself when they were courting, stories Damon had heard before but had forgotten. Jackie had brought out his baseball card and coin collections for her to see. As for Rose, she and Mia behaved as though they had been friends all their lives, exchanging the sly knowing looks of conspirators.

"Your mom tells me you're quite the ladies' man at school, Jack," Mia teased. "Two girlfriends, is it?"

Jackie lifted a shoulder. "I can't help it if girls like me."

"She says you take after your Uncle Damon."

"Maybe." He shrugged again, coloring.

"Then there's more than just two girls in the picture," his grandmother remarked.

"Ah, ha! The truth will out!"

"Hey, help me out here, Jack!" Damon exclaimed, but the boy ducked his head, grinning, and excused himself to go outside. There was still enough daylight to shoot a few baskets.

"He's at that age when the opposite sex holds a guilty and unfathomable fascination," Rose observed fondly after her son had left.

Mia was looking at Damon as though she had never outgrown that stage of life. "Tell me more about Father Casanova here," she said.

"Well, for one thing, Damey had the eye for Lucy O'Shea," said Rose.

"When I was nine."

"Oh, no, I seem to remember a love note that was confiscated by Sister Rita in seventh grade."

"That's right, you know, Damey," his mother chimed in. "I had to go talk with Sister about you. It was quite the scandal."

"Everything was a scandal to Sister Rita," he said.

"A rather precocious note, unless I'm mistaken," Rose persisted. "Something about breasts, wasn't it?"

"'Thy breasts are like two lilies.' Lucy was in eighth grade," Damon remembered, smiling. "And she definitely had them."

Mia puzzled, "The Song of Solomon?"

"Not quite. I think Sister was less outraged by what I'd quoted than by the fact I'd gotten it wrong."

"Our Damey was popular in high school," his mother said to Mia. She added rather pointedly, "So was your Michael."

"Very popular," Rose echoed, with an edge to her voice that seemed deliberate. "Remember Patti Maher, Ma? She told me she felt cursed when both Damon and Michael left for the seminary. I suspect she was trying to console me, by putting my singular loss to the Church in perspective."

Her brother shifted on his chair, clearly uncomfortable.

"She never married, that one, did she?" their mother asked rhetorically, then sniffed, "Well, it's privileged she should have felt, not cursed."

"I'll be sure to remind her of that the next time I run into her at the Food Fair, shopping for one," Rose snapped.

"That was high school, Rose," Damon said in a placating, almost pleading tone. "Neither of us was serious about Patti."

Rose inclined her head in his direction for emphasis. "Precisely."

"Let me get this straight," Mia broke in, enjoying herself, "Michael and Damon dated the same—" She halted in mid-sentence, staring in surprise past the others.

A masculine voice behind them called out, "Some things never change." A man with glasses, in running gear and baseball cap, had entered through the back door with Jackie. Both of them were flushed and slightly disheveled, the man holding a basketball that he tossed off to Damon, hard. "He's still trying to steal my girl." His expression was bland; a bead of perspiration glistened on his upper lip as he managed a half smile.

Mia went to the man immediately and kissed him full on the mouth. It was only then that Damon's mother and sister recognized him.

"Michael?"

"Michael O'Shea!"

Doffing his cap, he crossed the length of the kitchen and dining room to give the old woman his hand. "Mrs. Keith, it's been a long time. I'm so sorry to hear about The Chief. How is he?"

"He's doing well, Michael. He's a strong man. He's holding his own."

"Rose?"

She smiled disarmingly. "It's good to see you," she said. "I'll put on fresh coffee."

Michael held out his hand to Damon. Dropping the basketball to accept it, Damon wished he could think of the right thing to say.

"Thanks for taking care of Mia for me," Michael said quietly; and as they shook hands, his eyes thoughtfully searched his friend's face.

Ridiculously, Damon felt his throat close in a bleak wave of panic that came and went in an instant. Rose was his savior, calling breezily from the kitchen, "It was my pleasure." She brought Michael a dish of bread pudding and pulled out a chair by way of invitation. "She and I shopped the bridal salon today," she said sweetly, and suddenly all awkwardness was over.

26

Wiping methodically, always with downward strokes and a light touch, careful not to pull at the skin, Rose Keith Kelly removed the last traces of make-up. She regarded her face critically, examining the fine lines around her eyes and mouth in the harsh light of a magnifying cosmetic mirror. There were times of late when she felt less like a lady of somewhat diminished allure than like a failed rodeo clown, all paste and rouge. Her skin had already lost much of the elasticity of youth; make-up only tended to accentuate that fact. She opened the jar of night moisturizer and began to apply it to her neck and face. All upward strokes now, smoothing, firming, working a magic that would last, if she were lucky, all of thirty minutes.

Gently, and with both hands, she dabbed a cool gel onto her closed eyelids. The act made her remember the blessing of the Shabbos candles, the ritual performed by Jewish women that she had found so lovely and endearing when Benjamin, a reform Jew with a healthy respect for tradition, had taken her to the home of Orthodox friends for Sabbath dinner. She had not spoken aloud of Benjamin for years, but with Mia today the words had spilled out, and with them so much more had come to mind. The past was the past, elusive and irreversible; she had learned long ago that it was self-defeating to dwell there. Still, much endured that was good to remember.

Everything about Benjamin had been different, everything. His profile, his accent, his heritage, his religion. It was that very strangeness, embodied in a kindred soul, which had infused their relationship with excitement and romance. Perhaps that was how it was for Mia, discovering Catholicism through Michael. Yet Mia had chosen to be with Father Damon and his big sister, when she could have been with Michael's people, learning all there was to know from big sister times four. Curious.

The O'Shea girls, each of them half giggles, half hot Irish temper, had made for a lively neighborhood in the old days. Maureen was nearest Rose's age, but Rose knew all of them well. It was Lucy's daughter Colleen, now pregnant with her first, who was the guest of honor at tomorrow's baby shower. They were good women, friendly women, anxious no doubt to meet their brother and uncle's bride to be. Yet Mia chose to be here. Even now she was here, still under this roof, and Michael back at his sister's.

No mistake, there was a tense undercurrent of discomfort among those three tonight. And before Michael had arrived on the scene, Rose had witnessed with her own eyes and ears a very different tension between Damon and Mia. They were attracted to each other, obviously; perhaps it was already more than that. Yet because she knew her brother as well as she understood herself and because she trusted her own instincts about Mia Rodgers, she was certain nothing had happened between them. Father Damon would sooner die than betray his sacred vows or his personal honor, and clearly Mia was a decent sort still struggling to know her own mind, her own heart.

Long accustomed to a wounded and admittedly cynical perspective, Rose had rarely considered the effect of Church authority upon the clergy who embraced and enforced it. Was it hard for Damey, as vital and affectionate as she knew him to be, to live year after year with the downside of what he called God's package deal? Or was his priestly celibacy, as she had long suspected, an acceptable, even glorified means to a selfish end? *See how good am I, how godlike, how much more I love the Lord by the measure of my sacrifice!* The selflessness of any priest was, in Rose's caustic estimation, a sort of selfishness turned inside out, a devotion to God and "the people" at the expense of the few who, by blood or bad fortune, cherished him for who—not what—he was. The few who might have the temerity to make innocent demands upon his time, upon his allegiance. And be disappointed.

She was brushing her hair now, too vigorously. Annoyed by the turn her thoughts had taken, she cleaned her brush and wondered if her hair used to come out this much when she was younger. She couldn't remember.

There was a lot she had trouble remembering these days, like how close she and her little brother used to be. *I mothered him from the time he was born,* she mused. *He was my living dolly. He was my boy long before there was a Jackie, and now . . .* It wasn't fair to judge him harshly because of the road he'd taken, no more than it was logical to remain bitter over her own situation. Jack Kelly would undoubtedly lie for her if she asked him to help with a church annulment. And it would definitely be a bald-faced lie for either of them to say they had entered the marriage not intending to be joined by God for all eternity, however naïve that intention may have been. God would know the truth, and God, she was confident, had forgiven them their failure. So what would be the point?

She tossed the brush onto the dressing table and, moving swiftly to the bed, poured herself the merest taste from the bottle in her nightstand. Just a thimbleful of brandy, really. Not enough to make her maudlin, just enough to help her sleep.

27

Sunday ended the weekend for Damon much as Saturday had begun it, with Mia and himself moving in opposite directions. Michael picked her up before breakfast. Damon would have missed them in any case, since he had left even earlier to assist with first Mass at his mother's church in Norfolk. From there he took his father Holy Communion and stayed at his bedside throughout the morning into mid-afternoon, until his mother arrived. She was exceptionally tender in her leave-taking of her son; and The Chief, in rare form, saluted him smartly.

Damon had already driven past their old house before coming to the hospital, had circuited the strange old neighborhood once so familiar. The schoolyard and the building that had been his high school were demoted now to middle school status. Everything looked smaller. The corner candy store he and his sister had frequented had been converted to office spaces. He could not remember, if indeed he ever knew, where the Winslow boy had lived, not even which block. The phone book held no clue; the names listed ran from Winslet to Winslo to Winter, not one with the spelling he sought. If Gary Winslow's family still lived here-abouts, their phone number was unpublished. He had done what he reasonably could do, he felt. It would be useless to go out to Eastern State in Williamsburg without an invitation.

Instead he drove back to Ocean View and spent the remainder of the day with Jackie, while Rose paid her hospital call and attended the baby shower. He and Jackie went out for pizza and pinball. After that they strolled the amusements at Virginia Beach, and brought back enough saltwater taffy and fudge for an army. The boy seemed glad of his uncle's company, and for Damon the time passed all too quickly. He wished with all his heart that they could become closer. If there was one thing he faulted Rose for, it was the way she reduced his persona to his priesthood and used that against him. He was still her brother; he loved her, whether she had left the Church or not. Why couldn't she accept him for himself, even though he remained part of it?

He came close to asking her that very question as they sat together in her kitchen Sunday evening, she sampling the fudge and he drinking a last cup of coffee for the road. But he only came close, because Rose asked a probing question of her own.

"What are you going to do about Mia?"

He looked at her, uncomprehending. She was smiling at him, regarding him with more kindness than she had shown him in quite a while. "She would be happier with you, I think. And she would make you happy. How can you marry those two, knowing that?"

He was suddenly a little lightheaded. Could she be serious? "I don't know anything of the kind," he said coldly, but the words were hollow even to his own ears.

Rose came to him then, folded her arms about him, held him tightly for a long moment, and kissed the top of his head. She said no more about it, indeed said no more to him at all before he left. She quietly sent Jackie to fetch his uncle's overnight bag, then went to her room and closed the door.

As he hugged his nephew goodbye, Damon realized that his sister's heart really had not changed toward him. She was still trying to propel him in the direction she felt best, just as she always had done all those years ago when they were children. It wasn't quite the parting he was looking for. But it was something.

The ride home with Michael was quiet. Mia had braced herself for some unpleasantness, in fairness to him had expected it; but he was unfailingly good to her. When he had first gotten her alone that morning he had asked her breezily why she had ducked his family to stay with Damey's. He appeared tolerant of her one-word answer, "Jitters," if not wholly content with it.

He had changed the subject to the breaking news back at the office, word that Lance Corporal Ferris had agreed to waive his right to a formal pretrial investigation, and that the command was moving ahead with referral of the charges to a general court-martial. That new information, coming late on Friday, had freed Michael for the weekend after all, but not in time to catch her before she'd left with Damon.

And Michael's sisters had also been good to her, she reflected, wonderful really. From the moment she had crossed Maureen's threshold and found herself engulfed in redheads, they had all been welcoming, friendly and considerate. Yet she hadn't felt quite at ease, as she had at Rose Kelly's; and it was not until Rose arrived, covered dish and baby gift in hand, that she had relaxed. Wildly ridiculous, she knew, considering she had known Rose only hours longer than the other women; but there it was. Some people you warm to immediately and some you can't help but keep at arm's length, without understanding why. Perhaps it was because Michael's sisters in a way stood in for his mother, and one was conditioned to be apprehensive about meeting the future mother-in-law. Perhaps the sheer number of Michael's relations—his sisters, their husbands, their children, the aunties by marriage—was overwhelming. Perhaps it was all of that, or none of it. Maybe my problem really is just pre-wedding nerves, she thought.

They were on the last stretch of highway, north of Richmond. "Stay with me tonight," Michael said. He had been silent so long that she was startled at the sound of his voice. He reached for her in the dark, stroked her leg up, down, his fingers tickling her inner thigh. Mia thought she ought firmly to say, "I thought we agreed," but she could not bring herself to do that. She ought to push his hand away, she supposed, but it was warm and it was wanted, and she could not.

Alone as ever on his own dark road, Damon felt a chill of the sort his Grandmother Keith would have likened to a footfall on his waiting grave.

Rose's remarks about Mia had struck his defenseless heart and had gone deep. He had tried praying, he had tried the radio. Nothing helped. He was lonely, as he had not felt lonely in a long, long time. The Chevy was forever changed for him, for one thing. The seat beside his would be now and forever her seat, not a place for the chance passenger, not a receptacle for whatever he flung there, but her seat. Her empty seat. He laid his hand on the rough upholstery and caressed it lightly. That didn't help, either.

28

President Ford had pardoned former President Nixon, and the nation had finally stopped talking about it. Summer had given way to autumn, but autumn's deepening chill had relented in the mid-Atlantic region, permitting as a respite the bewitching charms of a true Indian summer. One last mad fling with sun and cloudless skies before winter settles in to stay. At Quantico, children played outside base housing without sweaters or jackets, deaf to predictions of colds and flu. Marines on training bivouac in the field sweated in their combat gear, men running for PT went shirtless, and everywhere windows were flung open for relief from the steam heat which had been fired up on schedule base wide and could not be turned off.

The Globe and Laurel restaurant in Q-Town burned to the ground, taking with it a man's life and leaving a swath of charred apartments. Another rebel on mess duty had distinguished himself, criminally charged with "urinating into fruit punch later consumed by members of the Officers Wives Club." Despite the accused's claim that he had merely been seen toying with a meat snack in his pocket, he earned both significant brig time and a place in judge advocate lore, as the ineffective yet supremely imaginative "bratwurst defense" entered the local lexicon. Then Halloween came, and All Saints Day and All Souls, and still the weather was unseasonably warm, November in name only. November already, and still no date set for the Ferris court-martial. Quantico's first murder trial in recent collective memory would not be rushed.

The moment Lance Corporal Ferris on advice of counsel had waived the Article 32 pretrial investigation, conceding that there was enough preliminary evidence to warrant charges and the referral of those charges to a general court-martial, there was a sea change. The burden upon the government shifted from merely "showing cause" to proving his guilt beyond reasonable doubt. The admissions he'd made to Special Agent Kaminski were incriminating but hardly a full confession; and should he choose to plead not guilty, they would be worthless without corroboration.

Encouraged by the command's decision not to refer this homicide as a capital case, and cagey as though he'd spent all his brief career defending accused murderers, Charlie Dawson seemed to have learned the black arts of dissembling and stone walling from his client. Through a series of delaying tactics he continued to buy the time he needed to prepare a defense, saying only that Ferris was slowly recovering memory.

The Article 32 waiver had sent NIS back to the streets. Prosecutor Michael O'Shea wanted more, needed more, and he had made his needs known. Favors were called in; resident agents from the Philadelphia Navy Yard visited the dead girl's family and hometown associates, haunted her leave hangouts. Locally, NIS canvassed the battalion, the barracks, all of Q-Town. They retraced the movements of Jimmy Ferris and Beverly Anderson on the last days of her life, interviewed and re-interviewed their known contacts; and they entertained every amateur detective's theory. Agents had returned to the Chaplains Office so often the Cap actually remarked upon it, protesting to Harry Reiner that their presence was disruptive and, by implication, bad for appearances. All these redoubled efforts turned up very little in the way of useful information.

In contrast, their "man on the inside" at the Chaplains Office had garnered for NIS one arrest for distribution of LSD and two for the sale of marijuana. With the incarceration of "Smitty" Smithson and his two cohorts, the chaplains' already depleted enlisted staff was decimated.

The one administrative hope promised by Manpower, the corporal who was experienced as a chaplain's assistant, had arrived from Camp Lejeune under the cloud of an unresolved mast. Because of his protracted family emergency, he was granted humanitarian transfer to the West Coast shortly after reporting to Quantico. The powers controlling personnel assignments would not be moved; there was no replacement, no immediate remedy. That left on the side of the angels only an unlikely trio: Sergeant Diaz, a newly minted private fresh from boot camp, and Willie the Swoop.

"Why you gettin' all bent outa shape, Sarge?"

Cisco Diaz was a doomed man. There was no other rational explanation. Somewhere along the line, he figured, *el Diablo,* the devil himself, must have pointed a bony finger, singling him out for a life of torment. And with luck like that, all the saints his mother prayed to could not turn his fate around. He was doomed.

"What is it? Just because I'm outa uniform?" Willie persisted, honestly guessing.

Doomed. Cisco's existence these days was like a record with a stuck needle or a bad dream that kept repeating itself. He never seemed able to escape from this church or from standing tall in front of the Cap's desk, answering for foul-ups created by shit heads trying to pass themselves off as United States Marines.

"Out of uniform would be a tee shirt and jeans, man. What the hell is this?"

Willie looked injured. "These threads cost me more'n a month's pay," he said, "and they come straight from the Garment District, custom tailor made."

"You look like a pimp."

Injury dissolved into pride. "Really?"

"Totally unsat, man. What made you think you could get away with this?"

Willie spread his hands, resplendent with the customary gold. "It's a wedding."

"Yeah, but it ain't your wedding. And this ain't Vegas."

"I never been to Vegas."

"Then, it ain't Times Square, Harlem, whatever; you know what I'm saying. And there's something you got to understand about weddings, man. Almost always, they're run by the bride's mother. And at this chapel the bride's mother is almost always an officer's wife. And an officer's wife almost always thinks she's got that invisible rank at least two grades higher than her husband's. And there ain't no witch this side of hell meaner than a bad-ass officer's wife mother-of-the-bride."

Cisco looked up in time to see the witch of the hour standing in the doorway, listening in horror, her imperious stare taking in the phenomenon of the lanky black man in white tie and lime green tails but ultimately fixing on his own sergeant's stripes and the name tag fastened, per regulation, an eighth inch above his right blouse pocket.

Doomed.

29

The chaplains' alternate week Monday night poker games had all but faded into legend with the transfer of Pete McLaughlin. Tonight's get-together, hastily called for 1900 hours at the quarters of Father Theo Lurakis, was only the third since Mac's departure and the second that Damon had attended. Theo had encouraged him to liven the evening with a friend or two, so Damon had invited Michael, and Michael had brought with him none other than Special Agent Harry Reiner. The rest of the players were chaplains, Shorty Lawrence, a chunky redhead who towered over them all at six feet, five inches, the bespectacled, reserved and somewhat priggish Jack Devlin, and Percival Langston Hughes, lean and brown, who prefaced every introduction with the news that he preferred answering to his last name.

Theo and Mary Lurakis, veterans of making do with base housing, considered themselves fortunate this tour to have been assigned one of the more spacious and comfortable old white frame bungalows usually reserved for "bird" colonels and Navy captains. The card table was set up on the sun porch in consideration of the unseasonably warm weather. Space had been cleared among the potted plants for a sumptuous party spread and a pail of bottled Sam Adams on ice. Mary, a slight, wraithlike creature in apron and house slippers, moved quietly between kitchen and porch, dutifully keeping the platters filled with sausages, hot peppers and Greek olives, a spicy bean dish topped with feta, and torn pita for dipping.

"I raise," said Theo. The game was Seven Card Stud, aces high, with a modest pot limit. Already the Lurakis family coffers were $12.50 to the good. Father Mac had been right about their host's talent for a believable bluff. Swarthy and rugged as his wife was fair and frail in appearance, Theo wore a permanent smirk, smugly inscrutable.

Damon had also just upped the ante, with feigned enthusiasm—transparently false, no doubt. He didn't feel lucky at all tonight. He felt uneasy, somewhat restless and vaguely anxious. It might be the guilty discomfiture he'd felt whenever he was in Michael's presence, ever since the Norfolk trip. Or maybe it was the heat. A slight breeze was stirring, but little of it could be felt inside the porch enclosure. Harry Reiner had excused himself earlier and stepped outside, ostensibly to indulge his self-deprecated "filthy habit." The glow of his cigar was a steady red beacon near the southwest corner of the yard. Seeing no chance for improvement in his luck this hand, Damon folded and joined Harry outside.

"I wanted to ask," he began in confidential tones, "whether we'll be permitted to keep the services of Lance Corporal Johnson for a while yet. We're so short-handed right now."

"Sure. I mean, I don't see why not. He seems to like it there."

Damon breathed a sigh. "Well, that's a relief. Without him I don't see how we could manage. I thought his duties as an NIS agent might call him back."

Harry barely suppressed a snicker. "Willie's not NIS," he said.

"Pardon?"

"He's not an agent. He doesn't belong to us, per se. He's a C.I., a confidential informant." He paused for effect. "Otherwise known as a snitch."

Damon's jaw dropped. Had he actually said, "Oh, dear," or had he merely thought it?

"But as C.I.'s go, Willie's relatively benign. I mean, there's no felony charge or threat of legal consequences hanging over his head."

"No?"

Harry's grin was barely perceptible in the dark. "A couple years ago he was questioned as an eyewitness to a barracks shooting. He provided some incidental info that checked out on an older open case. After that we approached him about fishing for more—incidental info, that is—and he volunteered, more or less."

"I see."

"He's made himself useful, flushing out druggies; helped us out in a couple situations before yours. And he gave us a good lead on a weapons theft ring with ties to Fort Belvoir. Willie's your basic law enforcement weed; adapts well where planted and grows in the role. I think he enjoys it. The kid has a theatrical bent."

"I've noticed."

"Yeah, well." Harry took a long drag that made his cigar glow brighter. "Remember when you told me about the casualty call Chaplain Roberts made to Anderson's parents?"

"Yes, when I reported the crank calls."

"You said that he noticed the girl's stepfather seemed anxious about taking possession of her car."

"I remember that."

"I asked an associate to make background checks of the family. The stepfather had been involved in some shady deals in Pennsylvania and Jersey. We had him watched and, long story short, there were drugs secreted in Beverly's car. Packets of coke and LSD were hidden where anyone at this end who knew where to look could raise the hood and find them. She wasn't especially close with her parents, but once a month she'd get an out-of-bounds pass and drive home to Pennsylvania. Apparently that was stipulated by her stepfather when he gave her use of the car."

Damon was stunned to silence.

"Ferris may have been involved in the distribution, but we have no proof of that. We're not even sure Beverly knew she was transporting."

"Could that be tied to her murder?"

"So far, no connection." Harry stubbed out the butt of his stogy against the sole of his shoe. "I saw baklava as I passed through the kitchen," he said.

They rejoined the game just as Jack Devlin had come alive, gloating over his winnings. "The worm has turned. Please, gentlemen, be seated."

"Where's the beginner's luck tonight?" Michael lamented. "These guys are cleaning me out."

"The night is young, my friend," Theo told him. "We have yet to hear the first sea story."

Hughes was licking bean dip off his fingers. "I say we belay the sea stories in favor of true crime, seeing we have an expert here." He raised eyebrows at Harry Reiner. "What's the inside scoop on young Jimmy Ferris? What's going to happen to him?"

Harry never discussed an open investigation in a social setting, and felt chagrined to realize he had just done so with Chaplain Keith. Pending court-martial or no, he considered this case still open. "I defer to learned counsel," he said. "It's in his court now, pun intended."

Michael colored somewhat. He didn't much care for mixing business with pleasure, either. "All indications are that Ferris will be pleading guilty," he said, "probably before a military judge, rather than a jury of court members."

"And facing what, in terms of penalty?"

"Life," Michael answered soberly, clearly uncomfortable. He didn't relish being put on the spot, especially with people who most likely sympathized with the defense. "He's not facing pre-meditated murder, where the maximum could be death and the mandated minimum is life in prison. But he's still charged with murder under Article 118, and the maximum possible punishment for that is life imprisonment. If he were to plead guilty to a lesser included offense, such as voluntary manslaughter, and if the facts upheld it, the maximum would be 15 years in Leavenworth." He emphasized, "But that's not how he is charged." Michael hesitated as though he were going to continue. When he didn't, Damon asked, "Once he pleads guilty to murder, then, there's no going back?"

"Not necessarily. There's what we call the 'providency,' or the providence inquiry. The judge asks him questions, and his answers have to support his guilt legally on all points. If the judge feels the guilty plea isn't provident, or proper, he won't accept it. He'll enter a plea of not guilty on the accused's behalf, despite what Ferris says, and he'll require me to prove my case." He lifted a shoulder slightly to convey, I'm not the bad guy here. "Or if Ferris changes his mind, he may be allowed to withdraw his guilty plea before it's accepted. It's up to the judge. It's a matter of discretion. Judicial discretion."

No one spoke for a moment. Harry cleared his throat. "I believe it's my deal."

"If you want sea stories," Devlin began, "did I ever tell you about the time I was high-lining in the breeches buoy from my cruiser to a destroyer and they nearly lost me in the Atlantic?"

The chorus of groans signified that indeed he had told them.

"Well, if that's the way it is," Devlin huffed.

"I haven't heard it," Harry said. "What happened?"

Hughes muttered out the side of his mouth, "He was high-lining in the breeches buoy from his cruiser to a destroyer and they nearly lost him in the Atlantic."

"A cable fouled," Jack Devlin said. "Check."

"I'll open," Theo purred, ogling his hand.

"In for a quarter," said Damon.

"I raise."

"Likewise."

"I'm out."

Still mining for entertainment, Harry asked Theo, "What about last summer? Aren't you the chaplain who talked that Marine with the hostages into surrendering his weapon?" For Damon's benefit he explained, "Some NCO holed up in housing on Geiger Ridge for hours, holding his girl and her family at gunpoint."

"Shhh," Theo said, jerking his head toward his wife in the kitchen. "Upsets the boss."

"I heard that," Mary called out. "Mind yourself, if you want dessert."

Gleeful echoes rippled round the table, "Mind yourself, Father Theo, mind yourself."

"I'm out," muttered Michael. He leaned back, still losing and feeling a little disgruntled. "You know, I'm not at all used to priests who are allowed to be married." He was aware of a piercing cautionary stare from Damon, but it was the truth. History lessons on the Great Schism of 1054 aside, all he really knew about Eastern Orthodox Catholics was that they made the sign of the cross backwards and answered to a Patriarch instead of the Pope. "There ought to be a story in that," he said.

A weary "Ah, now," was heard from the kitchen.

Theo beamed. "A story it is," he said, "one of those truths stranger than fiction."

Something was slammed in the next room, a pot or a cupboard door, and Theo beamed all the brighter.

"Is Rome in or out?" he asked.

"In, and I raise," Damon said.

"I'll see that bet," murmured Devlin.

"Fold," said Hughes.

"Out," said Shorty.

The game dwindled swiftly to a competition between Damon and Theo, or as Theo put it, between Rome and the True Church. Theo postponed the showdown, tantalizing, his cards held lovingly to his chest. "In the Orthodox Catholic Church," he intoned, "a married man may be ordained; but a bachelor, once ordained, must be forever celibate. It is not unheard of, nay, it is commonplace—"

An ominous noise from the kitchen.

"—in the weeks before ordination, for seminarians to go from door to parish door, asking for the hand of the daughter of the house." He smiled benevolently. "In my case, I was blessed with the promise of my high school sweetheart. We were engaged all my last year in seminary."

His wife came to stand behind him then, thorny resignation twisting her mouth, a plate of pastries in her hands.

"But, innocent young thing that she was, little Mary called me to her home two days before our wedding and three days before my ordination—three days, my friends—to tell me she was having doubts; her dainty feet were cold. One of my classmates and dearest friends was already on the verge of nervous collapse because his intended had backed out of their understanding that very week." Theo had them in thrall. "We were talking on the sidewalk at the top of the steps that led down to her father's basement office." Although he seemed to sense Mary's presence behind him, he continued in a whisper. "I threatened to throw her down the stairs."

She set the plate down. "He told me, 'Doubt yourself. Doubt God if you must. But you can't doubt us. That's not allowed.'"

"Not my finest hour," admitted Theo.

"And not your worst," Mary said. She caressed the top of his balding head as she left the room.

"What have you got?" he asked Damon.

"A full house."

Theo displayed his cards. "Four of a kind, gentlemen. Once again the True Church holds the better hand!"

30

"Is there something I can do for you?"

Rose had noticed the man with the drooping shock of sandy hair—she was positive it had been the same person—loitering near her mother's house several hours earlier in the day. And now as she prepared to leave for home he was there again, conspicuously bent over in close examination of the compact privet hedge, as though he was inspecting the leaves for signs of infestation. In November.

He drew himself erect when she spoke to him. He was of medium height, maybe a couple inches taller than she, wearing faded jeans and a camouflage tee shirt under a bulky gray sweater. He pushed the wayward hair off his forehead and looked at her shyly, then smiled. A rather disarming smile, really. "This used to be the Keith house?" he asked.

"It still is."

His brow furrowed and he seemed puzzled.

"Can I help you?"

He began to back away, shaking his head, and she thought perhaps whispering to himself, still looking confused.

"Do I know you?" she called. "I'm Rose."

As abruptly as he had begun his retreat, he halted. His whole demeanor changed as he wheeled and paced forward again with rapid confidence, recovering the distance in the sidewalk between them. "I know your brother," he announced brightly, and stuck out his hand.

"You do?" she exclaimed. The handshake was firm, but his hand was cold, almost clammy. The weather was still unseasonably warm, but there was a chilly wind blowing in from the shore today. Close up, the cardigan he was wearing looked rather the worse for wear; a light jacket might have served him better. "How do you know him?"

"From St. John's."

Rose let go his hand, bristling involuntarily at mention of the seminary. That did not sound right. This person was not anywhere near Damey's age; he had to be at least ten years younger.

"We were there at different times," the man said. "He helped me get in."

"I see. So it's Father—?"

"No. No, I left."

"And you are?" she asked, meaning to hear his name.

"Reminiscing," he said. "It's remarkable how little this part of Norfolk has changed."

"I suppose." Actually she thought it had changed very much indeed. The man had dropped his eyes and once again there was a bashful air about him. "Father Damon is in Virginia again," she offered. "He's in the Navy, a chaplain at Quantico."

"I'll have to look him up." He was surveying her now, head to toe and back again, in a way that made her flush. "Listen," he offered, "would you like to go for coffee?" He was staring intently, but not at her face.

"What?"

"You know, a cup of coffee. We could talk. Talk over coffee." Then he murmured, "Rose," pronouncing her name as softly as an endearment, and his gaze appeared to be resting on her bosom. It was all very unsettling.

"No. No, thank you. I was just leaving. I have to go."

"Well, some other time, then," he said briskly, and abruptly walked away.

She watched him turn the corner. It had been a long time since a man of any age had looked at her like that, let alone a relatively attractive younger man. But there was something odd about him and his manner, something not quite appropriate. She waited until she glimpsed him behind the wheel of an older model sedan, driving up a cross street, before she got into her own car. "Some other time"? She never even got his name.

Michael picked up the nearest *Military Justice Reporter* volume and threw it against the wall. "Son of a bitch!"

Charlie Dawson, glad it hadn't been aimed his way, retrieved the book from the floor and replaced it on the Chief Trial Counsel's desk. "Jeez, sir, I guess I should have told you in a memo."

"Fucking bastard son of a bitch!" Michael swore, his temper winding down as quickly as it had flared. He knew he should apologize for his language, but the adrenalin rush was still with him. "When did he tell you?"

"He didn't, if you mean Ferris. I found out from Hutchins himself in a copy of a notice of appearance."

"Damn it, Charlie."

"I know. I know, sir. My reaction was pretty much like yours."

"I thought we were finally ready to try this albatross."

"Sir, so did I. So did Ferris, for that matter. It was his family, some aunt and uncle in West Virginia, who called the civilian lawyer in. Apparently it took them this long to raise the money."

So the Ferret had a family. Who knew?

"Well, this particular civilian will take every cent and then some," Michael predicted darkly.

"Yeah. It's a shame, really, more ways than one." Dawson excused himself from the office, leaving Michael to stew on his own.

This would set the trial schedule back at least a month, probably more. Jamie Hutchins and his delaying tactics were well known at Quantico.

Legitimately, he'd need some time to come up to speed on the case, but if true to character he would also file a slew of spurious motions just to see the wheels of military justice spin in place.

Michael respected a handful of civilian attorneys who specialized in military law, most of whom were former judge advocates. Any one of them might validly contribute something to the defense of an accused. A few were truly sharp litigators who fought well for their clients. Jamie Hutchins unfortunately was the other sort, the guy who muddied the waters at best, and at worst sat back, allowing military counsel to do all the work while he took all the credit. He was a local yokel whose "aw-shucks" courtroom style and ill-fitting polyester suits were part of a package designed to appeal to the average brig rat looking to beat the system. He was a hustler, an opportunist who chased down military police reports, trading on the ten years he had spent as an Army noncom and the modicum of success he'd enjoyed winning cases other men had prepared. How he hoped to win this one was beyond comprehension.

Michael hung his head a moment, dejected. He rarely lost his temper and was always disappointed in himself when he did so, particularly in front of subordinates. From a major that outburst would have been unseemly enough, but he had picked up lieutenant colonel less than a month ago and was now not only a field grade officer but was also two grades superior to Captain Dawson. Hardly an exemplary performance.

Before Charlie came in Michael had been nursing a churlish mood, anyway. Since his promotion to O-5 he had been feeling his middle age and had become prone to introspection; examination of conscience, they used to call it in the sem. He was beginning to view his life in segments and to wonder how many more chapters were left. Ahead of him there was perhaps one more promotion, to bird colonel. Or perhaps not; competition was fierce. And when he was passed over for promotion, there was retirement—but to what? Most successful judge advocates punched out at 20 years as O-4's or O-5's, some as O-6's, often with the trophy second wife, and they moved on to private practice or something less strenuous, say, in higher education or consulting work. The elect few who had attained the coveted brigadier general slot all seemed to become minor league CEO's or to remain happily, respectably unemployed, traveling and writing their memoirs. Michael didn't see even the most mundane of those scenarios in store for himself, certainly not the trophy wife.

His relationship with Mia had changed so much of late, it was increasingly doubtful that the marriage he had convinced himself they both wanted would ever come about. She was driving him crazy with her hot-cold, on again, off again behavior. He no longer felt he had a life partner he could depend on to stand by him, to want the same things he wanted. How could he, when he hardly knew what he wanted himself?

In some strange, convoluted way the insertion of his religion into the mix had served to pull them apart, rather than bring them closer together. It wasn't merely the sex; he could endure a degree of abstinence beforehand for the sake of the sacrament. It was more than that. They had lost the closeness that had made their match special. He no longer knew what she was thinking, and she didn't seem to care any longer what was on his mind.

Absurd and juvenile as it had to be, he couldn't dismiss the nagging intuition that Damon Keith had something to do with it. Damon also was recently promoted, to commander. He and Mia had been invited to the ceremony on the quarterdeck, where Damon asked Mia to step forward and assist Captain Stannard in pinning on the silver, just as she had assisted the Staff Judge Advocate at Michael's ceremony. That didn't sit well. Not well at all.

"Sir?"

Maryann Phillips was tapping on his door jam. "Do you have a minute?"

"Sure. Come in, Lieutenant."

She perched warily on the edge of an armchair, as though poised to flee the moment she was dismissed. He gathered his voice had carried moments earlier.

"I talked with Smithson in the brig this morning," she said. "He has some information about the Ferris murder case."

"And?"

"And he was hoping to deal; a more lenient pretrial agreement in exchange for what he knows."

Michael stared at her, stony faced.

"Unfortunately, from a negotiating standpoint his information is more valuable to the defense than to the prosecution."

"Then tell Captain Dawson."

"I already have, sir. He said he'd inform his new co-counsel." She made a face. "But I suspect Mr. Hutchins already knows; seems he interviewed Smithson last week, without my knowledge."

"But no sale?"

"No, sir. Smitty said he was satisfied with his military defense counsel." She looked pleased with herself. "Could we take this to the convening authority, maybe sweeten my client's deal a little bit?"

"That depends. What's the information?"

"He says that he slipped Ferris a tab of blotter acid that night at The Sentry Box, just dropped it into his beer while Ferris was in the head. Apparently this is a reliable method of introducing LSD to potential customers; one hit whets the appetite."

"And?"

"And before Smitty could explain the high his good buddy was feeling, Beverly Anderson came in. He gave them some space, and a little while later they were gone." She paused, biting her lip. "He didn't know Ferris apparently had already taken amphetamines. He says he feels really bad about what happened."

"I'll bet."

"So?"

Michael shifted his focus to the stack of law books on his desk. If she only knew how much he wanted to throw something again. "Let me think about it," he said.

31

Thursday mornings at Lejeune Hall began with mandatory field day for all work sections. For Damon that meant an unremitting frontal assault on three of the five senses: In the nostrils, combative odors from sour mops and strong detergent, floor wax and Brasso, all vying for attention through a pervasive cloud of cigarette smoke. In the ears, the rasping scrapes of penknives in corners, coaxing up layers of old wax; the drone of commercial buffers on asphalt tile decks, and the muted hum of vacuums overhead, sucking the week's dust from topside carpets. On the tongue there was the inhaled taste of airborne Pledge. And if it was fortuitously the Thursday after payday, eventually there was the savory combination of sausage, pepperoni and string cheese on Tony's hand thrown crust with secret sauce, delivered as reward for a job well done. There's nothing like the aroma of pizza and Marine Corps coffee to neutralize the antiseptic stink of clean.

And this was in fact pizza week, and it was his turn to buy. He had gladly ponied up, confident that their tiny staff would do a creditable job field-daying the office spaces. Sergeant Diaz had proven that much when he and Willie had managed a small band of casuals in readying the chapel for Marine Corps Sunday. Damon was especially proud of Willie Johnson. The Swoop had badly wanted a walk-on role in the Birthday Pageant at Butler Stadium. He had fervently coveted the dapper uniform of The Marine of 1812. But Willie had swallowed his considerable disappointment when told he could not be spared from duty for rehearsals, and he had "turned to" smartly.

There would be two unclaimed slices of Tony's best to be shared among the troops today. Father Roberts would be covering noon Mass at Memorial Chapel as well as taking communion afterward to patients at the hospital. Damon was himself trading the dubious delights of field day for those of prolonged visitation at the correctional facility. If he ate lunch at all, it would be institutional fare with his little flock of Catholic inmates in the brig's dining hall, after making himself available for the Sacrament of Penance. The men often were eager to share confidences and news of home over their meal, happy just to talk with someone from the outside. Rarely did they discuss with him the acts that had brought them there, or their strategies for leaving confinement; they had lawyers for that.

But before heading to the little chapel to hear confessions, Damon would follow his routine on Thursdays and Sundays. He would pay a private call on Lance Corporal Ferris.

Jimmy Ferris had become less guarded of late, but it was a new openness not to be misconstrued as sociability. He remained demonstrably resentful of the chaplain's attentions. He just appeared to be more relaxed about it. His demeanor was still wound tight as a coiled spring. Damon noticed a contained edginess; Ferris had been biting and digging at the skin around his thumbnails until they were bloody. Whenever he spoke—and he was speaking quite a bit these days—his conversation seemed hollow and false. Whatever his game, he wasn't fooling Father Keith.

The priest was acknowledged with a nod of the head this morning. Ferris seemed eager to tell him, "I got me a lawyer." A tense grin, showing straight, small teeth. "Civilian lawyer. Gonna get me outa here."

"Out of the brig?"

"Outa solitary. Into general pop."

"Well, that's news. Are you sure?"

A dismissive flip of the hand. "It's a motion. He says it's up to the judge, but he'll get me out." Ferris's eyes narrowed and his voice dropped. "We got a witness, too," he said confidentially. "Now we got options."

"A witness?" Damon glanced up at the surveillance camera. "What kind of witness?"

"Somebody was there that night, watchin' us and gettin' himself off in the bushes."

"Somebody—you remember this now?"

"That's right. Somebody was there. I think it was this guy that was hangin' around when we come out on the sidewalk in front of the Sentry Box, and when we started walking up the hill. He was staring. At—at her, you know? I remember I hollered, 'Hey, cowboy!' and he disappeared into the shadows, away from the streetlights. But I think he still followed us, because somebody was there."

Damon felt a frisson of apprehension at the back of his neck and raised a hand to rub it down. "You called him 'cowboy'?"

"Because of the way he walked, you know? Bowlegged, like."

Damon stopped rubbing and passed his hand over sudden perspiration on his upper lip. "And you can find this witness, or your lawyer can?"

Ferris rewarded him with another tight grin. "Well, that's up to NIS, ain't it. That's their job."

Jimmy watched the chaplain go, after he had said his words over him. He was remembering a lot more these days than the watcher in the trees. Back in the hardscrabble hills he came from, what the do-gooders liked to call Appalachia, there had been no shortage of Bible thumpers. None of this man's tribe, none of the wine-into-blood mumbo jumbo, but plenty of fire breathing holy rollers and mealy mouthed missionaries. The summer after he found out his pa had just lit out when he came along, not been killed in a cave-in like he'd been told, his ma sent him to the missionaries to do their skivvy work, get three squares and be saved. Only the preacher man with the sissy ways tried things on him, tried to make him a sis, too. I wasn't having none of that, Jimmy remembered. He bit the bastard, and as soon as he could he lit out, just like his pa. He never forgave his dead ma for that summer. And why should he? She never forgave him for being born.

32

Father Mark Roberts, absorbed by the intricacies of the latest encyclical from Rome, looked up from his reading only when challenged by a persistent rapping on the jamb of his open office door. He resented the intrusion but did his best to render unto Caesar with charity, forcing a frosty smile. "Yes?"

"I'm looking for Chaplain Keith." The burly captain who filled the doorway fairly radiated irritation.

"He's not here just now," Father Roberts said.

"So I've been told."

"Is there something I can help you with?"

"I want to make a complaint."

"About?"

"About Chaplain Keith," the captain snapped. Patience apparently was a virtue unknown to him.

Father Roberts set aside his reading material and reassessed the intruder. Older than the average Marine captain, vaguely familiar, obviously angry. He glanced out the window at the unseasonable strength of the sun and consulted his wristwatch. The Cap would be at his outdoor office.

"The Staff Chaplain isn't in, either, I believe."

"I know that, too," the man said. "I need to know who else Keith answers to."

This was truly bizarre. Father Keith was not the type of man one could easily imagine making enemies. "For?"

"Overstepping," was the terse answer. "Church matters."

Roberts considered a moment before answering, reluctant to encourage the man. But the information sought was readily available elsewhere; no point in obfuscation. "That would be the Military Ordinary, who's the Archbishop of New York. Or Father Keith's civilian bishop. Richmond, I think. But can I ask what this is about? There may be a misunderstanding."

"There's no misunderstanding."

"But 'overstepping'? Some misunderstanding as to his duties, or as to Church law or teaching?"

"He advised my wife to get a divorce," said the captain, and had he not turned abruptly on his heel and left, Father Roberts would have been at a loss for a response.

"You wanted to see me, sir?" The young MP stood nervously in front of Harry's desk.

"Yes, Lance Corporal. Stand easy."

The Marine abandoned his edgy carriage for deer-in-the-headlights wariness.

"I wanted to ask you about this parking citation you wrote. It was a long time ago, but the date happens to be the night of the Beverly Anderson murder. Can you recall anything about it?"

The file copy was studied carefully. "Yes, sir, I remember this." The lance corporal relaxed and looked up expectantly.

"Well?"

"Well, sir?"

Jesus H. Christ. "Well, what do you remember about it?"

"I remember I wrote it up because that's officer housing, sir. I reported the parked car because it had an enlisted sticker, and a long expired sticker, at that. Like years. And no visitor pass showing. It was parked there for hours. Me and my partner patrolled the area all shift, and on the third time around I wrote the citation."

"The third time around?"

The young man colored a bit. "Yes, sir. We figured to cut whoever it was a huss, you know? A little slack. I mean, there's infractions and there's infractions. Parking in officer territory don't seem like the crime of the century. Sir."

"No, it don't," Harry answered sardonically. "Do it?"

"Sir?" The boy had gone all Bambi again.

"That's all, Lance Corporal, you can go."

The MP narrowly missed bumping into Betty in his haste. "Excuse you," she said, shaking her head, annoyed. She presented a slip of paper to her boss. "The registration trace you wanted."

"Thanks, Bets." Harry read the notation with no sense of surprise, improbable though it seemed. He'd had a gut feeling all along.

33

Hot, burning hot, when it should be cold. That can't be right, except it be a sign. For did not the prophet say, "Behold, the day cometh that shall burn as an oven . . . and I saw as it were, a sea of glass mingled with fire . . ."

The sins of the flesh are also a fire, an all-consuming fire that will not be quenched. The ungodly will atone for these deadly sins through the fires of damnation!

Yes, hot when it should be cold. Unnatural heat, unrelenting heat, suffocating heat. And the darkness of sin where there should be light. It was time for judgment.

It was time to be bold. It was time at last to act.

Much as Damon wished that God's good gift of Indian summer could last just a little while longer, the natural signs were unmistakable and now were officially confirmed by the Air Station Weather Service: There was a cold front on its way. The dawning sky was tinged with blood. *Red sky at night, sailor's delight; red sky at dawning, sailor take warning.* The air was heavy, weighted with humidity, the wind steady from the east. The temptation he felt pulling at him was palpable.

While away from Quantico on temporary duty, an usher at Memorial Chapel had entrusted to his favorite chaplain's care his beloved catboat, berthed in a slip at the Quantico Marina. Damon's desire to celebrate that trust and get out on the water—once, only once, please Lord, before the days of frost and the feverish work tempo of Advent—was at war with the sense of priority entrenched in his conscience. It was, after all, Sunday morning. Father Roberts was assigned Mass at the brig, but tradition dictated that Damon pay his customary call there as well, particularly upon Lance Corporal Ferris. And that was part of his dilemma.

He was still troubled by the bizarre encounter in the confessional and the assumptions he had made. Under seal he had told Mac about it and of his suspicions, and thereby he had inadvertently also told NIS. His version of the facts was out of the bag. Why not then inform Ferris, or his lawyer? On the other hand, Gary Winslow was confined in a mental health facility and physically could not be in two places at once. Should the investigative waters really be muddied by his implicating a sick man? A man whom only intuition and nagging self-reproach told him was guilty?

The secondary part of his problem, and by far the more unsettling to his conscience, was his deepening closeness with Mia Rodgers and a corresponding coolness from Michael O'Shea.

Since ordination certainly, and to a degree since childhood, Damon had enjoyed serene confidence that the Holy Spirit would see him through every test in life. He fully expected to meet each turning in his destiny with unwavering faith. It had upheld him in seminary. It had sustained him in Vietnam. But of late he found that he could not think clearly; more upsetting, he could not easily focus in prayer. He felt he had lost something of himself, something vital and real.

Often it seemed as though he were watching his own daily existence in a movie or a dream, seeing from afar and reacting passively. Drifting like a rudderless ship. He was certain that what he felt in his heart for Mia and the distance, real or imagined, between himself and Michael was at the core of his problem. And he firmly, if naively, believed there was no subject under heaven that could not be talked out among friends. In this one thing, he told himself, he could take initiative, act decisively. They could talk this through. He could regain control of his thoughts and his feelings, and thereby again, with grace, command his own life.

It was with that determination that he telephoned Michael after breakfast and asked him to go sailing with him in the early afternoon. He thought he could detect reluctance in his friend's voice, but the invitation was accepted.

Noon Mass ran long, and afterward there were more than the usual number of parishioners congregated on the steps of Memorial Chapel, eager to speak to Father. Damon saw that the rough weather pennant, rather than the oversized Sabbath flag, was now flying at Lejeune Hall, and he was more eager than ever to get to the usher's boat. He congratulated a couple newly engaged, while in his roving imagination already he felt the romance of the tiller in his hand, the damp breeze in his face. He admired and blessed a newborn soon to be baptized, but in distraction his mind was anticipating the luff and snap of the cat's sail in the rising wind. He and Michael would have a good sail. A short one, given the certainty of a coming storm, but a fine one.

By the time he disrobed and drove from the chapel through Q-Town and arrived at the marina, the sky was darkened with gloomy nimbus clouds roiling from the west. The water was gray, becoming choppy. Small craft warnings were out. Sailboats and motorboats were heading in from the Potomac. And beside the boathouse the sailor waiting forlornly in the wind was not Michael.

"He was called to Headquarters, Marine Corps," Mia shouted, looking about to cry. "I had already packed a picnic lunch for the two of you." She nudged a wicker hamper at her feet. Large drops of cold rain were starting to fall, pelting their heads.

Damon's confusion was even greater than his disappointment. *Why, Lord, why, when I had the best of intentions?* Lightning split the horizon, with simultaneous thunder that shook the earth. Raindrops were coming faster with each second of hesitation, falling driven and hard. Mia raised a hand to her cheek to wipe away rain or tears, and looked to him for direction.

"Have you eaten?" he asked.

"No."

"Run to your car, then, and follow mine." He picked up the hamper and carried it to the Chevy.

Retracing his route up Potomac Avenue, he exited the base, taking the civilian roadway that ran parallel to the Medal of Honor Golf Course. He was careful to check his rearview mirror periodically. Rain was sheeting the back window now, but he could make out Mia's headlights. He needed to keep her in sight because she had never been there before, had never visited the logical place for them to go, the one spot that was near and private and, discounting the appearance of impropriety should they be seen, safe. His little bungalow on Fuller Heights Road.

"I'm so angry with Michael," Mia said. She was trembling, with fury or with cold. They had darted from their vehicles to the overhang at Damon's front door but had nevertheless gotten soaked, and it was chilly inside the house. Damon had flicked a light switch to confirm that the storm had already knocked out the electricity.

He brought her a bath towel and a clean oxford shirt and began to coax a fire on the hearth. For privacy she moved out of sight into the kitchen, still talking. "He constantly does this. He breaks promises, he changes plans, he drops out, he never has time for—for anything but work."

Finally the kindling caught, and he added a stout log that settled into place in a shower of sparks. Mia reappeared in the doorway, for all the world resembling a 1950's bobbysoxer in blue jeans and a man's white shirt, the sleeves rolled to her elbows. "No time for us," she said. "And now for you. It's unforgivable, really."

Damon glanced up from the hearth. "Nothing is unforgivable," he said quietly.

"Yes, Father," she responded, with barely a trace of resentment in her voice and with wry emphasis on "Father." She cleared her throat, obviously marshalling better thoughts. "Shall I set out the lunch?"

"Please. I'll clear a place on the coffee table, and we can eat right here, by the fireplace." He made a clean sweep of it, depositing a pile of paperwork in a chair, and excused himself. By the time he returned from his bedroom in fresh clericals sans collar, she had moved his sofa cushions to the floor and spread a feast: Cold chicken, boiled eggs, cheese biscuits, pumpkin pie, a thermos of coffee and one of milk. He grinned in appreciation. "Now, this is better than a picnic on Chopawamsic Island!"

"I should think so. There's nothing there, you know."

"I know." Nothing but sand and driftwood and, likely, cigarette butts and beer cans.

"Sad to say, I was stranded there once," Mia said, pulling a face. "Marooned. Went on a motorboat ride with some Marines, male and female, who had no thought for returning to the mainland until the liquor was gone. Never felt so helpless in my life."

"Not good, feeling out of control," he agreed.

They bowed their heads for grace. After prayer he asked, "Is that why you're so angry with Michael?"

She bit her lip and looked about to cry again. "I suppose so."

Damon realized with a jolt that he wanted nothing more than to take her in his arms and give comfort. *Lord, guide me, help me offer mediation instead.* "You said he was called away?"

"Yes. There's a new case from Security Guard Battalion, something about the theft of specimen currency from a safe at the Paris Embassy. The State Department is in an uproar." She added grudgingly, "Whenever State is involved there are hoops to be jumped through."

"So you believe him?"

"Of course I believe him. I just wish it were different. I wish he wasn't always so unthinking, so quick to push his personal life aside in favor of—of—"

"Duty?"

Mia shrugged her shoulders, exasperated. "Okay, yes." Lightning and thunder erupted, alarmingly close. "I shouldn't expect you to understand. You're two of a kind."

Damon silently thanked God for the subtle trigger in that insight. "You're right. And not to be too preachy, but sometimes our difficulty is in understanding where our greatest duty lies."

They ate and drank ravenously, listening to the storm rage outside. Hail was using his roof for a kettledrum, and whenever the wind changed there was the scraping of branches on window glass. From this unusual vantage point near the floor, for Damon the room assumed a surreal quality, given the sudden lightning flashes in a contest with flickering firelight, and with Mia seated beside him. Most especially with Mia here. Conversation, when the storm subsided a bit and they were ready again to talk, turned to the court case that concerned them both. He asked, "Will this be your first murder trial?"

"Oh, no. The first in a long while, but my fourth, actually. There was one during my very first year as a court reporter, when I was still in a probationary period, in training." Mia frowned. "I had some awful nightmares. The autopsy photos, and the bloody clothes in an evidence bag. It stayed with me."

"Anything similar to this?"

"Not really. That first one was a grudge killing, a barracks disagreement gone horribly wrong. The other two were rape-murders." She fell quiet again for a moment. "But there's one thing all murder trials seem to have in common. It's the horrible feeling you get, like a weight pressing down on your chest, on your heart. At least, I know that's something I have experienced each time. I think it's because of the enormity of the crime, you know? Of the sin committed. Man's inhumanity, all that. Does that seem strange to you, or silly?"

"Not at all. I've felt much the same way at times, privy to confession," he admitted. "Burdened."

"Yes."

Before they were finished eating he found himself, against better judgment, telling her about the strange phone calls and the mystery man in the confessional. It was amazingly easy to open up to her once he had started. He told her all of it, of his certainty that the man was Winslow and why he was sure, about the tap on Father Mac's phone and Agent Reiner's dismissal of his worry, and now of Lance Corporal Ferris's claim of a witness and all that could portend for Ferris if by some miracle his own farfetched theory was correct.

Mia listened intently and sympathetically until he was done.

"But Damey, it isn't impossible," she said, smiling. "You may be entirely right about Winslow."

"What do you mean?"

"If it was a voluntary committal, rather than court ordered, he may be free to come and go from Eastern State."

Yet another jolt to his nerves. "How do you know this?"

"From testimony I've taken, primarily. People who are there voluntarily are permitted to check themselves out periodically "A.M. A." Against medical advice. Also, I know because I had a great aunt who was manic-depressive. She committed herself to a private hospital but would sign herself out on holidays to visit us. It's not unusual. Damey?"

He was on his feet now, pacing and rubbing down the sudden, familiar tension at the nape of his neck. "God forgive me," he exclaimed, "all this time, wasted. All this time, Lance Corporal Ferris has been in the brig. I should tell him. I should tell Agent Reiner."

Mia scrambled to her feet and caught him by the arm. "You can still make all that right," she said. "You can tell NIS. But you should also understand that it may not make a difference." She was peering into his face anxiously. Never before had he been so close to those lovely gray eyes. "Winslow may have done all this simply to punish you. He may not have been there at all."

He considered a moment, searching the face he found the more beautiful for its compassion. He had wanted to clear the air with Michael. Perhaps he could do that now with Mia. Her forehead, lined with concern, was at a height even with his lips. On impulse he kissed it softly. He took both of her hands in his. "Let's sit down again. There's something else I want to talk about."

She sat obediently, smiling with expectation. Would it be an exaggeration to say the woman was suddenly radiant? No, he decided, it would not. And did that elate him? Yes, God forgive him, it did.

"We've come as far as we need to with your religious instruction," Damon told her gently. "We don't need to meet for that anymore."

Her face fell somewhat. "What, I—I don't I get a test?"

"No test. If you want to make a profession of faith, you're ready."

"Oh, I do."

"Then you can, and you and Michael can set a wedding date."

Mia dropped her eyes.

"Mia? Michael still wants the marriage?"

"Yes." A clap of thunder startled her, but she did not raise her head. "As far as I know, he does."

Damon felt that tension and thrill of fear again, this time in his gut. *Dear Lord, you know me, I'm your servant. Please guide me.* He drew a deep breath. "And do you?" he pressed. She was hunched over, her hands folded in her lap. "Do you want it, Mia?"

She looked up at him finally, eyes glistening. "I—I think I do. It's complicated." The tears she had been holding back since he first spied her on the windy dock flooded her cheeks now, more quickly than she could brush them away. "Oh, Damey! Father! As long as we're telling secrets, I have one of my own."

34

Doctor Sam Hennessy's voice over the telephone shook, conveying his obvious embarrassment and alarm. He was apologizing profusely for all the difficulty NIS had had in reaching him. "I was just about to call the chaplain," he added hastily.

As for Harry, he couldn't disguise his impatience, nor his anger with himself. How could he have allowed this to happen? He had heard "mental" and taken much too much for granted. Why hadn't he pressed for more information, asked about Winslow's ability to check himself out of that damn hospital?

"I've already spoken to Mrs. Kelly, the chaplain's sister," the doctor was saying. "Tried that number first, since it's local. It sounds like Mr. Winslow may have accosted her recently, in Norfolk."

"What's that?" Harry shot a glance at Father Keith, back on the visitor's chair and appearing as worried and uncomfortable as the first time.

"From her description of the man, his manner and what he said—"

"Was he threatening?"

"No, not in the conventional sense."

"Come again?" Harry was losing what little patience he had before coffee on a Monday.

"She said she didn't feel threatened. But given what I know about Mr. Winslow's obsession with her brother, perhaps she should have. You must understand," Doctor Hennessy added quickly, "all this about Father Keith's guilt and retribution for it, all that, is very old news. I had no idea that after so many years it was more than an abstract. A psychic metaphor, if you will, for the sinful fall of man, and of course transference of Mr. Winslow's own shame, particularly regarding anything sexual."

"Yeah, well—"

"Until Housekeeping cleaned his room during another absence Saturday evening, and found some of his meds that he'd obviously skipped secreted under the mattress, and Father Keith's crumpled phone message for me in the wastebasket—"

"Yeah, yeah, I understand, Doc. Who'da thunk it, right? You keep notes, do you, of your sessions with Winslow?"

"Going back to his admission in 1969, yes. But if you want to see them, you'll need a court order, Agent."

"Not a problem." Harry winked his thanks at Betty, who had brought him a saving cup of joe, and another cup for the chaplain. "One point of curiosity, Doctor. All these times away from the hospital, where did you think he was going?"

Hennessy sighed audibly. "There was a brother. He used to visit Gary fairly often, and then when the brother moved from the immediate area he left an old sedan for Gary's use. Mr. Winslow led me to believe he was using the car to visit his brother in Fredericksburg."

"The brother's name?"

"William. But I tried the contact number Mr. Winslow had put in his file, as well as calling Information up there, after I spoke with Mrs. Kelly this weekend."

"Let me guess," Harry posited, now fortified by several scalding gulps of coffee, "a dead end?"

"Yes," he doctor replied. "And I trust that's merely a figure of speech."

"Honey, you ready to order?" Marie glanced over her shoulder at Tony, who was exhorting her with seriously pursed lips and acrobatic eyebrows. This character, with his cammies minus insignia and hair too long for active duty, had already hogged a booth for nearly an hour, reading what looked like a New Testament and toying with a menu.

The would-be customer raised his gaze about level with Marie's chest, something she was more or less accustomed to; D cups had their own fan base. But he kept silent, something she was not used to, not in this joint at dinnertime. The minute it was dark out, the Sentry Box neon in the front window kicked in, and the noise level inside ramped up. People got talkative when their workday was over and they could "freely imbibe," as Tony liked to put it.

"Or are you waiting for someone?" she asked politely.

The young man beamed up at her then. "You might say that."

"Well, how about I bring you something to drink?"

Even that suggestion seemed to give pause, while his eyes drifted back to her bust line.

"Iced tea? Coffee? A beer?"

"I'd like a cup of coffee," he said, suddenly decisive, "and a slice of pizza."

"Now we're talking. Pepperoni okay? Or would you like the house special? A buck extra, but it's got everything."

He seemed to have shot his wad on decision making. This was wearing on her last nerve. "I'll bring you a house slice," she said. "You'll love it, everybody does." Marie scribbled the order and turned on her heel before the weird little guy could change her mind for her. Tony just didn't pay her enough.

"Mia and Damey, sitting in a tree, K-I-S-S-I-N-G. First comes love, then comes marriage, then comes Mia with a baby carriage!"

Such a silly, childish singsong rhyme. But there was nothing at all childish about this. Damon's mouth sought hers hungrily with deep and soulful kisses. His lips then trailed to her neck, his breath hot and moist on her skin. All this while he was awkwardly caressing her body through her clothes with one hand, fumbling at her buttons with the other. She helped him open her blouse and freed her breasts, guiding his lips to them.

Kissing the top of his head, she moved away, unbuttoned and pulled urgently at his shirt. But there, caught in the tangle of curly dark hairs on his chest, lay the St. Patrick medal just like Michael's. It made her flinch, seeing it again. Strangely, it seemed to be luminous, picking up and reflecting ambient light. As she stared at the medal, it started to glow brighter and brighter, until more than merely glowing, it was becoming white hot, smoldering, beginning to sear its imprint into the flesh over Damon's heart.

She woke in a panic, breathless, flushed, horrified and oddly sad. For a long miserable moment she held her aching head. Then she groped on the bed through the darkness, and found Collette's fur. She pulled the cat close to her. And for this once, rather than launching the usual indignant struggle to be free, the animal relaxed, becoming pliant as the woman wept, allowing itself to be clutched and stroked and, at long last, cradled like a baby.

35

Come, O Sanctifier, Almighty and Eternal God, and bless this sacrifice prepared for the glory of your Holy Name.

It was Tuesday night. Two days since Mia had confided in him and sent him spinning, a day and a half since his return visit to NIS, a full twenty-four hours since Michael had called him late Monday with his excited news that, infrequent though opportunities had been, his champion "swimmers" had succeeded in making him an expectant dad. Two days that seemed to Damon like two years.

His duties today had not included the Mass, but like many priests of his generation, he felt a day was incomplete without it. Rather than use his Mass kit at home, he had come to the chapel to commune with his God. And come not merely to the little Blessed Sacrament Chapel at the rear of the building, but to the main chancel itself. He needed a large altar tonight, a cavernous arena for the enormity of his emotions. He had kept the minimal security lamps on within the darkened church, and had lovingly lit the sacramental candles, creating a small pool of warmth and light. He had brought forth the chalice and ciborium, the cruet tray and linens. Behind the altar he had turned the brass cross from its smooth Protestant design to reveal the corpus on the reverse side. He had made all things ready, and then in the vesting he had prepared himself.

It is truly right and just, proper and helpful toward salvation, that we always and everywhere give thanks to You, O Lord, holy Father, almighty and eternal God, through Christ our Lord.

There was solace in the knowledge that, although his voice echoed through the empty sanctuary, he was not alone. God was with him, of course; and surely somewhere in the world at this very moment a brother in Christ was praying the same prayer, sanctifying the same offering, living the same holy sacrifice. In a great cathedral, in the humblest of missions, in a hospital or a prison, in the privacy of his own rooms, or in the open air, a fellow cleric of the universal church was celebrating the Eucharist. The thought was comforting in its magnitude and in its intimacy. The priesthood, lonely though it might be, was a brotherhood like no other.

You always create, sanctify, fill with life, bless, and bestow upon us all good things.

His raw jealousy of Michael felt different now, rather like joy and grief commingled. His tender affection for Mia remained, but that too had undergone a transformation that was near miraculous. Almost from the moment she had entrusted him with her secret, sharing gladness freighted with fear, he had begun to see her differently; and the shift in perspective was oddly freeing. The fact that she carried a child was a visceral reality, proof of a physical union far removed from his own life experience. He had counseled couples often enough on the "Madonna effect" of pregnancy, but now he truly understood it. He loved her, of that he was certain; but he no longer desired her. She was a mother; she, the baby and Michael were a family now, an option closed to him. He could be a part of each family yet belong to none, to paraphrase Lacordaire; he was a priest forever. And he was clear on this now: even more than he loved Mia, he loved being a priest.

As often as you shall do these things, in memory of Me shall you do them.

No matter how often he repeated them, the words were never stale, for the truth in them renewed itself with each Eucharist. Their simplicity and beauty were ever fresh, as though the Lord were breaking bread with his disciples in the here and now, saying for the first time, "Do this in remembrance of me." Damon lost himself in the reaffirmation of his faith each time he celebrated Mass. The cares of the day were surrendered to God, as in total concentration he became God's instrument. Time was suspended while he consecrated the bread and wine. The mystery of the sacrament had never disappointed him.

Lord, I am not worthy that You should come under my roof. Speak but the word and my soul will be healed.

Having consumed the precious body and blood, he was quiet in a prayerful clarity of mind that went on for untold minutes. The chapel was silent as only an empty building meant to be filled with human activity can be. But as he made the ablutions, cleansing the chalice, polishing it with the purificator, he thought he heard something, sensed movement in the shadows.

"Ask for a blessing, Father, for you have sinned." This time the voice was loud, distinct and familiar; the figure slowly moved in its rocking gait into the candlelight.

Damon raised his eyes and met those of his accuser with a serenity that surprised even himself. "Gary," Damon said softly. "I suppose I've been expecting you."

Winslow was dressed in sneakers and camouflage greens that looked sweat stained and too small for his body, and he was holding a K-bar knife. Feeling remarkably calm, Damon pointed at it.

"You've brought that into God's house? That's not like you."

Winslow raised the blade and looked at it, blinking convulsively. "Retribution is—"

"But don't you remember what our Lord said when he gave us the Our Father? 'If you forgive men their transgressions, your heavenly Father will forgive you. But if you do not forgive men, neither will your Father forgive your transgressions.'"

"No! It's time," Winslow said, "a time to reap—"

The heavy metal thud of a closing outer door sounded and reverberated. Special Agent Merle Parks was already advancing up the center aisle of the nave, his left shoulder harness and holster visible beneath his flared suit jacket, his right hand at the ready. His badge was held high in his left hand. "NIS! Drop the weapon!"

Police presence produced the adrenalin rush that confrontation by Gary Winslow had not. Damon stepped away from the communion table and moved closer to his would-be assailant, whose attention was riveted to him and oblivious to the intrusion. "Please! Gary, listen to me. I didn't betray you in the way you think I did."

"Shut up!" Winslow was rounding on Damon, still stress blinking, twitching his head in an effort to clear it perhaps, but brandishing the knife as though he well remembered his combat training.

"I have wronged you, it's true," Damon said, "by sin of omission, and I ask you to forgive me for that."

"Padre, that's not helping." Parks was at the steps of the altar now, and for the first time Winslow appeared aware of him. He began crouching somewhat in fighting stance, gazing wild eyed from priest to cop and back again.

Suddenly a dark shape erupted from the ghostly dimness to the side of the sanctuary, streaking past a fluted pillar and seemingly flying catlike through the air to tackle Winslow high, above the waist. The two fell sideways together, thrashing for possession of the knife that had been knocked free on impact. It tumbled down the carpeted steps and was kicked aside by Agent Parks. Winslow's staccato yelps, "No, no, no, no!" echoed as he was finally pulled to his feet, and swiftly both arms were wrenched behind his back.

"Hot damn, Swoop, I didn't know you had it in you!" Agent Parks exclaimed.

Lance Corporal Willie Johnson flashed a golden smile as he presented his prisoner to be cuffed. "Whaddaya talking? I'm a Marine, ain't I?"

Shaking his head in disbelief, Parks couldn't suppress a smile. He pulled a rights card from his pocket and began an advisement, stumbling a bit over adapting Article 31 rights to a civilian detainee but delivering the gist admirably.

Damon descended the altar steps to thank Agent Parks and Willie. Gary Winslow, after his initial spasm of frustration, had quieted strangely. More frightened than menacing now, Damon thought; his face held a vestige of the fanatical ex-seminarian Damon remembered. The mouth was slack with confusion, the eyes that had once held such promising eagerness were pale green and watery. Winslow held those eyes tightly closed when the priest touched his forehead, making the sign of the cross. "Please forgive me," Damon said again, "as I forgive you, in the name of the Father, and of the Son, and of the Holy Spirit." No one could tell him that wasn't helping.

36

Michael O'Shea had been running by the glow of streetlamps along Barnett Avenue since O-dark-thirty. Now that the sun was rising above the trees on Waller Hill, he broke for the sharply inclined road behind the barracks buildings that bypassed the old abandoned brig, to circle the hard way back to Lejeune Hall. He felt the burn in his legs and lungs, felt his heart pumping with every stride, and kept on going, his body on autopilot but his head focused.

With Gary Winslow in police custody pending escort back to Eastern State Hospital, he had been assured by Harry Reiner that the prosecution could now effectively respond to Jamie Hutchins's extraordinary request for production of Jimmy Ferris's mystery witness. Reiner had questioned Winslow extensively and had pulled a 180, no longer doubting the culpability of Lance Corporal Ferris. He was newly convinced that Winslow had been at the scene, had witnessed the murder, and had supplied the confessional stole after the fact. If Winslow were closely monitored until the trial and received all his meds, extracting competent court testimony to that effect might be possible. Or might not. The court-martial would go forward mid-January in any event, ready or not.

And by mid-January he would be an old married man. Old, if the burn in his chest was an indicator, and very much married, on authority of his overachieving, ever amazing friend Damon Keith. Damey had called on him with a bottle of Jameson's in one hand and a church calendar in the other, oozing passionately somber advice on devotion in marriage. "You have to make time for her," he'd insisted fiercely, "you have to make her feel secure, let her know she and your children will always come first. Before work, before the Corps, before yourself."

"Before everyone but God," Michael repeated aloud as he rounded a curve in the pavement and the sun caught him full in the eyes. A wake-up call? Okay, he'd give Damey that. It was what Mia had been trying to tell him for months. And hell, he knew they were right.

And so it has come to pass, he had realized this morning, that God and his best friend have accomplished in short order what he had failed to do for half a year. The Almighty, with that most common of miracles, procreation; and Damon, through his extraordinary influence on the intended bride: They had set a wedding date.

It was all figured out, and largely without his help. He could only marvel at the plan, which he was assured would proceed like clockwork. Little more than a week from now, Mia would make a profession of faith privately in the Blessed Sacrament Chapel, followed by her first confession. She would receive her first communion at their wedding Mass that same morning of Thanksgiving Day. A small gathering, informal and intimate; his sisters would be there, Cassie Martin and her husband; Maureen's husband would be best man. Mass would be followed by brunch at the Officers' Club.

He and his bride would drive with Mia's mother to Norfolk. Late that afternoon they would join his sisters and their extended families at a favorite restaurant for a traditional holiday meal. Mia had joked that what she would save on a fancy gown and a tiered wedding cake would pay for the champagne, the pies, and cranberry sauce laced with brandy. Maureen would host his new mother-in-law for the weekend, while the happy couple relaxed in luxury at the Williamsburg Inn. The newlyweds would return Mrs. Rodgers to Richmond on Sunday morning, on their way back to Quantico. They would make their real honeymoon trip later, during the Christmas stand down. He would return early in January refreshed, to push the Ferris general court-martial to completion two weeks later—and he would take care all the while not to neglect his beloved. Of course he would.

And she was his beloved, now more than ever. Maddening, confounding, but utterly lovable. And frightening. If anyone had told him six months ago that he would now be approaching the marriage he had so wanted with a new ambivalence, even trepidation, he would have scoffed. Sometimes of late he reflected on his short, tranquil stay in seminary with something akin to nostalgia. He supposed he would never understand women.

Pausing near Lejeune Hall for a few cool down stretches before heading for the showers in the basement, he thought he saw Rose Kelly, or someone who looked like her, striding with purpose across the parking lot. Damon had it easy, he thought, with only his birth family to complicate his life. No entanglements, no responsibility for anyone but himself. No heartbreak.

With the element of surprise in her favor, Rose presented herself in her brother's office with the determined grace of a lioness closing upon its kill. She'd had her hair cut shorter and lightened somewhat. Together with soft makeup and a trim new navy suit, hemline slightly higher than usual, it was a younger, more eye-catching look, and she carried it off with authority.

"I'm here to help Mia with wedding preparations," she announced. "Mom has Jackie for a couple days. You can put me up, right?" She gave him a swift kiss on the cheek and, without waiting for an answer, delivered her bombshell. "Mia wants me as her matron of honor. And I'm doing it," she added defiantly.

It crossed Damon's mind later that he must have been agape as Marley's ghost. "Rose," was all he could say.

"I know better than you how long I've been away from the church, and how far away, and that the official witnesses to the ceremony are supposed to be Catholics in good standing. But if you have qualms you can always have someone else sign the register. Right?"

"Rose."

She pulled herself tall, all five feet, three inches at attention, and jutted her chin in determination. "She wants *me*, Damey."

He smiled at his sister and found the presence of mind to kiss her back. "Naturally she does," he said.

While her matron of honor was crusading on her behalf Mia was on her knees in her en suite bathroom, alternately puking, retching, and gagging over the porcelain bowl. If this is what it's going to be like, she thought crazily, I'm paying for my sins. Out of the corner of her eye she saw the cat watching her intently, and in spite of the puke she felt like laughing. I'm really turning into a Catholic, if I'm thinking in terms of sin at a time like this.

Rose Kelly was coming over this afternoon. She had told her on the phone that she was bringing with her on approval from the bridal salon three "becoming possibilities" in winter ivory—a tailored linen suit, a silk and lace two-piece dress, and a jacketed dress trimmed with cream embroidery. A comedown in Rose's mind, no doubt, from the clouds of white organza Mia had tried on months ago; but to Mia, just what the doctor ordered. Doctor. Ugh. She would have to find one. Or perhaps she would make use of the naval clinic. After all, very soon she would qualify as a military dependent. So much would be different.

She rinsed her mouth with water, used mouthwash, brushed her teeth and rinsed again. Collette remained watching, patiently waiting. At least this way, Mia had decided, we will be spared a mountain of details before the wedding. There will be no engraved invitations, no fussing over catering choices, no angst about registering for gifts. It was not really a loss, to her mind; the simplicity suited her. She didn't want to wait. She had thought long and hard, had prayed about it. No child of hers would one day be counting months on fingers, wondering how big the shotgun was. As a young girl curious about her parents, her own interest in calendar dates and their implications had bordered on obsession. Her tight-lipped mother still deflected questions. Her dad, her dependable rock—her angel—had made loving reassurances. But Mia had always speculated about the marriage of two so disparate souls and, whenever they openly argued, felt sad and inexplicably guilty. There would be none of that for her child.

Besides, months of planning would not make the ceremony itself any more beautiful. She was sure of that. Cassie had told her that a horn of plenty replete with fresh vegetables, gourds, nuts and fruits would be on the main altar; Cass would see to the cornucopia herself, as was her custom. The Altar Guild would provide the customary baskets of asters, mums, and gladioli in autumn colors. Mia need only add a couple vases of yellow roses to complement the bouquet she would carry, and the sanctuary would be quite resplendent. The organist had already agreed to come early Thanksgiving morning, and Damey had suggestions for music. Damey. She really must remember to call him "Father Damon" more often now.

It was good luck that today's docket was empty and she could call in sick this morning without guilt. Everyone needed a mental health day once in a while. She splashed water on her face and toweled off vigorously. Going to the kitchen to put the kettle on for tea, she noticed that the cat followed, still scrutinizing her every move. Mia turned finally and bent closer to her furry shadow. "It's all right, Collette," she said quietly. "I'm okay."

The ginger cat pinched her eyes shut for a moment to signify her understanding, then moved regally to the front door to be let out. Her work here was done.

Harry Reiner was in a sour mood. He'd had to cancel plans with Marilyn a few times—okay, more than a few—and now she wasn't returning his calls. That was one of the troubles with a May-December relationship, he supposed. If old man December doesn't deliver, she "May" get her jollies elsewhere. Well, nothing lasts forever. He'd been drumming his fingers on the telephone receiver, trying to decide whether another attempt was worth it, when a woman in navy blue captured all his attention.

"Mrs. Kelly, is it?" he asked, rising.

Rose shook hands and introduced herself.

"I wouldn't have taken you for Father Keith's sister," Harry said.

She reddened a bit. "No, there's not much resemblance, is there? Looks or otherwise."

Harry grabbed the cushion he often used to ease his back and placed it on the visitor chair for her. "Please," he said.

They discussed the reason for her visit. "It's not that it has a direct connection with the Anderson case," he told her, "it's more like, it fills in the background for me, and confirms that he was pursuing his obsession with the chaplain while he was free on earlier occasions."

"I see."

"He's due to be picked up and returned to the hospital in an hour. They should be ready for us about now."

He took her to a room where she could view a physical lineup of young men of similar height, weight and coloring, without being seen herself. She had no trouble pointing out Gary Winslow. Had she not recognized his features, his demeanor and his anxious darting eyes would have given him away. "That's him, number three."

Harry thanked her, shook her hand again, and realized suddenly that he wanted to delay her leaving. "I could use a break. Want to go for coffee?" he asked.

Rose reddened again, and started to laugh. "That's what he said." She tipped her head toward the viewing glass.

"Oh, yeah."

She looked at her wristwatch. "It's nearly lunchtime, Mr. Reiner."

"Harry."

"Then please call me Rose. Nearly lunchtime, and I had a long drive this morning, Harry. I could use a sandwich. And maybe a beer?"

He grinned and grabbed the lady's elbow to steer her toward the door. "You're my kinda girl," he said, and began to hope it was true.

37

Mia, Rose and Cassie were gathered around Mia's dining room table, congratulating themselves on all that had been accomplished. The creamy silk and lace two-piece dress that was chosen as wedding attire and the tailored ivory suit that would be the bride's traveling outfit were hanging upstairs, safely encased in garment bags. Both had been modeled with élan this evening and awarded two thumbs up. The bridal bouquet and accompanying flowers were already ordered, the music suggestions discussed and approved. Arrangements had been made with the Officers Club for reserved seating at brunch and with the restaurant in Norfolk for a large private room in the late afternoon for a sumptuous family dinner. Come Thanksgiving morning, Cassie would help Mia with hair and makeup. Her husband Joe would pick up Mia's mother at the train station, and Joe's best friend would serve as their semi-professional photographer. Maureen would bring something old, the prayer book Michael's mother had carried at her wedding Mass. Lucy would provide something new, the gift of a mother of pearl rosary. Rose had the borrowed and blue requirements covered with a string of cultured pearls and a garter, respectively. So there was nothing left to do now but celebrate with an impromptu party. Virgin Mai Tai's, baked brie with French bread, and petit fours, a strange but wholly satisfying combination.

"Okay, I thought you were gutsy before," Rose said during a lull in laughter, "but tell the truth, Mia. The Catholic Church, marriage and a baby too? You're ready for all of this at once?"

Mia didn't hesitate. "I'm scared witless," she said, setting off a new burst of hilarity.

"Good answer, girl. If you'd said otherwise, I'd be worried."

"You're ready," Cassie assured her, reaching for another little cake, "you're fine. But I don't know, Mee," she offered mischievously, "is getting married on Thanksgiving really such a good idea? I mean, you'll always associate the word 'husband' with 'turkey.'"

Rose hooted. "Your point being?"

Mia was feeling a deliciously cozy, ebullient warmth. She studied the swizzle stick in her drink. "Are you sure there's nothing in this?"

"I wouldn't do that to you," Rose said. Her mind's eye flashed on the sexy bald detective who had bought her lunch the day before. Sixteen years sober, he'd said. "Or to little Mikey or Michelle there," she added, nodding toward Mia's tummy.

"Omigod, Mee, have you picked out names?"

She wrinkled her nose. "No, no, Cass. It still isn't that real to me, despite the morning sickness."

"How is Michael with it?"

"He's been wonderful. He'll make a great dad."

"And my brother, the father?" Rose asked quietly.

Mia looked at her quizzically and knew her color was rising. "He's been very supportive."

Cassie chimed in, "Father Keith is great with children. He's always the first choice with the parents for baptisms."

Without quite knowing why, Mia wanted to change the subject. "Michael is agreeable to moving in here, which is a great relief to me. I didn't want to lose my house."

"It's a beautiful home," Rose agreed. "I'm glad for you. How many bedrooms are there?"

"Three, although the third one is tiny. Just right for a nursery. Would you like a tour?"

"You bet."

On their way up the staircase they were passed by a furry orange streak, coming down. Cassie, who knew her way, had barged ahead to turn on lights and close closet doors.

"Colette's the only uncertainty," Mia said. "That cat may decamp for the neighbor's once Michael is here to stay, and then a baby." She looked back from the stairs to see Colette gazing up at her. "But I rather hope not," she added wistfully.

Rose put an arm around Mia and gently turned her round. "Are you truly happy, then?" she asked softly.

Mia sensed the importance of the question and the sisterly concern from whence it came. She paused thoughtfully before answering. "It's what I've wanted, all of it. And it all finally does feel right."

Rose kissed her new friend on the cheek. That didn't quite answer her question, but it would have to do.

Damon had turned in early but found he couldn't sleep. The more he tried to channel his thoughts toward peace and grace, the more they slipped stubbornly back to frustration and unease. He had perused the ordinary for the nuptial Mass before retiring, and the words about love and submission were now mixed up in his mind with a kaleidoscope of images. Michael with Mia, Ferris with Beverly, Captain Brady with Martha, Winslow with any woman. *How do so many people get it so wrong, Lord?*

He had heard from Father Mac today, calling from Great Lakes to inquire about progress in Lance Corporal Ferris's case. It was Damon's impression that the phone taps had been abandoned, but still he was guarded in his responses. He did not tell Mac that he was facing censure from his bishop in the matter of the Bradys, a misunderstanding that had taken a regrettable turn. And then Mac asked about Michael and Mia.

"O'Shea called me with his news, very excited," he'd said. "He's a good man."

"The best."

"I always liked him. And I understand that you grew up together?"

"That's right."

"He told me Miss Rodgers is entering the Church the same day."

"Yes."

"As I recall, she had little interest in religion before they got engaged. I hope it's a true conversion; no buyer's remorse, for his sake."

"It is. It is." Damon had felt the hairs on the back of his neck rise and tingle as Father Mac spoke. He had listened carefully and watched Mia closely for long enough to know. If you are open to it, sooner or later the prayer that is the Mass speaks to your soul, and you fall in love. He knew love when he saw it.

"Well, Boy-o, it's a grand thing. A grand thing."

It was that. And yet there was that residual sense of loss, the vague wistfulness of the outsider in matters of the heart that would not let him rest. He turned on the lamp beside his bed. He had not experienced a bout of insomnia since Vietnam, and in those days it had not been caused by the horrors of war, which he'd borne with the help of the Holy Spirit, but by the aftereffects of Nuoc Mam sauce and Bah Muy Bah beer. He turned his book again to the page that addressed two become one flesh and began formulating his wedding homily, until that moment came when he felt himself floating up to the ceiling, body and soul, and finally sleep claimed him.

38

Thanksgiving Day dawned seasonably cold and crisp, not a cloud in the sky, a happy portent that all of Mia's careful planning would pay off handsomely. Someone once said that it's not a wedding until something goes wrong, but that was not so in her case. Her special day was truly charmed, and the highlights would be etched deeply in her memory for all time:

Not a hint of morning sickness! Her mother, so beautifully turned out and in an expansive if teary mood, sharing tales of her own wedding day. The organist, on time and on key, the music heavenly. The amateur photographer, organized and amazing. And Willie "the Swoop" Johnson, riding a wave of gratitude and granted dispensation from the uniform of the day, tending the altar in his finest white frock coat, to the amusement of early guests.

She would remember that Father Damon embraced her after she made her profession of faith, and that he was kindness personified in the confessional. That she walked the white linen unrolled in the crimson aisle with confidence, drawn by Michael's beaming face; that the rings were not fumbled, nor did either voice falter in repeating the vows. At communion the host, fresh and delicate, dissolved on her tongue even before she could be sensible of its taste.

But perhaps best of all she would remember that while dear Damey's hand moved in cruciform above their heads as he pronounced a final blessing upon them as man and wife, she realized with the whole of her being that from this moment forward, her life was irrevocably changed. Nothing, positively not one thing, would ever again be the same.

Damon was thinking much along similar lines as he stood on the sidewalk outside Harry Lee Hall a few hours later, watching the small caravan of vehicles pull out, led by Michael's beribboned and soaped coupe. Toasting the happy couple had been the easiest part of the morning for him. He could speak his heart under cover of tradition, and his heart had been full.

"Excuse me, Commander." The colonel who headed Manpower, he of the granite-like features and Italian surname, approached him, looking oddly discomfited. "A word?"

"Yes, of course." Damon consulted his wristwatch, nonetheless; he had an ecumenical service of Thanksgiving at one and a Mass at three.

"This is difficult. I don't know if you're aware . . ." the colonel's gaze wandered over the priest, at once reluctant and earnest.

"Yes?"

"The Brady business has become common knowledge among your congregation."

Damon wondered how the colonel would know that; he had never seen him at Mass. As though reading his thoughts, the gentleman offered an explanation. "My wife, at an Officers Wives Club tea."

"Well, that's dismaying," Damon said. It was also disappointing. And destructive. "There has been an unfortunate—"

"Look, Father, Brady's an ass." The colonel managed an embarrassed smile. "No one who knows him gives it credence. I just thought it fair to give you a head's up. Apparently he has petitioned the Chief of Chaplains, because word has filtered through staffing channels that you will probably be replaced. You should know, you soon may be getting orders."

Damon felt a pang in his chest. Reflexively he glanced back in the direction his friends had gone, but the little caravan had already disappeared down the hill. He thanked the colonel for his concern and walked to the Chevy with lead in his step. The sun had retreated behind scudding clouds. The day of gratitude to God had turned cold indeed.

39

"And still under the sun in the judgment place I saw wickedness, and in the seat of justice, iniquity. And I said to myself, both the just and the wicked God will judge, since there is a time for every affair and on every work a judgment. Ecclesiastes 3:16." And can I be complacent, and should I be complicit, for shall I not also be judged? No one can tell me the answer. I must look within myself, and therein waits a judgment more terrible than any from on high.

Jamison M. Hutchins, Esquire, prided himself on having built a comfortable law career on the Down and Dirty D's. It was a phrase he'd coined early on, inspired by the four F's that had well served him and his buddies as kids in the Army: Find 'em, Fool 'em, Fuck 'em, Flee 'em. The four D's of defense in his personal rulebook were Deny, Deflect, Divert, Defeat. Lance Corporal Jimmy Ferris so far had been giving him trouble with the first one.

He scratched his head, then absently smoothed his feathery comb-over and, as the information he'd been reading from the newly delivered discovery packet sunk in, he began to grin from ear to ear. He could not believe his extraordinary good fortune. A certified squirrel had fallen out of the nut tree and into his lap.

He picked up a mechanical pencil with tri-color leads and began doodling in the margins of the accompanying memo he'd received from trial counsel. The layered triangles he scribbled became Christmas trees; those were his specialty doodles this time of year. At one lower corner of the triangle, the late Beverly Anderson. At the other, his estimable client. And for the star at the topmost point, the unknown quantity that was Gary Edward Winslow, mental patient. It was a fact, indisputable: No matter how many pretty decorations were on a Christmas tree, the eye was always drawn aloft to a really bright star.

The Advent season settled on Quantico its traditional aura of rising anticipation. The noon bell song from the Memorial Chapel tower switched from "Panis Angelicus" to "O Come, O Come, Emmanuel," which was soon to be exchanged for a joyful medley of carols. Fresh pine boughs graced official archways and doors throughout Mainside, rendering even the meanest barrack a more welcoming place. Along roadways, the leaping stag stenciled on deer crossing signs sported its annual bulbous red nose. Personnel offices throughout the command were inundated with leave requests. And Chaplain Damon Keith, still adjusting to awkward changes within his small circle of familiars, felt pressured by a mounting uncertainty as his naval career remained in limbo.

He was also fighting a touch of influenza. At least that's what he thought it was; he hadn't been to sickbay, given his workload. He was well aware of the perils of self-diagnosis, but all reliable indications were that he had picked up a bug. He was getting plenty of fluids, slept when he could. If the TV commercials for over-the-counter remedies held any truth, he reflected grimly, he would live.

On the third Sunday of Advent, filled with the rosy hope of *Gaudete,* Damon went to the Correctional Facility determined to get through once and for all to Lance Corporal Ferris. They met at a white Formica topped table in an interview room, one of the perks of Jimmy's move to confinement within the general inmate population. His cockiness had grown exponentially.

The prisoner rested his elbows on the table and smirked with satisfaction, settling his scrawny chin in his hands and regarding the chaplain coolly. "Not that I ain't glad to have a visitor, Padre, but you know that I've heard it all before."

Undeterred, from his chair pulled well back from the table Damon made eye contact and held it patiently. "Remember the first time I came to see you, Jimmy?"

"Sure."

"When you told me about you and Beverly in the back of the chapel?"

"Doin' it. Yeah, I remember."

"You said she told you that she didn't care if God Himself saw."

"Yeah."

"She said that because she wasn't ashamed."

"I dunno." His bottom squirmed a little on his chair.

"But I do. I'm telling you, Jimmy, I do. She wasn't ashamed because she loved you, and she thought that love would make it all right. In God's eyes, that is. And you know God sees everything."

"Whatever." Ferris sat back and folded his arms.

Damon drew a ragged breath. "She came into the Sentry Box that night to tell you about the baby, didn't she?"

Ferris shook his head slowly, clearly suffering a fool. "Why don't you quit trying to play me? You want to play me like a fish on a line."

"I'm not trying to play you." Racked with a coughing spasm, Damon covered his mouth with his handkerchief and slid his chair yet farther away. "I'm not trying to play you. I'm trying to make you think."

"That's what I got a lawyer for," Ferris snapped. "He can do the heavy thinking."

Damon sighed. He was more tired than he'd realized. "She came looking for you to tell you about the baby. There would have been no other reason. And what she wanted you to know about the child was that it was yours. I want you to think about that, Jimmy. I just want you to think."

Ferris was becoming agitated and morose, as he always did eventually when the subject of the dead girl was broached. Looking away, he reared back in an effort to slide his own chair from the table in feigned disgust, forgetting it was bolted to the floor. He grinned crookedly. "Christmastime, and that's the best you can do, Padre? No candy cane in your pocket?"

"No candy cane." Damon rubbed his temples. His head hurt.

"You look like shit, by the way, *Sir*. You got a cold, you shouldn't be coming around, spreading it here."

Damon tried to choose his words carefully. "Time is getting short, Jimmy. I know you remember more now than you did at first."

Ferris shot him a look that would melt glass.

"I understand about the drugs and what that can do to a man's judgment. But I also believe you're man enough to take responsibility for your actions."

Ferris stood up and signaled a guard that visitation was over.

"Think. I'm sure that's what Beverly would want, Jim. I know it's what God wants."

Damon watched as Ferris was escorted from the room and did not look back. "I'll be praying for you," he called, as the door was closing.

He sat for a while longer, mentally fingering a rosary decade but ultimately praying an S.O.S. Help was needed here, for Ferris, for Winslow, for the truth, whatever that might be.

Back on his rack in general pop, Ferris did allow himself to think, and the effort made him tense. When you come right down to it, he thought, me and her, we had a lot in common. We both come up rough, and nobody ever gave us much, not even the benefit of the doubt. Captain Dawson had told him about the stepfather's stash in her car, and about Smitty's trick on him with the blotter acid. What chance did either of us have? When did we ever catch a break? Always somebody looking to take advantage of you, looking to profit at your expense. Speaking of which, in another quick hour he'd be escorted back to the interview room; Hutchins would be showing up, him and his shiny suit and sweaty handshake. When you come down to it, Ferris thought again, there had been advantages to solitary. An hour would have been more than enough time. He felt like working off his mood with some purposeful exercise. And a nice shower.

40

The O'Sheas settled into married life more naturally than either had thought likely. A sort of rhythm grew out of their daily routine that was sweetly soothing. Each of them found contentment in the smallest things, a leisurely breakfast, a backrub, shared reading time before bed. Mia found that an abrupt change in plans or Michael's occasional delay at the office was not as upsetting now as before, because she was never truly alone. She was serenely aware that he was with her always in the child she carried. Perhaps because of the enchantment of firsts as man and wife, or perhaps because their home became a haven, they delayed their honeymoon trip to Disney World until well into the New Year.

The jury that was Collette remained out, reserving judgment on the new tenant who had for so long inspired scorn as a mere visitor. She had been content to spend her share of the wedding week with the neighbor while her favorite and the interloper disappeared. And then they were back, and new habits clouded memory of old, and days grew colder and shorter, until glorious Christmas with its toys and tasty treats came at last—as naughty cats and boys and girls learn—ready or not.

With the last of his obligations fulfilled on Christmas Day, Damon dragged his weary body to the row house in Norfolk and its familiar fresh balsam tree ablaze with Depression era baubles and cascades of old-fashioned tinsel, where he slept fourteen hours straight in his old childhood bed. Upon waking he submitted gratefully to the ministrations of his mother, ultimately emerging from a fog of Vicks vapor, steaming soup and "good hot toddy" a new-made man. He repaid her with the gift she had requested, which only he could provide: A Latin Mass in the living room. Vatican II in general and the English liturgy in particular had been a blow to his mother's nervous system from which she had never fully recovered. His father was content with a new briar pipe.

Eventually beneath the tree he found what his mother told him had arrived by "special delivery," their old code for mysterious packages that evoked the North Pole. It was a stout box artfully wrapped in heavy silver paper topped with a sand dollar and gold ribbon. There was a formal card from "Lieutenant Colonel and Mrs. Michael O'Shea" attached, with a personal note in Mia's hand: "Found the first two books at an estate sale, ordered the latest from the UK. We think you'll like them. Happy Christmas." Inside were three Aubrey/Maturin novels by Patrick O'Brian, each also lovingly inscribed. While the balance of his holiday leave was consumed with discovery of the world of HMS Surprise, Damon felt no special delivery could have pleased him more.

Time seems to speed up when events we dread loom on the horizon. Such was the case at the turn of the year. Anxious to move on, the nation breathed a collective sigh on January first, when John N. Mitchell, H. R. Haldeman, and John D. Elrlichman were found guilty in the Watergate cover-up. Leave papers expired at Quantico, and the base stirred to life again like a surly sluggard, only somewhat hung over.

While the chaplains strove to keep Christmas cheer alive through Epiphany, Father Keith received his official letter of censure from the Richmond Diocese, copy to Captain Stannard; as expected, it cited a lapse in judgment that had "given rise to scandal."

The wheels of military justice resumed their creaking circuit from stratagem to obstruction and back again. Returned from his Florida trip, Michael cringed to hear from Vic McManus that Jamie Hutchins had been "nosing around," hinting at an alternate theory of defense and "leaking credibility from every orifice." As January picked up suspenseful momentum like a rolling snowball, Gary Winslow and his doctor were under subpoena and Ferris's guilty plea was in doubt. The only constant was choice of forum. He wished to be tried by military judge alone.

In his windowless office at the Washington Yard, Captain Isaac Hawkes, Navy Judge Advocate General Corps, tossed aside his updated general court-martial docket to answer the phone. It was Maggie, his wife of 25 years, who didn't trust him to remember a goddamn thing on his own. They were supposed to take their daughter to Charlottesville and on to Farmville this weekend, to look at prospective schools. It was too early in the year, but you couldn't tell Maggie that, or tell her much of anything else. With a savage flourish he ground out his fifth cigarette of the day. Unfiltered Camels, seductive poison. He wanted to quit. He had been trying to quit, God knows.

"I know, baby doll. I know. One trial at Annapolis on Thursday is all, and even if it runs over it won't jeopardize our weekend, you have my word on that. You go ahead and reserve the motel rooms." He held the receiver away from his ear, regretting having stubbed out that cig. "A suite would be okay, that or two rooms. She's a grown girl, after all, and we can afford it, for God's sake." Maggie could be obtuse at times. "Okay, baby doll. I'll see you tonight."

He picked up the docket again and scrutinized it. The case that really piqued his interest was the homicide scheduled for the following week, down at Quantico. Murder of a young woman Marine. It didn't get more serious than that. His daughter was nearly the age of the victim, if he wasn't mistaken. Damned if this wasn't the type of offense that made him miss the old system, before the Manual for Courts-martial was revised in '69, or even yearn for the "rocks and shoals" that was well before his time. Nail the bastard to the yardarm. Make him walk the goddamn plank. Too many rights these days, too many lawyers.

The phone rang again. He sighed. "Ramada Inn is fine, Mags, I don't care." That Ramada would put them within a stone's throw of two furniture outlets; he could read his wife like a book. "I'll see you tonight, okay, doll? Got to get some work done here."

Rocks and shoals, that was the ticket; rocks and shoals was legend. All of his bench cases, his own deliberations, unfortunately were in the here and now. Absently he looked around the room, at the tasteful watercolors his wife had chosen, the family photographs, the plastic plant, the framed JAG poster, the walnut plaque with the brass gavel. He sighed again. It didn't matter how plush the carpet was, this goddamn windowless hole in the wall was claustrophobic. He needed another cigarette.

41

This time it was Michael who called on Damon, with a bottle of good Bourbon and a baguette under his arm. "I saw the light and figured you'd still be up."

Damon looked questioningly past his friend into the cold dark of Fuller Heights Road.

"It's just me," Michael said. He was wearing running shoes and a leather jacket over gray USMC sweats. "I heard about the diocese. Thought maybe you could use a stiff one."

"Can't say no to that."

The remnant of a fire still glowed on the hearth where he'd been dozing sitting up on the couch, his breviary fallen aside. Damon stirred the embers to life, and added a few more scraps of wood. They settled before the re-born blaze in easy chairs, with iced drinks, buttered crusty bread, and some of the cheddar from his fridge. Damon was reminded immediately of another fire and of a picnic on the floor, but he pushed the memory from his mind.

"I could go down there," Michael offered suddenly. "Once the Ferris court-martial is over I could visit the Richmond chancery, speak on your behalf."

"Not necessary." The whiskey was more warming than the fire, or maybe it was the companionship. "It was a misstep on my part, and a misunderstanding on the part of others. I think they know that. But thanks."

They drank in silence for a moment or two, watching the flames rise and fall. "The trial is day after tomorrow, right?"

"That's the rumor," Michael said. "I'll be glad to see the end of it."

"I had a call from Gary Winslow's doctor, intimating that it might be best if I stayed away. But I can't do that."

Michael raised a quizzical eyebrow.

"I've told Ferris I'll be there," Damon explained. "Not that he cares."

Michael buttered another chunk of bread. "The defense still hasn't indicated whether they're going to contest the charge, so we have to proceed as though he's pleading not guilty. We'll have several witnesses ready to testify about the history between the accused and the victim and their last known activities, a witness who can tell us Ferris was doped up, some witnesses who saw them leave the Sentry Box together. The medical examiner will be standing by to describe the marks on her neck from hands, rather than from ligature, and to say that the blood typing of the fetus matched that of the accused. And Gary Winslow can describe what he observed from his hidey hole and how he placed the stole." He drew a long deep breath. "But Winslow's appearance is dicey. The civilian lawyer has the notion he can throw blame his way, if Ferris pleads not guilty. On the other hand, Harry Reiner thinks just having Winslow present there on the periphery as a potential witness could push Ferris to plead out. It's a mixed-up mess. I've interviewed the poor bastard since he's been back on his meds. He's not going to admit to something he didn't do, but he could easily be discredited on the stand, and that might be enough to raise reasonable doubt."

Damon stared hard at the whiskey in his glass and the way the fire made it look like liquid gold. He wondered whether he should pursue the subject. "I feel responsible," he said finally. "For Winslow's involvement. For whatever twisted reason, he was there because of me."

Michael downed his drink and responded gruffly. "Because of his obsession. Not because of you. Hell, Damey, it's not your fault. Let it go. Some things you have to leave up to God, and learn to live with the outcome."

"Is that how you practice law?"

Michael grinned. "Affirmative." He glanced above the fireplace at the ship's wheel with a clock face. "I should go home." He grabbed his jacket and they headed for the door, but halfway there Michael turned. "There is one other thing." He wore a somber expression now, and his eyes behind the rimless lenses looked misty. "I never really thanked you," he said. "For Mia."

"The lessons? My pleasure."

"No, I don't mean that."

"What, then?" Damon asked warily.

Michael coughed self-consciously and cleared his throat. "We—we've talked about it, she and I," he began with some hesitation. "We've given it a lot of thought, and we've decided that when the time comes, we'd like you to be godfather."

An electric rush of relief. "I'd be honored," Damon said. "I may not be here, though, for the baptism."

"Understood. I've heard about that, too. But there's more that I want from you, Damey, and I probably should ask you now." Michael took another long deep breath and swallowed hard, his brow furrowed, his lips pursed. He looked every day of his 42 years yet as artless as the boy altar server he once was. "I want you to promise, if anything ever happens to me, you'll take care of Mia and the child. Not just the spiritual aspect, but really look out for them."

Damon was too stunned to speak.

"My sisters and their husbands are great," Michael continued earnestly, "and they'll come to love Mia in time. But I think you already do."

"I—"

"Please. I know. If the day ever comes that I'm not able to, I want you to take care of our girl for me, Damey."

He was filled with emotion and could only nod in agreement. And they did something then, which they had never done before in all their lifetime acquaintance. They managed a hug that began with an awkward handshake but ended in backslapping, prodigal affection.

After Michael had gone, Damon rested his head against the closed door. *God writes straight with crooked lines.* He felt in his chest that a burden had been lifted.

42

There was a lull in the trial proceedings, not that the proceedings had gotten very far. Lance Corporal Ferris had made his choice of forum officially for the court-martial record and now appeared to be in a *sotto voce* tug of war with his civilian counsel, presumably over his plea. Mia took a discreet sip of water and held her Stenomask ready. This morning had been for her just as such courts-martial had always been before. She felt the burdensome weight of circumstance when a human life has been taken and another life, the life accountable for the crime, hangs in the balance. A crushing weight, fiercely oppressive, almost numbing in its somber intensity.

As the moments of waiting dragged on she found herself staring at her surroundings. Perhaps it was imagination, but to her mind Courtroom One looked particularly impressive today. The faux walnut paneling, vinyl that peeled from its seams here and there, betraying cinder block beneath, had been wiped clean floor to ceiling, and apparently strategically repasted. Old Glory and the fringed Marine Corps Flag on their eagle-topped staffs in brass stands flanked, as always, the raised bench with its JAG Corps and Marine Corps Seals; but today the colorful flags seemed a little bit brighter. The bench, the railing of the bar, her scarred old desk and the oaken counsel tables had all been polished. This was a humble room, but there were times when it held a magnificent dignity, much as if it had been fashioned from mahogany and marble. Those were times when the justice meted out was truly fair and right.

Judge Hawkes caught her eye and mouthed, "Do you need a recess?" She shook her head no, but her free hand went instinctively to her belly as though seeking reassurance from her constant companion. Hawkes frowned and announced, "Counsel, we'll take ten minutes." In the suppressed din that followed he leaned over the bench and asked, "How far along are you?"

She looked up in surprise. "Not quite three months. You can tell?"

He smiled, "Been there, done that, in a manner of speaking. Congratulations."

"Thanks. And I'm all right."

"I know," he said, still smiling. "I need a smoke."

His Honor withdrew to chambers. Michael had already left the courtroom. Mia considered making a beeline for the women's head; it was wise to do so, since it might be a long while before another bathroom break. Looking around, she noticed the accused watching her—staring, actually. She could not bring herself to smile at Lance Corporal Ferris this morning, although she remembered him as a presence, usually sullen and unhelpful, in the Chaplains Office. She nodded at him instead. He did not return the acknowledgment.

Expressionless, Ferris turned away from the counsel table that he shared with Captain Dawson and Jamie Hutchins and scanned the spectator section behind the bar. There were few people back there now, but before the recess there had been a middle-aged woman, small and slight, who shared the same narrow features and hard dark eyes as he, and a tall man with her. His aunt, and the uncle he had never met. There appeared to be no one for her, from the victim's family. No one for Bev.

"This general court-martial will come to order," the military judge announced. "Counsel, have you had sufficient time to confer with your client?"

"Yes, sir."

"And are you prepared to enter pleas?"

Hutchins, still in some agitation, delivered a low Hail Mary to his client's ear, "Are you sure about this?"

Jimmy Ferris twisted in his seat to glance behind him once more and met his aunt's hopeful gaze. She and her husband had mortgaged their house to buy him this old turd in a leisure suit. Nobody had ever done that much for him before. The public seating area was full up now. He recognized the cowboy sitting there in the second row, along with his shrink or keeper, whatever. And standing in the back was the chaplain, the one visitor he'd had in six months other than his lawyers. Gotta hand it to him, that man was one persistent sonofabitch. Probably still expected him to hit the deck on his knees.

He turned forward and looked again at the court reporter, pregnant but not showing much, just like her, like Bev. It was suffocating close in here. He wished they could open the windows. A puny little bird was outside, jumping around in the bushes. He'd like to throw the window open, startle it and make it fly away.

"Yes," he said finally to Hutchins, and was barely audible. "I'm sure."

"We're ready, your Honor," Hutchins said.

"Accused and counsel, please rise."

All three stood and faced the bench. Jimmy knew this was an important moment, one he'd remember the rest of his life. He wondered why he didn't feel anything. It was like he was hollow. Not scared, not sad, nothing. Just empty.

"Lance Corporal James W. Ferris, United States Marine Corps, how do you plead?"

He sensed all those eyes drilling the back of his head, one pair in particular. They were blue, they probably saw into his soul, and they were stubborn.

"Guilty," Hutchins answered for him.

And it was all downhill from there.

Mia could tell that Captain Hawkes was having a problem with the providency. He needed to be convinced of the accused's guilt on all points, particularly his capacity to form intent, or he would have to reject his plea. There was much ambiguity here that was troubling; even she, with no legal training, could see that.

"Lance Corporal," the military judge said, "let's go back to the act itself."

Ferris emitted a long sigh that could be heard throughout the courtroom.

"You were sufficiently impaired that you suffered memory loss for weeks afterward."

"Yes, sir."

"Yet you can now remember choking PFC Anderson until she expired?"

Ferris huffed another short sigh of frustration and cleared his throat. Other than that, he betrayed no emotion. "Like I said, it come back to me little by little. I remember choking her at first as part of the sex. We wasn't into scarfing. I mean, I done it myself, plenty of times. But not her and I. She was scared of it."

"And by 'scarfing' you mean erotic, or autoerotic, asphyxiation?"

"Yeah, that."

A barely perceptible nudge from Captain Dawson under the table.

"Excuse me, yes. Sir. That's what I mean, yes, sir. I knew she didn't like it, but she'd been playing up to me, about the baby and all, wanting me back, so I started to, anyway, and she let me. But then she panicked, I think, because she was hitting me on the arms. And I was glad she was scared." He huffed again, deep in his throat. "At some point she seemed to relax, and instead of stopping I kept on, and on until I knew . . ." His voice trailed off.

"So you forced the PFC—"

"No, sir," Ferris said emphatically. "There was no forcing. I didn't force her, I didn't have to. There was no struggle even with the scarfing, until the last, and that was just . . ." His voice trailed off again.

"I'm sorry? You have to speak up, Lance Corporal. 'That was just'?"

"To breathe."

The military judge flushed, not a good sign. "I see," he said evenly. "So you went too far? It was accidental?"

"No." Ferris was emphatic. "No, sir." Again with the sighing, but he appeared to be gathering momentum. "I was high as hell, and for a long time I drew a blank. But I do remember now. I know I was mad; I know I wanted her dead. And it wasn't just from being high. I was still mad at her after I was sober." He was silent a moment, perhaps to steady himself. "I didn't want a kid, a kid that might not even be mine. I didn't like the way that made me feel, like a chump." He paused again, drawing in breath.

"You know how you can love a person and hate them at the same time? Well, mostly I remember hate. And I remember wanting to be rid of her. So I wouldn't have to feel that way anymore."

Following the boilerplate script that covered the elements of the offense, Captain Hawkes then asked the necessary questions of law that reduce a pernicious crime against God and nature to a series of banalities.

"Lance Corporal Ferris, do you agree that Beverly Grace Anderson, a Private First Class in the United States Marine Corps, is dead?"

"Yes, sir."

"Do you admit that her death resulted from an act you committed?"

"Yes, sir."

"And do you admit that the killing of PFC Anderson was unlawful?"

"Yes, sir."

"And finally, do you admit that at the time of the killing of Miss Anderson it was your intent and purpose to kill her or to inflict great bodily harm upon her?"

"Yes, sir."

"Is there anything further you wish to tell me about this offense, Lance Corporal?"

Until that juncture Ferris had been downcast, but he finished with his head up, jaw set, speaking loud and clear. "I did it," he said, matter-of-factly, "and sorry don't change what is. But owning up, it's the right thing."

The silence of deliberation that ensued went on long enough that Mia noted on the record the approximate time it had started. Charlie Dawson was squirming, nervously clenching and unclenching his fists under the defense table. Jamie Hutchins, the gasbag, looked like a deflated balloon. Michael was grim, staring at the floor. The woman who resembled Ferris was crying. Damey—Father Damon—glanced her way, his face drawn and ashen. Mr. Winslow's eyes were closed, his lips moving silently. His companion from Eastern State stared vacantly, apparently lost in thought. The accused was looking out the window.

A small brown bird, a thrush or a sparrow, was perched on the box-wood outside. It began a signal to others of its kind at intervals, one call, two calls . . . three . . . four. It flew away. When finally the military judge spoke again, twelve minutes had passed.

"The guilty plea is accepted," he said.

43

Lance Corporal Ferris got 18 years in Leavenworth. It could have been a lot worse for him; but Cassie, bent over her desk and getting a cramp in her writing hand, wondered if it was enough. She had sat in the back of the courtroom that afternoon, after the guilty verdict had been announced, to hear the defense's case in extenuation and mitigation. Jimmy's aunt testified about the death of his unmarried parents, the many foster homes he'd lived in. A psychiatrist talked about physical abuse at a young age. But lots of people have crap childhoods, and they don't grow up to do murder.

He'd be middle aged when he got out. It was hard to picture a middle-aged Jimmy Ferris. Beverly, the laughing girl she remembered from last Easter, was robbed of that, and of so much more. Cassie glanced at her half-finished crochet work in delicate pink and blue, occupying a chair in the corner of her office. In 18 years the baby Beverly Anderson had been carrying would have been grown; any financial obligation Ferris could have been held to would likely be over. She wondered if that had factored at all into the judge's sentencing.

Mia had rushed to her office during the noon break in the trial to give her the news that the guilty plea stood, which she called anticlimactic. And in quiet moments since that day they had discussed the sentencing. Mia had told her there could be an appeal later on, but all that legal detail, like the military judge's reasoning, was beyond Cass; she didn't really try to understand it. An appeal based on ineffective counsel or some such, Mia said, or possibly the complication that some of Jimmy's intoxication was involuntary. Even though intoxication wasn't a defense to murder, unless it made you crazy.

And that was another thing that bothered her. She didn't expect anything for herself from Gary Winslow, for all that happened years ago. That was over and done with. But if he was well enough to come to court, why couldn't he have apologized to Father Keith?

"What are you doing?"

Father Roberts had come in unnoticed and was now standing over her. She thought it should be rather obvious what she was doing. "I'm writing reception invitations by hand for General Swaggart," she said.

"Shouldn't that be his secretary's job?"

"Thank you!" She set aside the pen and the ruler she used as a straight line guide. "She and the aide farm them out. Apparently that's not what they're paid the big bucks for."

He nodded, admiring her work. "You do have very nice handwriting."

"Thanks again."

As usual, Father Roberts looked like God's gift, while completely clueless about it. It was clichéd, but what a waste. Oddly annoying, in her present frame of mind. "I thought that maybe after the last time I'd be spared, but no dice."

"Why, what happened the last time?"

"I wrote 'the honor of your presence is required,' rather than 'requested' on a few."

"On purpose?"

"Not consciously."

He seemed interested. "So what happened?"

"Oh, a little public humiliation and a big do-over, that's all." She took another fake vellum embossed with the MCDEC seal from the stack and started to write again. He continued to hover.

"What's that?" He pointed at the shapeless lump of pink and blue yarn.

"A receiving blanket I'm crocheting for my friend, Mia O'Shea." she said. "When I'm not writing invitations. On my lunch time, I might add."

"That's nice."

She had to smile. This was Father Roberts making an effort. It was almost comical, the sociable change in him since he'd learned he would be flying solo for a few weeks, until Father Keith's relief arrived. Clearly, he was terrified.

"Can I get you a cup of coffee, Father?"

"No, thanks, I'm good."

And he was, too. A good man, that is. He was no Father Keith, nor even another Father Mac, but he tried. She shouldn't be hard on him; he meant well.

"But is there any of Father Keith's going-away cake left?" he asked.

So that was it. She motioned to the Tupperware on a corner of a worktable, out of anyone's line of sight when the door to her office was opened all the way, as it was now. "Help yourself," she said dryly. She should have known better than to believe she could take some of the cake she had baked herself home to Joe and Joey.

That was what really perturbed her the most today, the fact that that they'd had to bid "fair winds and following seas" to Damon Keith so bloody soon. And all over what was only some commonsense advice to a woman who was obviously better off for taking it. She knew that the odds were against Father Keith's ever having yet another, a third tour here. A snowball's chance, actually. It was like being taken for granted for noon phone watch, or being burdened with busy work. It wasn't fair.

The young priest cut himself a discretely narrow slice of cake, leaving enough to take home if she hid the container better. He spoke with his mouth full, uncharacteristic of him. "Ullree mishim."

"What's that?" she asked irritably. He was beginning to get on her nerves.

He swallowed. "I say, I'll really miss him." Somewhat abashed, he smiled at her faintly before drifting toward the coffee mess in the waiting room. "I honestly will."

Cassie brushed a tear away before it could fall and ruin her meticulous work. It was just not fair at all.

44

It was 0800 and damned cold, with the smell of snow in the air, but for once Harry Reiner was glad to be caught at headquarters by the call for attention to colors. He stood stock still on the sidewalk behind Lejeune Hall while the bugle recording blared. He was facing the general direction of the flagpole at the front of the building and had covered his heart with his hand, even though from here he couldn't see the flag being raised. Out of the corner of his eye he had spied Chaplain Keith at the rear of his Impala, rendering a military salute. That was why he was glad of the timing. He had wanted to catch the chaplain before he left Quantico.

When the last notes of reveille faded he strode over, his right hand outstretched.

Chaplain Keith had a good, firm grip. "Harry! Good to see you. Are you coming or going?"

"I'm on my way in, meeting with trial counsel about a case from the Paris Embassy." He indicated the bags and boxes in the trunk of the Chevy as its lid was closed. "No need to ask you the same question. I'm sorry to see you go."

"Don't be too sorry," Damon responded sheepishly. "I'm finally getting sea duty, something I've wanted for a long time. That makes me a little like Br'er Rabbit thrown into the briar patch."

"Well, all right, then. You stopping inside?"

"No, I'm done. My official sendoff was yesterday. I was just here this morning to grab a couple things from the office, say my final goodbyes. I'm ready to head out."

"Well, then, it's luck I saw you. I've been meaning to phone and ask you something personal. I have some leave time coming to me . . ." As Harry talked, Father Keith was gazing over Harry's shoulder toward Lejeune Hall. A strange expression washed his face, naked emotion almost like grief. Harry turned and looked in that direction, and noticed a figure in a window, her hand raised against the glass. Mia Rodgers—no, O'Shea now—if he was not mistaken. Nice woman. Attractive woman, a stand out even when she wasn't wearing bright red.

He didn't think the chaplain had heard him. "Father?"

Chaplain Keith waved hastily and swallowed hard, turning his attention back to Harry. "I'm sorry, you were saying?"

"Just that I have some leave coming up, and I thought I might try Virginia Beach off season, maybe look up your sister. Would you mind?"

He had the priest's full attention now, a soul searching, piercing blue gaze that Harry did his best to meet steadily. "No, not at all," Chaplain Keith said after a moment, and offered his hand again. His eyes flickered toward the window once more and Harry looked, too, but the lady in red was gone.

Harry still had a few minutes before his meeting with Mike O'Shea. He stayed in the chill morning air just a bit longer to watch the chaplain drive away toward his future, past the stalwart brick chapel that stood across the winter parched parade field like a bulwark against hopelessness. He felt both sad and euphoric. There were no banks of votives in military chapels, he knew that much—they were against fire safety regs—but for the first time in years, damn if he didn't feel like lighting a candle.

EPILOGUE

The view from Father Kelly's office was especially beautiful this evening. The sun was setting in the Blue Ridge, casting a mellow glow over the burnt umber, scarlet and gold of hardwoods splashed liberally throughout the landscape. Contrasted against the deep near-black of evergreens, they were like the work of heaven's paintbrush. People traveled to New England or drove the Skyline Drive for this kind of autumn beauty, and he had it all right here beyond his window. There were days when he didn't much enjoy teaching theology to seminarians at Vianney, days when he wished his vocation had taken a different course, but this wasn't one of them. His was a dream job, cushy yet challenging, and only about three hours from his mother, should she need him.

"Day dreaming again?" It was old Sheffield, head and shoulders inside the doorjamb and holding onto it as though he needed help staying upright. Which maybe he did.

"Not really, Monsignor. Just enjoying the sunset."

"Well, it's last call in the cafeteria, my boy. Thought maybe you'd join me."

"I will be happy to, in a moment. I just need to send this correspondence to print," he said, pressing the appropriate keys.

"Beg pardon?" When it came to computers, Sheffield was the last holdout on the faculty. Not necessary, he'd say, not when the curricula is two thousand years old.

Father Kelly raised his voice over the printer's electronic grind. "I'm printing out a letter of recommendation for one of our graduates. Do you remember Jason Connors? He was ordained, oh, five years ago."

Old Sheffield passed a tremulous hand over his mouth and chin, as he often did while thinking hard. "Prematurely gray fellow, lax in Greek?" he asked at last.

"Yes, sir, you've placed him precisely. He's done well at his first two parishes. Lost a brother in Iraq while he was still in seminary. He's applying for the military chaplaincy."

"Ah, commendable."

Father Kelly pressed enter and turned his laptop so that the monsignor could see the screen. "Connors was thinking Army, which is fine, but I believe I've nudged him toward the Navy," he said, as the Chaplain Corps web site was pulled from cyberspace for Sheffield to see.

"Is that the Internet?" Old Sheffield held opinions about the Internet, none of them complimentary.

"Yes, Monsignor. Look here." Two more clicks and a page appeared that was devoted to Chaplain Vincent Capodanno. "You've heard of this priest, surely."

Sheffield squinted slightly and nodded. "Vietnam," he said.

"'Died in 1967,'" Father Kelly read aloud, "'while providing aid to wounded men on the battlefield during Operation Swift.' He had three Purple Hearts and was awarded the Congressional Medal of Honor posthumously."

"Yes."

"And in 2006 he was declared a Servant of God."

"The first step in the canonization process, yes." Sheffield said. "A saint one day."

"I think so."

Undeterred, the monsignor pointed at the clock on the wall. "Last call, Jack. It's lasagna night."

"Right, Monsignor. And garlic bread. I do hope there is some garlic bread left." He logged off and sent his laptop to sleep mode. One last look out the window, where light was fading and the rolling hills to the west, as the dusk gathered, looked rather like the sea. If you grow up near the ocean, you tend to look for it everywhere.

The old man had preceded him down the hall; he had to hustle to catch up and fall into step. "My uncle was a Navy chaplain, you know, in the Vietnam days."

"I seem to recall that, yes."

As they walked together Jack smiled broadly, recalling the family stories and cheered by the thought of how Uncle Damey would grin at what he was about to say: "Father Vince was a friend of his."

AUTHOR'S NOTE

Like most works of fiction, this book is the product of the author's imagination, informed by the author's experiences. (Welcome to my world, circa 1971.)

There was no greater inspiration to me than my lifelong friend Chaplain John J. O'Connor, who became a prince of the Church and Archbishop of New York. The Cardinal never lost his humility or his sense of humor. He was unfailingly supportive, always urging me to "keep writing." It was Chaplain O'Connor who nearly fell into the ocean from a breaches buoy. While Chief of Chaplains from 1975 to 1979, he approved establishment of the Religious Program Specialist rating for enlisted personnel in the U.S. Navy. The motto of his episcopate was "There can be no love without justice," and he was quite fond of quoting the proverb, "God writes straight with crooked lines." The character Damon Keith is patterned after Father John.

The Reverend Keith Ramey was also supportive of my writing. He provided the poisoned wine example as background on the sanctity of confession. His advice on building Damey's personality was, "Keep him real by giving him flaws." The nervous habit of rubbing his neck and a touch of claustrophobia were the best I could do.

The character of Father Roberts was influenced by my boyfriend Robert E. Maher, who was later ordained and became a monsignor and Vicar General of the Brownsville Diocese. Bob's devotion to Christ was intense, he played a 12-string folk guitar, and he did indeed have the voice of an angel.

Theo Lurakis is a blend of two Eastern Orthodox chaplains: Michael Frimenko (married to Mary), who bravely handled a hostage situation; and Robert M. Radasky, who loved to relate his threat to kick fiancée Betty downstairs on the eve of their wedding. Father Radasky became Roman Catholic late in life.

All these dear people are gone now. That is what happens when you take 40 years to finish what you have started.

Tony's Italian Kitchen/The Sentry Box, Our Lady of the Harbor High School, and St. John Vianney Seminary are fictitious. The wilted lettuce and "knockwurst defense" court cases? The working girl named Joy who stiffed Uncle Sam for witness fees? The chaplain's assistant who "did it" with his girl in the choir room? All true. And the unlikely character of Willie the Swoop was a real person, whose surname has been changed. A year or two after he left military service, someone sent the chaplains a clipping and photo from a New York newspaper, much to Father Frimenko's delight: "Look, that's him! It's Willie! That's our Willie the Swoop!" The man pictured was looking sharp, wearing a Marine Corps uniform . . . with rank insignia and medals he had never attained.

Donna Lee Davis became Catholic at Marine Memorial Chapel in 1969. Her 33-year career at Quantico included six years as Chaplains Office Secretary and 27 in court reporting within the military justice system, most of them as Senior Court Reporter. Upon retirement Donna was awarded the Navy Department's Meritorious Civilian Service Medal. She has twice self-published poetry, *Sheer Poetry* in 1981 and *Sheer Poetry Revisited* in 2007. Her short fiction has appeared in the international magazine *Carpe Articulum Literary Review* (2010), print issues and online, and has been short listed for the *Chicago Tribune*'s Nelson Algren Award (2007).

Donna is proud that she was born in Philadelphia, but she has been a Virginian since sixth grade. She lives in Hartwood.

ALSO BY DONNA LEE DAVIS:

HERE IS THE CHURCH:
A History of St. Mary Parish

SHEER POETRY REVISITED

Visit Donna online at
https://www.thebriarfields.com

Find out more about Chaplain Vincent Capodanno
and his Cause for Canonization at
https://www.facebook.com/capodannoguild/